COPY
KAT

COPY

KAT

KAREN KIJEWSKI

A PERFECT CRIME BOOK
DOUBLEDAY
NEW YORK LONDON TORONTO SYDNEY AUCKLAND

A Perfect Crime Book

PUBLISHED BY DOUBLEDAY
a division of Bantam Doubleday Dell Publishing Group, Inc.
666 Fifth Avenue, New York, New York 10103

DOUBLEDAY is a trademark of Doubleday,
a division of Bantam Doubleday Dell
Publishing Group, Inc.

All of the characters in this book are fictitious, and any
resemblance to actual persons, living or dead, is purely coincidental.

Book design by Tasha Hall

Library of Congress Cataloging-in-Publication Data
Kijewski, Karen.
Copy kat / by Karen Kijewski. — 1st ed.
p   cm.
"A Perfect Crime book."
I. Title.
PS3561.I364C66   1992
813'.54—dc20   92-14482
                                                    CIP
ISBN 0-385-42096-X
Copyright © 1992 by Karen Kijewski
All Rights Reserved
Printed in the United States of America
December 1992

3   5   7   9   10   8   6   4   2

For Michael, Luciene, Aimée, and Jennifer.

ACKNOWLEDGMENTS

I was a bartender for almost twelve years. I know hundreds of drinks. I have served thousands of them.

Each drink has a drinker. I met a lot of people across the bar and across the years. I've forgotten some of the names, but not the faces, the stories, the conversations, not the drinks. This is my thank-you to all the interesting, delightful, and generous people I met and came to know.

And to the occasional others: the rude ones, the crude ones, the Neanderthals? This thank-you is for you, too. I never forgot that I didn't want to be behind a bar forever. You never let me.

COPY
KAT

1

I didn't recognize her without her clothes. She looked drab, diminished somehow.

Death does that to you.

I meet his eyes finally. It was easier than looking at hers, but not by much.

"It's not pretty." A statement, not a question. She was the "it." His voice was as dead as the woman.

"No. Autopsy photos never are."

I looked at the drab skin of the young woman against the stainless steel table, the gutters and drains for body fluids an ugly reminder of violence and death. Her hair looked darker in the photo than it probably was in daylight, her skin paler than it had ever been. The bullet wound in her chest was round, neat, and tidy.

And final. The period to her life.

I tried to hand the pictures back to the old man but he wouldn't take them.

"You needn't do this," I said gently. "Perhaps I could get us some tea?"

"I have other pictures."

He didn't point them out; he didn't need to. They were everywhere: on the top of the old-fashioned curio, the mantel, the lace-covered piano, hanging on the walls, and displayed on the coffee table. A number of them were lying facedown, or turned to the wall.

"But when I look at those I just remember her the way she was. I remember her and I care for her and I don't want to do that." He shook his head violently.

"No, ma'am. I want to hate and I want to look at her dead, violated by them who took her life and then by them who saw and talked her over like she was so much trash washed up in the gutter. And then—" His voice was harsh and his breath came in torn gasps as though he'd been running to the point of pain and beyond. "Then they slashed her up from top to bottom, peeled her scalp back, chopped off the top of her head—"

The words were jagged now, sharp-edged and dangerous. His throat filled up and cut them off. He was choking on hatred, I thought.

Maybe he had a right.

He had a reason.

His hands, large with bone and the remembrance of muscle, the knuckles swollen and oversized by a lifetime of hard work, lay on the quilted comforter in his lap. A hand reached out to me, blindly at first and then grasping for the autopsy photos. He held them without looking at them.

"These pictures make me hate and I want that."

It was like a song, a song of loathing. I stood and walked to the door, turned reluctantly. It would have been easier just to walk out.

"You need someone else, Mr. McAlister. A minister, a friend . . ." I stopped. I didn't know what he needed, or who; I didn't have the answer. "But not me, not a private investigator." My hand dropped to the doorknob, a luminous glass one that had turned violet over the decades.

"*Please.*" He pushed the back of his hand across his eyes, then ran his fingers through his thinning white hair. When I entered the house twenty minutes ago, it had been carefully combed. It wasn't now. "I don't like this neither. I want justice done, that's all. I can't outrun the sorrow. I can't get through what's past, through the hate."

He made it sound like a physical place, a geographical location: The Hate. I could see it, too easily in fact: a marshy, swampy place littered with fetid matter, mined with decaying things. Bubbles of swamp gas and stink would catch at you, miasmas dance in your face. There would be red, not just red but blood, rivulets, rivers. . . . I sucked in my breath hard and shook my head sharply.

His eyes watched me. *You see, you know,* is what they said: The look was as clear as the spoken words would have been. And I did. I knew that place, and I knew I didn't want to go back there. I was running from something too, blood-red nightmares that licked at my heels even in the daytime.

I didn't answer the question in his eyes, just the spoken one—the easy one, not the one about justice.

"No, I do background and corporate investigations, an occasional insurance scam, that sort of thing. Not this. I'm sorry." I turned again to leave.

"Please. I need help. Tea? You offered before. . . ."

I came back and stood in front of him without speaking. We stared at each other.

The sun streamed in the windows and the air came alive with dust motes. The light had to be right before you could see them, but they were always there. Like hatred, or anger. Or love. You couldn't see it, necessarily, but it was there.

"All right," I said. He smiled but I was stern. "I'll make tea. I make no promises."

"But you'll listen to my story?"

"Yes."

"It's enough."

He followed me into the kitchen and showed me where things were. It had been a woman's kitchen once, with curtains, handmade potholders, framed canning labels, and knickknacks. Now it was his: sloppier, dusty, and with adaptations to accommodate the wheelchair. We drank the tea out of heavy chipped white mugs. He liked his tea strong and bitter so I made it that way. I had to add sugar and hot water to mine to get it down.

He grinned at me. "Us tough old farts can drink about anything." His eyes measured me. "You might say it's a tad early to be putting brandy in your tea?"

"I might," I agreed. "And I might not."

5

So we had brandy in our tea. It makes the storytelling easier some-times. I thought to myself that it would be harder now to walk off.

It was. I was right.

And I didn't.

"She was my godchild."

That was the beginning, simple, neat, and tidy; tidy then, for that moment in time, but not ever again. I listened quietly as he told it.

"Her name is—was—Deidre." His eyes darkened as he changed verbs. "She was only twenty-nine. I loved her very much when she was a child. Deedee, we called her. I didn't know her as good as an adult. What I knew I didn't always like. Or understand.

"Oftentimes she changed in front of my very eyes. I never knew who she was. And, if I knew one day, goddamn if she wasn't something different the next. Something I might recognize, something I might not. It was a puzzle, it was. I couldn't understand and it made me mad. She couldn't, or wouldn't—was no way of knowing—explain." His voice was flat and dark and matched his eyes.

"I'm doing this for the child, and because . . ." He stared blankly into his tea cup. ". . . because she died before we could make up. I want that. I want to make it up to her."

He slammed his fist down on the kitchen table, making the mugs jump. Me, too. I caught mine in time. His, empty now, fell on its side. That explained the chips.

"I am a crippled old man, powerless to save what I love."

The words were as bitter as the tea. He stood the cup upright and poured more brandy. I shook my head at the offer.

"Mr.—"

"Call me Tobias."

"What child, Tobias?"

"Named Toby. After me. Three years old." He sipped at the brandy and I waited. Finally he smiled ruefully. "Forgive me. I'm an angry old man."

"And sad."

The smile faded, his face locked up. I had overstepped a boundary.

"Deidre was killed. It's been four months and more now. She was shot as she made her way home from the restaurant and bar she and her hus-band, Matt, own. She had twelve hundred dollars in a cash bag and it was taken. No struggle. Maybe she knew the person. Maybe the person came upon her suddenly, surprised her. It don't make sense to me. Why not just take the money and be done with it?"

"Why kill her?"

"Yes."

"Would she have fought for the money?"

"No. She was a sensible one. Money is money. A life is a life."

"Have the police—"

"Ha!"

He slammed a closed fist on the table again. I saw it coming this time, was ready this time. I grabbed for his mug too, and thought it remarkable that he had any crockery left at all.

"They *say* they're still looking, but they're not. They *say* the case is still open, but . . ." He shrugged.

"A homicide case is never closed, Tobias, not until—"

"I know, I *know*." His voice was impatient.

I nodded. "Okay. What do you want from me? Private investigators don't solve murders; cops do."

He leaned forward, his hands gripped on the wheelchair arms. "I want you to be my eyes and ears. And legs," he added harshly. "And I don't want you to go into this looking like some damn investigator."

My eyebrows went up.

He grinned. It was more like a grimace. "Take a vacation, maybe, or look for a job, or—hell, I don't know, do what you want, that part's up to you.

"Just talk to people, see what you can find out. Her husband, her sister, her friends, see what you can find out. It's too late for Deidre, but I want the truth. And I'm worried about the boy. Pour more tea, would you? Please," he added abruptly, and the please was for more than the tea.

"The young ones have a hard enough time without—" He broke off and stared into his mug. "Do you believe in tea leaves?" His large hand swirled the mug carefully and he looked up at me.

"No."

"Death. These say death. My grandmother taught me. She said there was gypsy blood in our family back in the old country and she learned from them, learned to read fortunes. Don't know how good it works but it ain't evidence and it don't name names nor kick ass. That's where you come in."

I nodded. I was up to speed. I had the picture now.

"If it's the husband, I want you to pin it on him." He jabbed his hand viciously in the air as though he were holding a tack and a paper tail and playing pin-the-tail-on-the-donkey.

I guess I didn't have the picture. "Pin it on him?" I stood up. "I don't work that way, Tobias. Thanks for the tea."

"Hey, now." His tone was conciliatory; his hand reached out for mine and touched it gently. "Hey, now, don't git fired up. I'm an ornery old fool and I spoke out of turn. Sit down, do."

I did, but grudgingly.

He pointed at a picture under a magnet on the refrigerator door. A child smiled mischievously at us; there was a cloud in his eyes and a rip in his jeans. He was a beautiful child.

"You see?"

I did.

"It won't be cheap, Tobias. If I go undercover, live up there—"

He shrugged. "I don't care, miss. I don't look it but I'm wealthy, money in the bank and land rich. Money don't mean a damn thing to me, but the truth and that boy do. I can't outrun the sorrow no more 'n Deidre could, but maybe he can. I'll do my damnedest to help. Now, where do you stand? Will you help me?"

"Today's Friday. I'll start Tuesday."

"I thank you for it."

He leaned forward and reached in his hip pocket for an old worn-out and beat-up billfold. Laboriously he unfolded it, pulled out the bills, counted them, and put the wallet back in his pocket. He gave me ten one-hundred-dollar bills and wouldn't take a receipt.

"I don't do business that way, miss. I heard good of you, I like you." We shook hands. That was the contract, the agreement, the signing, the receipt.

"It's Kat, not miss."

"Suits me fine. You come back when you need more money, or to tell me how it goes, or even"—he smiled shyly, looking suddenly like Toby's kin—"jist to sit and rest a spell, to have you a spot of tea or brandy."

I smiled back and we sat in understanding and in silence.

"Here." He pulled a carton toward him across the kitchen table, heedlessly jeopardizing the mugs again. "This here is her, is Deidre's, stuff. I haven't looked through it, haven't touched it. She left it here, in the back room, because it was private and she trusted me. You see if it'll help; if not, I reckon we'll jist let it be.

"I wrote down the other, too: the names and addresses of folks, of who's who, and what's what, and where, some things the po-lice told me. Some pictures, too. You look through it, tell me what you need. You need more, I'll try to git it."

Before I left I looked at the pictures of Deidre, the ones Tobias had faced down or away. All I had were the autopsy photos and I wanted to know what she looked like alive.

The pictures showed me a woman with a slender build, shoulder-length straight blond hair, and bangs. She was almost pretty, striking was perhaps a better word, and vulnerable-looking in the earlier shots—like a kid who knows she's going to be the last chosen and least wanted for the spelling bee or softball team, and is trying to be brave about it but is hurting desperately.

In the later ones she was poised and self-assured. It was like looking at before-and-after pictures in a woman's magazine, only in this case it was not a fashion but a personality make-over.

There wasn't just one image or look. I was struck by that. Like a model, Deidre seemed to be posing, presenting a variety of images, personalities, styles. Except for the glasses. They were a constant. She hadn't worn them as a child, but as an adult she always had them on: dark glasses outside and rose- and violet-tinted ones in.

"Was she near or farsighted?" I asked Tobias.

"They weren't prescription," he said. "She just liked the look of it, liked wearing 'em."

I found that interesting.

I turned the pictures facedown again and he saw me out. Wheeling into the wind pulling at our hair and clothing he opened the car door for me.

"I thank you," he said.

I nodded.

"I don't say it often."

I nodded again.

"See you."

His still-powerful arms spun the wheelchair around and headed back to the old wooden house halfway hidden under the gnarled and twisted limbs of the valley oaks.

You can't outrun sorrow.

I thought about it as I drove down from the foothills into the Sacramento Valley and home. And I thought about what I was running from: the nightmares; the blood; the horror of killing someone I'd thought I'd known and hadn't, thought I'd cared for and had killed because otherwise he would have killed me.

I was running, but the nightmares were with me. Always.

You can't outrun . . .

Stepping into a twenty-four-hour job, an assumed life and identity didn't sound bad. I passed the exit to Newcastle off I-80 and stepped on the gas, picking up speed. Was taking on a new job to banish nightmares from the last one foolishness, like taking coals to Newcastle? The speedometer hovered at seventy, then climbed. Speeding wasn't the same as outrunning. I knew that, knew it wasn't the answer.

I sped anyway.

2

His hands ran up and down her bare arms, then cupped her elbows and pulled her toward him. She could feel the tremor in her flesh and the fear and anticipation in her heart.

His breath was hot on her skin as he bent over her; his lips left a scorching trail on her cheek. Her heart pounded.

"You're mine." The voice was commanding and she felt powerless to resist. Was this the love that she had waited for, longed for, hoped for?

His lips, rough and hot, took hers. She prayed that it was and surrendered herself. . . .

—unpublished fragment from Deidre Durkin's work

. . . .

There was a brisk knock, then the front door opened and slammed, making me jump. I looked up guiltily from the smudged, coffee-stained, penciled pages spread out on the kitchen table in front of me. It was five o'clock and I'd been reading Deidre's "stuff," as Tobias had phrased it, for two hours. A quick and familiar step pattered through the house.

"Kat? Katy, are you here? Where are you?" Charity stepped into the kitchen and flipped on the lights. I blinked. "You'll ruin your eyes," she said disapprovingly. "May I make a snack?" She headed for the refrigerator.

"Yes," I said, but hesitantly.

"It's not okay?" Her voice was quick, shy, hurt.

"It's okay." I walked over and hugged my oldest and dearest friend. "I just don't think there's much in there."

"What's new?" She sighed and opened the door. "Peanut butter, science project something—" She peered at it. "Ugh! Stale English muffins, moldy cheese. Really, Kat!"

"That's *blue* cheese." I was indignant. "It's *supposed* to be moldy."

"But not fuzzy."

I looked again. She had a point there; I didn't argue it.

"Oh, well." She looked at me bleakly.

"Charity, what's the matter?" I asked softly. Food is Charity's answer to stress.

"Wine?"

There was a weak thread of hope in her voice. I nodded and poured two glasses. She slugged half of hers down and wiped her mouth on the back of her hand. I gaped in disbelief. At five feet two, with smooth blond hair and a Madonna smile, Charity is a model of manners and decorum, a nationally syndicated advice columnist with the manners of a yuppie, not a farm girl.

"Let's get a pizza."

"Extra large?"

"Yes, with everything. Maybe two."

Uh-oh, bad sign. She finished her wine and poured more. Another bad sign. I smiled; I couldn't help it. Bad move. She frowned at me.

"It won't work, Charity," I said gently. "Even two extra-large pizzas with everything won't make it go away."

She started crying. *Rats!* I thought, but wisely didn't say.

"Yesterday was my birthday."

"Yes."

I knew that; she knew I knew it. I had taken her out to lunch, made a fuss with flowers and a present. Once, years ago, I'd forgotten her birthday. Once was enough. She was still crying. A glimmer of the situation was filtering in.

"Al—" She stumbled over the rest of her sentence, then sobbed out, "He forgot!"

Uh-oh. *Maybe he wasn't, after all, the love that she had waited for, hoped for, prayed for.* Deidre's words. I couldn't get away from them.

"Forgot?" My voice sounded incredulous.

"He didn't call even, not until this morning and *then* he didn't say he was sorry or *anything*."

"What did he say?"

"Nothing."

I stared at her. It didn't sound like Al, not at all. Al is a nice guy, considerate, thoughtful, very fond of Charity.

"Nothing?"

"Well . . . I hung up. I was mad, Katy. Excessively so."

Until I met Charity I had no idea an advice columnist could manage her life so badly.

"He was going to cook dinner for me. It started off as a joke because he can't cook, but he said he would barbecue. It was so sweet. And make a salad and garlic bread. His garlic bread is *divine*. And then—"

She broke off and I stared out the window. It was the barbecue that did it, that snapped my mind into line. "The news last night—"

"Kat," she wailed, "how can you be so unfeeling? Who *cares* about news?"

"There was an eighteen car pileup." The silence was sudden. "On Highway Fifty." Her eyes became deep and unreadable, then blanked out like stars on a foggy Sacramento night. "A tanker truck went over taking four cars. Three people died, a bunch more on the critical list.

"He's a cop, Charity, Highway Patrol. Do you know what they call burn fatalities?" Her hand flew to her mouth. I was relentless. "Crispy critters. Even if he'd been able to get away, and I'm sure he couldn't, barbecue might not have been the most appealing—"

She gagged, retched deep in her throat, and ran for the bathroom. I started after her, then stopped and leaned my head against the wall. It was cool and comforting, nonjudgmental; it didn't talk back. I was still there when Charity tottered back into the room.

"Kat?"

"Call him," I said, and pushed her toward the phone. "Then we'll go for pizza." I picked up my glass of wine and headed for the front room. And sat for a long time.

"Katy?"

I looked up and smiled at her.

"Rain check on the pizza?"

"Sure."

"He's going to make me dinner. A salad." Her eyes filled.

I thought about cool crisp greens, celery, radishes, tomatoes, onions, peppers, both red and yellow—

"And ice cream for dessert." The tears spilled over. "He said he was sorry and that he couldn't help it. He didn't forget at all. Oh, Katy, I felt like such a jerk."

Good, I thought, but—again wisely—didn't say.

"He has a present for me and *everything.*"

"I bet," I said, and watched her blush. Charity's the only person I know over fifteen who blushes once, sometimes twice a day.

"You know that bottle of champagne in the fridge that you've been saving for a special occasion?"

"Mmmm," I said, not really paying attention, not quite catching the drift.

"It'll be perfect. Thanks, Katy." She leaned over, champagne under her arm, brushed my cheek with hers, and was gone.

The silence now was much louder than before she had come. The memories licked at my heels as I tried to speed up, to outrun, to dodge, to get out of Dodge, to do anything at all. And Deidre's pencil-scribbled words about love and longing played in the flames and blood in the helter-skelter of my mind and refused to calm down, go away, or listen to reason.

Business as usual.

I have an office thirty minutes away in a slightly refurbished Victorian in midtown Sacramento. I went to it. I couldn't go undercover for a week or two without taking care of business. That's what I told myself, anyway.

At seven o'clock on a Friday night I was the only one there. It was peaceful: The phone didn't ring, the clock had stopped ticking four years ago. I finished up two ongoing reports, answered a stack of business letters, and started paying bills. I didn't have to be at the airport for another two hours.

Somebody knocked at the front door but I ignored it. During the day the heavy old wooden door with stained glass panels is unlocked, affording easy access to any of the four offices within. Now it was dead-bolted. Seven is way past office hours.

The knocking continued. The shouting started. "Yo, Colorado, I *know* you're in there."

I didn't recognize the voice. I signed a check giving the Sacramento Municipal Utility District, aptly called SMUD, twenty-seven dollars and thirty-two cents of my hard-earned money, then started to sign over some to Kwik-Kopy (they could copy, even though they couldn't spell). The noise stopped.

When the phone rang five minutes later my heart sank. Hank couldn't get away. He wasn't coming in from Vegas tonight after all. I picked up the receiver and bar noises moved in, filling up my mind. I heard pool balls click and beer bottles slam. It didn't make sense. Hank wouldn't call from a bar.

"Hey, Colorado, how come you don't answer your damn door?"

"Kat Colorado Investigations," I said in a brisk, toneless voice. "Please call Monday morning after nine or leave a message now." I paused, then beeped.

"Aw, Kat, for chrissakes, gimme a break. It's Murray and I need to see you. Now. You can't beep for shit either—it wouldn't fool a drunken sailor."

"Oh. Well, fortunately I don't get many calls from drunken sailors. Or criminal defense lawyers."

"Can't hear you." There was a shout, a crash, and the sound of breaking glass in the background. "Five minutes, Kat, that's all I ask."

"No!" I shouted so he could hear me.

"You want a hot dog? Sauerkraut and mustard?"

"No!" I shouted again, this time into a dead receiver.

I let him in against my better judgment but I wouldn't eat the hot dog. Judgment held firm on that. 1–1. I've had more impressive scores.

"What do you want, Murray?"

He grinned and wiped mustard off his chin, then started in on the hot dog he'd brought for me. "Hey, Kat, where are your manners?" he chided me. "What happened to Hi, Murray, how are you? What's up?"

"Someone with his mouth full, mustard on his face, and sauerkraut between his teeth is commenting on my manners?"

It was a purely rhetorical question. Murray ignores anything that doesn't interest him, another reason I loathe talking to him.

"I'm fine, thanks, and you?"

"I—"

"Yeah, well, let's move it along, Kat. I got a case I need a sharp investigator like you on."

I shook my head.

"Hey, you don't even know what it's about yet."

"Yes, I do."

He looked at me in disbelief. "Naw. News travels fast, but not *that* fast. I only picked this case up yesterday."

"Murray, you have some slimeball you want me to make look good, don't you?"

"Tsk, tsk, Kat. A man is innocent until proven guilty, entitled to a fair trial, and with the best possible defense—"

"What's he charged with?"

"Homicide."

I shook my head.

"Just listen, Kat."

I asked a question instead. "How many priors?"

"That's not relevant."

"I'm not a jury. How many?"

"Three."

"What?"

"Receiving stolen property, burglary, rape."

"Slime," I said. "I won't do it."

He grinned. "The money's good."

"Sleeping at night is better." Not that I was, but that was another story.

He stuffed the last of his/my hot dog into his mouth, balled up the waxed paper and napkins, and took aim for the wastebasket.

"No way," I said warningly. "Take that smelly stuff out with you."

He grinned and tossed it in.

"Two points. Wish I could turn you around, Kat, make you see the real world."

"Did you try to get him off the rape, too?"

"No, they had someone else. Too bad, there were a couple of points where—"

I got up, picked up the wastebasket, and stuck it in the hall. "I'm putting the trash out now, Murray; that means you."

He grinned at me, picking his teeth with a frayed toothpick. That Murray, what a class act.

"Outta step, outta time, outta date Colorado. Winning, winning fair and square, is what counts. You only want the good guys to win."

"I only *help* the good guys win," I corrected, but my voice jumped. Thoughts, too.

He heard it. "Tough call, Kat. Nobody's God."

I nodded. It was a tough call and I wasn't always right. It's why I wasn't sleeping well.

He tossed the toothpick at the wastebasket and missed. "See you. Call if you change your mind."

"Hold your breath, okay, Murray?" He laughed.

I finished the bills, then wrote a few notes to family, friends, and associates explaining that I would be out of town for a week or so. I made a mental note to talk to Timmy, my twelve-year-old neighbor, about caring for the animals.

And it still wasn't time to leave for the airport. Damn.

I fidgeted a bit, then pulled a five-by-seven spiral notebook from my purse. The papers in the carton Tobias McAlister had given me were a

16

motley assortment: folders, notebooks of several sizes, loose pages carefully sorted, numbered, and clipped together. I had thought at first it was a diary, but I didn't think so now. It seemed to be a novel, or parts of a novel or novels. Some bits were fragments, others whole sections or chapters. All were romance. I opened the notebook at random.

> Her hands reached out imploringly for him and then stopped. It was only a picture, not a flesh-and-blood man, not a living, breathing, loving person. Tears filled her eyes and her heart filled with longing. What did it matter? she thought in despair, and why did she bother?
>
> Her hand reached out again, not to touch, to bring him close, but to place the picture in the silver frame facedown. She couldn't have him anyway. She never had. She never would.
>
> Would she ever find her heart's desire?

3

My heart's desire was one of the first off the plane. For a big man he moved quickly and with an easy fluid grace. He dropped his carry-on to pick me up and swing me around, words in my ears, kisses on my face. Was this what Deidre longed for?

"Hey, Katy."

"Hey, Hank."

We smiled at each other, kissed again, and started for the exit. It doesn't take long to walk out of Sacramento Metro Airport. The car was parked at a meter fifteen yards from the terminal door. It's the kind of thing I love about Sacramento. I unlocked Hank's door, and he tossed the carry-on in the back of the Bronco and climbed in. It's the kind of thing I love about Hank.

"You look tired."

"Mmmm." He fished a cold Dr Pepper I'd put there for him out from between the bucket seats and popped the top. "Good. Thanks, sweetheart."

"Work?" I asked.

He nodded.

"Want to talk about it?"

"Not now, maybe later."

So I let it go. Hank's a detective with the Las Vegas Police Department. Sometimes he brings the job home with him, sometimes not. We let it work either way. His hand rested gently on my neck. I could feel the shivers down my back.

"Have you eaten?" I scooted off I-5 South and onto I-80 East.

"Yes." He grinned wryly. "Airport food, but it'll do. You made dinner?"

I shook my head and we laughed. Hank's the cook, not me. "I made cinnamon rolls though." I can't cook but I can bake, and I bake often for Hank. Betty Crocker had a point.

His finger traced my cheekbone and touched the corner of my mouth. I changed lanes recklessly and a big rig flashed its lights at me. It was probably a four-letter word.

"I'm glad you're here, Hank."

"Why, Katy?" His voice was soft, gentle, loving.

I cut across three lanes for the exit I've been taking for years and had almost missed. Stressed out, I can't drive for shit. Hank noticed it but didn't say anything. Another reason I love him.

"Bad dreams still?"

"Yes."

Then we meandered across Sacramento County to my part of Orangevale. Hank finished his Dr Pepper and squashed the can into an unappealing looking mass of metal. He was thinking of my nightmares, I knew. We pulled into the driveway. As I climbed out Hank whistled.

I grinned. "Nice, huh?" My little wooden, two-bedroom, old-fashioned white-with-blue-trim house was splashed with yellow. Last December in a wild moment I'd bought two hundred daffodil bulbs and six cauliflower plants. The daffs all came up and the snails ate the cauliflower. There you go.

Hank put his arm around my shoulders and hugged me into him as we walked to the gate. Ranger, my Australian shepherd, whined and danced with excitement at the sound of our voices.

The house was warm still; I'd built up the fire carefully before leaving.

Hank put another log on and I got a beer for him, a glass of wine for me, and a dog biscuit for Ranger. We plopped on the couch and stuck our feet out toward the potbellied stove, drank, kissed, and didn't talk. Hank had taught me that, to love and learn to be together again before talking. He finished his beer, took my wine glass, and headed for the kitchen and refills. Ranger thumped his tail hopefully, thinking of biscuits.

Hank reappeared with drinks but bypassed me for the bathroom, then I heard water running into the bathtub. Eventually I got up and wandered that way. The place smelled like a spicy tropical jungle whorehouse, hot water foaming into all the bath oils Hank could find.

"Hank—"

"Uh-uh, into the bath with you, you're wound tight as a top, Katy." He started unbuttoning my shirt. I shrugged it off and stepped out of my jeans and into the water. He sat on the edge of the tub ruffling my hair, splashing my back and talking small stuff.

"Hank, I want to tell you about—"

He kissed me, he handed me my glass of wine, he rubbed my back; he wouldn't listen to me until later. Fine. Two can play that game. I unbuttoned his shirt, splashed him, pulled him into the water with me.

I am the first to admit that taking off more of his clothes would have been a good idea. We should have let some water out of the tub, too. Still, that's hindsight, a damn sight more forward-thinking than love.

I didn't get much sleep that night, but not because of nightmares. When I finally drifted off it was with Hank's arms around me, daring the nightmares to approach. But they didn't. Lines from Deidre's notebook slipped in and out of my consciousness as I lay on the edge of sleep. Vaguely I remember wondering at them and thinking that perhaps she had never known love and wrote in the hopes of finding it.

But now she was dead. She never would.

Hank's arms and warmth tightened around me and I sighed and slept. Dreamlessly.

I awoke in the morning to kisses, coffee, the smell of cinnamon rolls, and a warm house. Shameless indulgence has a lot going for it. Show me where to sign. I would have dozed off again but Hank showed up with the cat, the dog, and questions.

"Scrambled eggs or an omelet?"

I shook my head. He raised an eyebrow. "I don't think I could, not without working up an appetite, anyway."

He grinned. "You want to climb into your running clothes?"

Not exactly. I stretched out, hooked a finger into the belt loop on his jeans, and pulled. It beat running by a bunch.

After working up an appetite we had omelets and cinnamon rolls. Hank poured another cup of coffee and asked me if I wanted more juice.

"Okay."

I held my juice glass out in Hank's direction and read.

"Hey, listen to this: *Dear Charity*—OUCH!"

The kitten had jumped for my lap, missed, and was sliding down my bare leg with claws extended. I grabbed for him, muttering wildly, then tossed him at Hank. They sat and listened to me whimper and then read:

Dear Charity,
We had a fairy-tale childhood but recently, after our parents died, Sis found family records detailing theft, murder, prison time (San Quentin!), adoption, illegitimacy—all this in our family tree. She's agog and wants to find out more. I want to forget it, burn all the stuff, and pretend it never happened. Help! I'm sick at heart over this.

Desperate in Duluth

Dear DD,
This is one fairy tale that won't have a happy ending. You could ask Sis not to tell you what she finds out but she probably will anyway. You're right: Truth hurts. Buy earplugs. Plan to wear them and drink warm milk at night so you can sleep.

Charity

"How important is—Hank!"

The kitten stood on the kitchen table, its two front paws on Hank's plate, lapping up a puddle of milk. His oversized, fuzzy ears twitched back at the sound of my voice and he started lapping faster. Hank picked up the kitten and the plate and put them on the floor.

"How important is—?" he asked.

"Truth."

"Important, but everybody's truth is different." Hank got up for another cinnamon roll.

"Yes. That's the problem."

He nodded. "I've spent a career in law enforcement trying to prove, if not the truth then at least a truth based on solid evidence: a car theft was committed by X; Y ran a credit card fraud; Z killed his business associate.

But what you build up from evidence is not the only 'truth'; that's why we have extenuating and mitigating circumstances. And the emotional reality for an individual is often very different from all the rest of it."

"Do people lie a lot?" I got up and walked to the refrigerator for a bottle of diet Dr Pepper. Cold caffeine. Yum.

"People?"

I stood next to him, my arm around his shoulders, swigging pop. His hand ran up my bare legs and under the tee shirt of his I was wearing.

"You don't. The people I deal with do."

"A lot?" I sat on his lap.

"A lot, often, and for a variety of reasons." He kissed the tip of my nose. "Here's an interesting one. It was a homicide case. The defendant was trying to establish an alibi by claiming he spent the night with a neighbor friend. She denied it and denied any sexual intimacy with him. She wasn't lying about him not being there—we turned up evidence to place him at the scene—but she was lying about the issue of intimacy. Why?"

I slugged down some more pop. I knew. I understood. "She was ashamed."

"Yes. Not just in front of us, or the courtroom, or the public, but in her own eyes."

Yes.

"She couldn't accept that, out of loneliness or need, she had slept with a guy who murdered an innocent old man for thirty-two dollars, a bag of Cheetos, and an opened bottle of Jack Daniels." I could understand that, too. "It was devastating to her sense of self and self-worth. So she lied."

"Her real need was not to fool you, but to create a 'truth' she could live with?"

"Exactly. And she did. I watched her perjure herself and she was one of the most believable witnesses I've seen, because by then *she* believed it. People do that all the time; not necessarily to defraud, but so they can live with themselves."

We were silent for a while. The kitten showed up again and mewed. Hank picked him up and dumped him on our laps where he purred loudly and with abandon. I patted him absentmindedly.

"Does this have anything to do with your new case?"

I nodded.

"What?"

"An old man named Tobias McAlister hired me." Hank waited patiently for me to answer the question. "To find out the truth."

I stood up abruptly and stepped on the plate Hank had put on the floor for the kitten. Gingerly I picked my foot up, sticky now with frosting from the cinnamon rolls. Then I sighed and sat back down on Hank's lap.

"The truth about what?"

"His goddaughter, Deidre, died early one morning almost five months ago in the parking lot of the Pioneer Hotel, a restaurant/bar she and her husband owned in Grass Valley. It was just before Christmas. She left the bar at two-thirty, alone and carrying a cash bag with twelve hundred dollars and a number of credit card receipts and checks in it."

Hank shook his head.

"She was shot once in the chest with no signs of a struggle. Only the cash was taken. There was a thorough investigation done as far as I can tell, though Tobias claims the contrary. She, her family, and the business were liked and respected throughout the area."

"What did the cops turn up?"

"I don't know for sure yet—I haven't talked to anyone directly involved—but apparently nothing substantial. No witnesses, no spending spree by an unlikely person, no one suspicious hanging out in the bar that evening or around that time."

"The husband?"

"Home with the three-year-old. Nothing to support that after the kid went to bed at eight, but nothing to contradict it either. Said he was reading a book."

"Katy—"

I knew what was coming, so I rushed heedlessly into where-angels-fear-to-tread territory. "The field's wide open with possibilities. Homicide in the commission of a robbery seems the most likely, but it's only the beginning. The husband was rumored to have a girlfriend; the victim's sister was fiercely competitive, maybe jealous; her brother-in-law was a not entirely innocent bystander and—"

I paused for dramatic effect but needn't have bothered. Hank was scowling at me, not waiting with bated breath.

"And Deidre had a very active romantic life, mostly fiction and fantasy, I think, but—" I shrugged "—maybe not."

"Kat."

Uh-oh, I was Kat now and he spoke in his tough cop voice. Still, it takes more than that to scare me. I stood up and narrowly missed the plate on the floor. Luck. I'm a quick study, no question about it.

"Kat, this is a homicide. A citizen, even a private investigator, has no place in a homicide investigation."

"Not an ongoing one, no." I agreed with him. "But this one's on the shelf gathering dust. Come on, let's jump in the shower and decide what we want to do with our day." I leaned over and tugged on his elbows.

He growled at me. What a tough guy. I kissed him and kept pulling.

"I hate it when you do this."

"Yes." We've been together for a while and this was not news to either of us. "I'm not crazy about your job sometimes either." Ha. That might shush him up for a bit.

"Katy—"

Good, back to Katy. "I'm not going up as a private investigator either."

"What, then?"

"Tobias wants me undercover, vacationing, looking for a job, something."

"Vacationing in Grass Valley in May?"

Stretching it a bit, I agreed, but not that much. "No, working would be better."

He raised an eyebrow.

"I'll look for a job as a bartender. It's been a while but, like bicycling, it's something you never forget. I'll be up to speed in no time." I danced a little in place, in anticipation.

He almost smiled. "You're looking forward to it."

"Yes. It's different for me now. And a challenge. A relief, too."

His hand touched my cheek gently.

"I get to step out of my reality for a little while, to be somebody else besides me, to look at somebody else's life, not mine." Deidre's words floated through my head, startling me, haunting me.

Wouldn't it be wonderful to be a heroine in a novel, to live a life that someone made up with perfection, charm, and symmetry? To believe in a world where lights always turn green, the good guys win, and love lasts? Wouldn't that be something?

Would it? Perhaps not, or only for a while.

"It will even be fun being behind a bar again."

Hank stood up, looking worried, then stepped back onto the plate and broke it. Aha, *two* quick studies. He looked chagrined, but I don't care about things like that. Plates are easy to replace, easier than broken dreams. Or hearts. So I shrugged off the broken plate.

"I've got to do something, Hank," I said softly. "I'm going nuts."

"The nightmares?"

"The nightmares," I agreed.

"You had to kill him, Katy; he would have killed you."

"Yes. I know, but it doesn't make it easy." Nothing to say to that one, for either of us. "I've got to get through the nightmares." I held out my hands helplessly. "I live with the shots in my ears, the blood, the replay of those scenes every day. It's eating me up."

His eyes were dark and unreadable. "Come to Vegas, Katy. We'll—"

I shook my head. "I have to do it on my own. Mostly." I reached for him. His arm encircled my waist, strong, sure, safe. God, I love this man.

"You don't have to do it on your own. You *can't* do it on your own. It's out of control, Katy, and you're out of control with it. You're not facing things: the killing, the issues between us, the nightmares. You're trying to run away from it."

Running, dancing, dodging, hiding, limping, I was doing it all. *You can't outrun sorrow.* You can't? I could *try.* It *might* work.

"Katy, a cop kills someone, he/she goes through counseling. It changes you. You think you're so tough you can do it on your own?"

This is an old argument with us, and yes, I do. Mostly.

"The nightmares, Katy. It's something inside trying to get out, to get help."

"I'm doing that," I said evenly. "I'm picking up the pieces, I'm going back to work. Life goes on."

He shook his head. "Listen to yourself: 'It will be good to go under-cover, to be someone else, to get away from me.' "

I covered my ears with my hands like a child. It hadn't worked then; it didn't work now.

His arms were around me, pulling me in. Then he put his hands on my wrists and drew my hands away from my ears. "Get help, Katy. Quit running."

I stared out the window. I would have said something but I couldn't think of anything. Nothing great, nothing even so-so, nothing at all. I didn't think it was a good sign.

"I'm going to put it on the line, Katy."

I *knew* that wasn't a good sign.

"I won't support you in this—too much is at stake. You're in a world of hurt, one of the walking wounded, and you should not be out there looking for a killer."

"You can't stop me." Oh, great, I was not only thinking like a five-year-old, I was talking like one.

"No."

25

"I can do what I want." Eight-year-old. There's progress for you.

"Yes."

"And I will." Twelve. Well, at least ten. I was picking up speed, no question.

"All right."

"Okay, good, fine, that's settled."

"We know where we are," he agreed, but he didn't look real thrilled about it.

And I didn't like the sound of it. "Where?" Six. Damn.

"I won't support you in this." His hands cupped my face. "If I could stop you, I would. But I can't. If you do it, you're on your own."

How can I make love stay, now and forever? How?

"But you love me."

"Yes."

"You *can't*," I wailed, back to eight again, maybe five.

"Yes. When you love someone you don't help them self-destruct. Get help, Katy."

"Hank!"

We'd just been through a bad time where we hadn't been together. No way I wanted to do that again. We were apart a lot physically and geographically, in space and in time. That was okay, that was easy as long as I had him in my life, in my mind and heart.

"Get help, Katy."

"I'm doing it this way. It'll be okay."

I was stubborn. And afraid. And I'd already chosen. I wasn't necessarily trying to do, to be these things. It just was. Sometimes things are. That night he held me but it didn't keep the nightmares away. In the morning he left.

I was on my own.

4

"I've looked for you for a long time."

"Have you?"

She looked up at him through lashes that sparkled with tears.

"I was afraid I'd never find you."

His voice almost broke.

"But you did, you have."

She fell into his arms, felt his heart thudding heavily, wildly against hers, and knew this would be the night of her dreams.

. . . .

Tuesday midmorning I sat trying to get into character, or yawning and drinking coffee, depending on your point of view. By ten-thirty I was packed and in character, a character, anyway: Kate Collins.

I didn't dare go as Kat Colorado. Too distinctive—all right, too odd—too recognizable. And I was known in my field, by name if not by face. Kate is my given name though I've never used it much. Nobody else has either since my mother died. Collins is Charity's last name. It was familiar and close enough to my name so I might even respond to it.

By eleven I was doing seventy in the center lane on I-80 East and reciting my lessons: *Hi, my name is Kate Collins. I'm new in town, looking for a place to stay and work.*

I felt freer than I had in three months. Kate hadn't shot someone she'd known and cared for, hadn't seen the splash of blood and the last spurt of a life. Kate was a bartender making a new start. I laughed out loud and turned on the radio.

At Auburn I left I-80 and got on Highway 49 named that way after the 1849 gold rush. I was in gold country. The weather was misty, off and on rainy, and gray. Everything was green but not for long. Soon the brown California summer would be here.

The radio station faded in and out on "Good Girls Don't Cry" and then "It's My Party and I'll Cry If I Want To." Was the DJ making a statement? And I thought then about how the things Deidre had written spoke for her now that she no longer could: smiles, tears, and heartthrobs; fantasy and romance.

I had a hunch about Deidre. I imagined she would prove an elusive will-o'-the-wisp character. And then, if pinned down, a chameleon, changing her colors, her persona, rewriting the script before your very eyes. Only a hunch. Okay, a hunch and the photographs I'd seen at Tobias's house.

I wasn't doing seventy anymore. North of Auburn much of Highway 49 is curvy two-lane, not valley terrain, foothills. I poked along sedately behind a grandma in a battered Chrysler. A stud behind me in an orange Prelude and a hurry kept gunning the engine to ride my bumper, then falling back, then gunning it again. It seemed to be his only trick but he didn't tire of it. Grandma and I held up pretty well.

It had been open country at first, fields with oaks, farm houses with barns. I passed an old stone house with a metal roof. Fire danger is fierce in the hot dry California summer and many of the old wooden houses are gone. There was an occasional picket fence, but barbed wire or split rail was more common. Trucks, farm equipment, and junker cars with For Sale signs on them were parked in driveways and on side roads. We Californians love our cars. Most places had piles of firewood, down now in the spring; some had flowers. The grass everywhere was lush and green.

I hadn't been paying attention to time and mileage, but it wasn't far, I knew it by the countryside. First the pines had started closing in on the fields and oaks, and now at this higher elevation, they were dominant.

I pulled into Grass Valley, "Grass Valley—♥ of the Gold Country," a huge sign painted on a building told me. The heart had once been painted a deep gold. The sign was old, weathered, and accurate. Beneath today's charming, quiet, and quaint streets and houses, more than 960 million dollars of gold had been extracted by The Empire Mine and other nearby mines in times past.

It was 1:30. I found a room at the Sleepy Niner Motel, picked up a local paper, and went into a bakery café for lunch and to read the want ads. Nobody wanted a bartender. Yet. Kate, the optimist.

That afternoon I walked around Grass Valley and Nevada City, "Queen of the Northern Mines," three miles down the road. They were both gold-mining towns and the history and charm is still there in restored gold miners' cottages and the classy Victorian homes of the owners and merchants, now bed-and-breakfast inns.

Nevada City's gaslamp-lit downtown is a designated historical preservation district, and the Nevada Theatre is the oldest operating theater west of the Rockies. Museums, shops, and restaurants abound on the hilly and sometimes narrow and winding streets. I've been here a fair amount over the years. I love that sense of another time, another California. I was glad to be here now.

At six I headed back to the motel to sleep for a couple of hours. I don't do my best work running on almost empty and twenty-hour days. I got up at eight and dressed sharp—for me, all things are relative—in designer jeans, boots, a silk blouse, and a leather jacket. I was Kate and I almost didn't recognize myself in the mirror. All right! I had the undercover angle down for sure.

I'd walked past the Pioneer Hotel earlier, past but not into. It was not far from the older and more famous Holbrooke, a hotel with the oldest bar in the state and a guest register that boasted names like Mark Twain, Bret Harte, Lotta Crabtree, Black Bart, Lola Montez, Grover Cleveland, Benjamin Harrison, and Ulysses S. Grant, in a who's who of California and U.S. history. In a quiet moment you could feel that history, a resident not a visitor, here and throughout the area.

The Pioneer had been Deidre and Matt's place, if you can really own something that is so much older and more knocked-around than you, and was now Matt's. I liked the look and feel of it right away. It wasn't a hotel anymore but a restaurant and bar, a wooden structure surrounded by old brick buildings painted cream or white with trim in yellow, green, and red. There were benches on the sidewalk in front of the Pioneer where earlier I had seen old codgers rolling cigarettes and sunning themselves. It was a town where people knew each other, said hello, and stopped to visit.

A nice town, but murder happens even in nice towns.

I climbed wide wooden steps leading up to an imposing set of carved doors that swung open effortlessly. They'd been truly hung, workmanship from another and bygone era, and decorated with ornate carvings and letters spelling out THE PIONEER HOTEL.

Inside a long, old, and scarred wooden bar ran the length of the room to the right, making a slight L at the faraway wall. To the left a number of tables, wrought iron stands with beat-up wooden tops, filled up space in a crowded but hospitable way. About a third had customers. All had flowers. In May? In Grass Valley? Welcome to the Pioneer.

The walls were covered in old-fashioned wallpaper—the kind with violets and overblown pale pink roses climbing an improbably rickety trellis—and with old bric-a-brac and photographs. It was real and was therefore pleasing rather than a faux period statement. A massive grandfather clock stood in one corner.

Echoes of the past hung here too, floated in the air and in the yesterday eyes of the photographs. Local talk had it that the ghost of a miner visited, perhaps resided, here. Elihu Ogden McCall had struck it rich and asked his sweetheart, Angel Murphy, to marry him. She accepted, but then, foolishly, he had been cheated out of his fortune, or lost it at cards; the story varied.

Angel, unable to live up to her name, had left him in a hot minute and, though it was to take years, Elihu set out to drink himself to death. Late at night sometimes he was seen at the bar wreathed in cigar smoke with a glass of whiskey cradled in his hands, sorrow in his heart. Sometimes, they said, the faint sound of a honky-tonk piano could be heard.

I had never seen him, but I didn't disbelieve. I didn't see him now, but it wasn't late enough. At the bar I sat down next to the waitress stand and just down from the bartender, a bar hot spot and central location. And very much in the present.

I settled in with an ease bred of familiarity and comfort, my elbows on the bar, my feet on the brass rail. Home sweet home. My face gazed back at me from an old mirror with beveled edges and a heavy gilt frame that was hung behind the bar. Another face edged mine out.

"Good evening."

"Hi."

The bartender looked two to three years older than I am, midthirties, light brown hair already streaked with gray, and a lopsided smile. Nothing quite matched; nothing quite made sense. There was even a scar. Yet he was very good-looking. It adds up that way sometimes. Gray eyes framed in sun- and smile-wrinkles looked down at me.

"What can I get you?"

"White wine, please."

He nodded, picked up a wine glass, and filled it. The house wines were on tap here. The liquid in my glass bubbled and frothed a bit as I stared at it glumly. Swill no doubt. Phooey. What good was it being on an unlimited expense account? I could hardly step out of my assumed job-hunting character and order the good stuff.

"One seventy-five." There was a twenty on the bar in front of me. He made no move to take it. "You're new in town." It was a statement, not a question, and it didn't make him a detective. In May, in Grass Valley, the tourist trade is just starting. That left business or new in town.

"Order, please." The waitress spoke before I could.

"Yeah?"

"Bourbon water, Scotch soda, vodka tonic, Tom Collins, snowshoe, brandy up, coffee back. That Jimmie gonna drive me crazy he tells me any more dumb jokes tonight, I swear."

The waitress was young and blond, pretty in a vapid, unformed way. She pulled the hair out of her eyes with a tired, almost fretful gesture and garnished the drinks as they came up. The bartender's movements were studied, careful. He poured with familiarity but not with ease or assurance. It wasn't something he did full-time or even all that often.

The sound of a glass breaking sliced into the jukebox music and my thoughts.

"Aw, *shit!*" The waitress grabbed a bar rag. "Jimmie, I bet. Shit! I'm cutting him off."

My interest in being a bartender declined. This part of it was depressingly familiar.

"Tonight the Bottle Let Me Down," Emmy Lou wailed from the jukebox. That, too, was familiar. Home sweet home? I had forgotten how quickly one can tire of "home."

"Damn."

It was spoken softly, to himself. I looked up, catching his eye without meaning to.

The bartender looked rueful and snapped his fingers. "I forgot one." He shrugged and grinned lopsidedly at me.

I looked at the drinks on the pour pad. "Snowshoe." It was automatic, years of training paying off. Even now I can't sit at a bar without memorizing a call order; it's a reflex that I have no control over.

"Yeah." He grinned again. "No wonder I forgot." He looked at me, an eyebrow cocked.

"Turkey rocks, schnapps float."

Emmy Lou and Jimmie were both singing now. It was easy to tell who was the professional. The waitress was back.

"Dragging a coffee, Matt."

Matt. Aha. The investigator in me perked right up. Matt Durkin got the coffee and another glass of wine for me.

"Thanks for the help."

"Sure. You don't have to—"

He dismissed my protest. "My pleasure."

"Thank you."

He put his hands on the bar and leaned toward me. I could see a small scar jumping in his left eyebrow.

"Are you a bartender?"

I nodded.

"Want a job?"

I nodded again.

"It's yours."

I had what I came for.

It seemed too easy.

5

She knew the instant she laid eyes on him, his body tall and hard, strong and perfect. His eyes drilled into hers and into her heart as well. He made no move to come toward her, to come close, to touch her. He didn't have to, she was his, for now and maybe forever. She knew it in that first instant.

. . . .

"Do you want references, a job history, that sort of thing?"

"Do I need it?"

I looked at his handsome scarred face. Maybe not. "You're the boss."

He shrugged. "I trust my judgment, first impressions. How much experience?"

"Six years."

"You don't look like you'd still be in it." Our eyes held for a long time.

"I just moved up here. Things changed for me and I'm trying to start over."

"Where are you from?"

"Sacramento."

"What's your name?"

"Kate Collins." I lied like a trouper, no hesitation, no stumbling. On one hand it was a good sign, on the other it wasn't. I'm used to predicaments like this. Unfortunately.

"Seven an hour, four nights a week, Tuesday through Friday. You come on at five, work to closing, usually around midnight, earlier if it's slow. You can have more hours in the summer when it picks up if you want them. Wear whatever you want. Jeans are fine. Okay?"

"Okay."

"Can you start tomorrow?"

"Yes."

He left to make drinks and I sipped on my wine and made my face go blank.

"Kate, this is Charlene."

"Hi! Hey, Matt says you're the new bartender." She grinned. "Hope you're faster than he is. On a slow night like tonight, it's no biggie but sometimes we get buried."

I smiled. "I'm fast." Correction, I thought wryly: I *used* to be fast.

Matt winked at me. "Three tables in a row and she's 'buried.' "

"Oh, you!" Charlene wadded up a cocktail napkin and threw it at him, missing, then drifted off to her tables. Jimmie was singing again. I hoped he didn't come in every night.

Someone fed the jukebox and the Police sang that wherever I went, whatever I did, they'd be watching me. Spooky. I shivered, then picked up the conversation with Matt the way you do with a bartender when there's a lull.

"A bartender quit on you?"

He wiped down the bar in front of me. "You could say that." Three men came in hollering for drinks and attention. "Look, can you close with me tonight? I'd like to walk you through our procedure."

"Sure." The grandfather clock bonged the half hour, nine-thirty. "I'm going to get something to eat. I'll be back. What time?"

"Eleven-thirty."

I left half a glass of wine on the bar and started to get up. Everyone was watching me. I wasn't just a newcomer anymore, I was the new bartender. News travels fast.

"Don't take you long, huh, Matt?"

The Pioneer got quiet fast. Even the echoes from the past stilled. I heard a drip in the sink as I froze in place, then glanced in the mirror at the guy who had spoken. He was stocky and nice looking, about fifty-five with clean, well-worn clothes—old jeans, and a wool shirt. His hands were wrapped around the full beer he'd been nursing, his pale eyes on Matt.

"Naw, I'd say it sure don't." He answered his own question.

"Why don't you just leave it at that, Bobbie," Matt said evenly.

"I don't reckon I will, Matt. I was a betting man I wouldn't have bet you could move so fast. You go through the ladies real damn quick, don't you. Pretty ones, too." His pale eyes flicked over me.

Like Lot's wife, I was frozen in place.

"Nothing against you, miss. You're new in town, I know that. New in town and probably a nice gal looking for a good job. But this ain't it."

"That's enough, Bobbie."

"I don't reckon it is. You see, Deidre had a lot of friends here. She was our bartender. There ain't none of us happy about what happened to her. A lot of us got our ideas about it. Maybe not from the first, maybe not right off. No. You got friends in this town too, Matt. I know, I used to be one of 'em. But not anymore. I seen too much now. The ladies, the other stuff." His voice was raspy with anger.

"Here's to your memory, Deidre." Bobbie swung his beer mug high in the air. "You were a damn fine lady, a helluva friend, a damn good bartender." He drank the beer in three swallows and stood. "I reckon I'll take my business elsewhere.

"Good luck, little lady." He spoke to me. "Stay on your toes now. Keep yourself safe."

The place was dead silent after he left. The walls at the Pioneer had witnessed a lot over the last hundred and fifty or so years. There was blood spilled here, passion, secrets, and betrayal; lovers found, friendships broken. The clock ticked. The faucet dripped. Dead silent.

Matt Durkin broke it. "Bobbie's entitled to his opinion," he said. "Anyone who agrees, he's free to go, no hard feelings."

The muscle in his eyebrow jumped and twitched. The words were okay, but his eyes were ugly, his mouth twisted, his shoulders squared off as if for a fight. He didn't wait to see if anyone would take him up on his offer.

"You lost a bartender, I lost a wife. Lost her, not killed her." His voice was low, deadly.

No one said a word. We were focused on survival, that's why, and were too smart to speak. Durkin looked like he could kill, was ready, eager even, just needed a reason, and anything would do.

I cleared my throat. "You got a minute, Matt, I'll take another." I had a half full drink in front of me.

"Yeah. Me, too."

"Shot of schnapps here, Matt."

"Gimme a coffee, okay?"

They spoke up one at a time. Matt's face relaxed but the muscle in his eyebrow jumped still. Somebody fed the jukebox. Matt made the drinks. Charlene got busy serving them.

"What the hell happened to your truck, Matt?" the coffee drinker at the end of the bar asked conversationally.

Durkin's eyebrow jumped again. He poured a short draft and drank it.

"Looks like someone shot the hell out of it—windshields all busted out that way. Goddamn kids or what?"

"Don't know," said Durkin. "Hell of a deal, though. Sure going to cost me." He put the empty glass down on the bar.

"They spray your truck at the same time?"

Durkin nodded. "Just about, I guess."

"Shot out your windows? Sprayed the truck? Spray paint?" Charlene asked. Durkin nodded. "What's going on, Matt? I don't get it. Who would do that? And why?"

"Kids, I guess."

"What'd they write?"

"Buy American." The scar jumped. *He's lying,* I thought.

"Huh? You have a Ford, don't you?"

"Dumb kids, I guess."

Charlene started to speak, then stopped when she saw Matt's face. I didn't blame her; I would have too. There was silence, then the jukebox whirred and a song about a stranger in the house came on. Nobody moved or spoke. I took a sip of wine, then slugged the rest down. What the hell. I got up.

Matt looked at me. "You coming back?"

"Yes."

His shoulders relaxed a little as he pushed my money back across the bar to me, a bartender's shorthand for thank you.

I was back at eleven-thirty, fortified by expectations, a sandwich, and coffee, but not as cheerful and excited as I had been. No kidding. The place was quiet. No customers. Charlene was wiping tables and Matt was washing glasses. He paused and tossed up a heavy pass-through section of the bar for me.

"C'mon back."

Charlene stuck her cash caddy in her purse, put her tray away, and tossed a couple of filthy bar rags on the bar.

"Night, you two."

Matt glanced up and a look I couldn't decipher bounced around between them. "I'll walk you to your car." His voice was hard, abrupt.

"Don't bother. Steve's here." That look again. She flipped a hand at me. "Bye, see you tomorrow."

Matt followed her across the floor, then locked the door. We worked our way through cleanup, accounting, and security. It was nothing I didn't know but every place has its own rules.

"You're quick," Matt said.

I nodded modestly. I am, it's true.

"And good?" he asked.

Another nod.

"You'll do fine here. Look—" A vein in his temple throbbed. He changed his tone with an effort, made it soft though he couldn't make it gentle. "Sit down and have a drink, okay?"

"All right."

He pulled out a bottle of decent white wine from the reach-in, opened it and set it on the bar with clean glasses. Poured for both of us, then tipped his glass back and drank slowly, steadily, emptied his glass and poured again.

"Hey. You drink that way, you might as well drink house white."

No smile, no nothing. I sat and ran my finger around the rim of my glass without drinking, wondering what I had signed on for.

"You asked if I wanted references?"

"Yes."

"Hell, I hired you without even knowing your name."

"Yes."

"I don't care. You won't stay long. Why should you? You're too smart, too pretty—" He'd been looking at his hands; now he looked up at me in the mirror. "Tall, slim, curly brown hair, and those green eyes. Don't see eyes like that often." He was looking straight at me in the mirror, then his eyes dropped to his hands again. "I'm just hoping you'll stay long enough for—" He broke off. "Why are you here?"

I was getting used to the abrupt conversational changes. "Here?" I kicked at the brass rail. "Good wine and the price is right, so-so company—" He almost smiled and I gave myself points for it. "What is this, Truth Night? Spilling Guts at the Pioneer Bar Time?"

"Why not?" There was something reckless about his eyes. "I am. No. You don't have to. Your life is yours, not mine. The job is yours, too." He refilled his wine glass.

I took a deep breath. I was going to have to tell a story sooner or later, it might as well be now.

"I'm not what I seem."

"Yeah. Who is?" He sounded incurious.

"I'm living a lie."

That one was greeted with silence. I stayed there for a while. I was still telling the truth so it was a nice place to be.

"And?" His voice was low.

And I started lying. "You're right, what you said about my not staying places real long. I'm on the run. A guy threatened me so I took off, left my life in Sacramento behind. For a while, anyway. Kate Collins isn't my name and I'm not a bartender, although I used to be. As I said, I'm not what I seem." My voice sounded clear, strong, and untroubled, and it said I was the kind of person he could believe, even telling lies.

He looked at me and I met his glance for a while before my eyes dropped, stumbling slightly over these lies and the lies to come.

"*You can't outrun sorrow*. My wife's godfather says that. I'm sorry for you."

I ignored it for now. I had lies to tell.

He touched my arm and his voice was soft. "That's rough."

I choked up a little, not because it was rough but because I felt cheapened by the lies.

He touched my arm again, undemanding, quickly. "Hey, you're here for a while, that's fine. Maybe we can help each other out. Your life calms down and I get things straight. Look, Katie—"

I shivered. He saw it.

"I'm sorry, that was presumptuous. May I call you that? You look more like a Katie somehow than a Kate."

"Kate would be better." I said it, but I couldn't look him in the eye as I did.

"Sure. Okay."

There was silence between us but it was the easy companionable kind now.

"Why?" I asked finally.

"Why?"

"Why don't you care? How do you know you can't outrun sorrow? Why did your bartender quit? Those whys."

"Yeah. Okay. Go ahead, skip the small talk."

I looked up quickly. There was a lopsided grin on his lopsided face. "You look nice when you smile."

He frowned.

"Of course, you wouldn't want to overdo it."

"Damn you, Kate." But his voice said he didn't mean it.

"It's the bar," I said. "In the early morning when the bar is closed, the register down, the shades pulled and the bartender on this side of the bar, that's when you talk, tell the truth. A truth," I amended. "There are too many to tell, of course."

He stared at me.

"You know," I continued, "we've both sat here before." A lot in my case; his too, I was betting.

He looked like he was going to say something but he didn't; he poured the last of the bottle of wine before he spoke.

"I know you can't outrun sorrow because I've tried and I'm a fast runner, Kate Collins or whatever your name is. I think, no, I *hope* you can face it down and walk away from it. That takes courage. Maybe more than I have right now, maybe more than I have anytime, but I can't face that either. Not right now. Hey, you saw what happened tonight."

The scar twitched. His shoulders squared off, tightened up.

"My bartender didn't quit. She was murdered. And she wasn't my bartender. She was my partner and a fill-in bartender for our business. She was also my wife and the mother of our child."

I drank the rest of my wine and set the glass down too suddenly, too sharply.

Matt got up, walked around the bar, pushed behind the stored fruit in the reach-in and pulled out another bottle of wine. He grabbed an opener off the back bar, then stood there, handing it to me finally. "She was only twenty-nine. Toby, our son, is not quite three."

I cut the foil and pulled the cork out with a pop.

"She'll always be twenty-nine. He'll grow up without her; I'll grow old alone."

I thought that highly unlikely but now didn't seem to be the time to say so.

"There's more."

Yes, I thought, there always is; that's what the bad dreams are about.

"It doesn't get better."

No. Often, all too often it doesn't.

"The cops think maybe I killed her. They can't prove I did it; I can't prove I didn't. Hell of a deal. And they're not the only ones, I guess. The damage to my truck? It was worse than I let on. It wasn't just that someone shot out the windows, though that's bad enough. It was that I was in the truck at the time. I was. My son was." His voice was hard and ugly.

"Who?"

"I don't know. I was at a four-way stop in a remote part of the county. I didn't see anything and I didn't go looking. Couldn't. Not with my son there."

"And the graffiti?"

"*Killer. Murderer.* Drawings of a gun and drops of blood. Ugly."

"Kids?" I didn't believe it, but I wanted to hear what he would say.

He didn't answer. I poured the wine. He came around the bar and sat next to me. We drank, slowly now, and thoughtfully.

"People here in town have known us for a long time. Nobody's come right out and asked if I killed her, though some of them maybe think like Bobbie. Some of them sympathize with me and my boy. Sometimes they bring casseroles and cookies, or home-baked bread. Sometimes they stay, visit, shoot the shit. They come in here now more than ever. This is a hot spot, Kate, Grass Valley's most recent murder site. Hell of a deal, huh?"

His voice was loud and hard. I flinched, but inside.

"I loved my wife."

That's what they all say, I thought, talking tough to myself. *You're a private investigator, Kat, a trained and neutral observer, a—*

"That's what they all say, I know."

"Yes."

"I didn't kill her."

I drank my wine. They all say that, too.

"They say that, too, I know."

I was silent. People watch too damn much TV these days.

He got up, walked around the bar, picked up a package of corn nuts, opened it and spilled them across the bar, then sat down again and we ate them. I rubbed the salt off on my hands and then rubbed my hands on my jeans. And drank.

"They don't ask me but they think it: *Did you do her? Did you take the money to make it look like a robbery? Did she die easy or hard? Was it worth it? Why did you do it? What kind of slime are you?* I read it in their eyes, in the way they walk and talk, in what they don't say. I pretend I don't see it but I do and it's getting to me. It's killing something in me like someone killed her."

I drank and did what *they* did: wondered if I were sitting next to a murderer, wondered if he could read the conjecture in my eyes, in my silence; wondered most of all if he guessed that I was pretending, too.

He poured more wine. We drank. I'd decided long ago that I was walking back to the motel.

"Who did?"

"Who did what?" he asked, his eyes hooded and dark. I thought the question overly ingenuous but wrote it off to stress and alcohol.

"If you didn't kill her, who did?"

6

She twisted the handkerchief through her fingers. "I thought my love for him would die."

"And?" her friend asked.

"It's stronger than ever." Her breath caught on a sob. "And then . . . then I thought I could kill that love but—but I couldn't." She broke down and wept.

. . . .

"I don't want to do that."

He picked up a corn nut, tossed it in the air, leaned back and caught it. Cute. Not like seals of course. They're really cute, clapping their flippers, smacking their tails, and barking. I do a pretty good seal bark imitation, too, but I held myself back.

"Do what?"

"Do what everyone's doing to me, speculate on the guilt of possibly—no, probably—innocent people."

"It's a good Christian sentiment and it makes you look like a swell guy, Matt, but it doesn't do a damn thing to dig you out from your hole, does it?"

Uh-oh. I sounded a whole lot more like an investigator than a recently hired bartender. His head snapped up. He'd noticed. Damn.

"No wonder people are after you," he said.

I flushed.

"Look, do you always talk like this?"

I nodded. "My mother named me after Kate in *The Taming of the Shrew*. I probably would have been a perfectly okay kid if she'd called me Amanda, or Jessica, or Julie—sweet, soft-spoken, never out of line, handy with the perfect sentiment instead of a smart-ass crack or a pushy question."

He laughed. Boy, he was a looker when he wiped that sad, beat-up, crashed-around-like-an-old-Ford-pickup-with-junk-and-empty-beer-cans-in-the-back expression off his face.

"Do you mind?" What the hell? I was pushing my luck anyway, might as well go for it.

"No," he said. "No, I don't. It's a relief. You're the only one who has spoken honestly to me since she was killed." He smiled wryly. "Except for her godfather. He said I goddamn well better not be the one who shot her, or he'd see I rotted in jail for it. That was at the funeral."

It sounded like Tobias, all right. I looked at Matt's profile, the scar in his eyebrow jumping and twitching. He poured more wine. It was that kind of a night. *In vino veritas?* I hoped for that anyway.

"Nobody believes I didn't do it."

"I'm sure your son loves you, trusts you, believes in you, though he's not old enough to put it that way."

"Yeah." There was a note of surprise in his voice. "Except for Toby." He thought about it. "What do you think?"

"That's not fair, Matt."

"No," he agreed, "it's not. I want an answer anyway."

"I don't think you did it." I was surprised to hear myself saying it, feeling it. *In vino veritas?* "But I don't know."

"And you'll be looking, wondering." It was said bitterly.

"Oh, yes, but everybody always does that about everything, so don't start feeling sorry for yourself. Right now you're doing that about me, looking, wondering."

"That's true." He sounded surprised. "It's natural, I guess."

"Yes, so try not to be so thin-skinned. People don't know and can't help wondering. And you're overlooking a big part of the problem."

"What?" His eyebrow had stopped jumping.

"Many, no, *most* women who are murdered are killed by a husband or boyfriend. It's something people understand."

"No!"

"I didn't say condone, and I'm still trying to get to the problem."

"Go on."

"If you didn't do it, it's one of *them*, somebody else's husband, or friend, or neighbor or—" I broke off, left it there. "You see?"

"Yeah. I do."

And it wasn't pretty.

"My friends—" He laughed uneasily and shrugged.

I nodded to show I heard the inflection on the word "friends" and understood.

"They're going for the stranger-in-town theory."

"Yes." I wasn't surprised; it's always a popular and comforting notion in a case like this. "Let me guess: A guy comes in for a drink at last call. Deidre lets him stay because he seems nice enough. He offers to walk her to the car and—"

"Only it couldn't have happened like that."

"Atta boy, Matt. Adjust that noose, tighten that knot."

He snorted.

"You don't know," I pointed out reasonably. "You said you weren't there."

"A couple of regulars were, though. They finished their drinks and left together. She locked the door behind them, they heard the dead bolt. Usually she would have left with them. I don't like her to leave alone that time of night. She didn't like it either, rarely did it. And here's what I *really* don't get."

His voice sounded unhappy and puzzled. I waited.

"We have a safe and the money should have gone in there. She *never* left with any money and everyone knew it. Hell, I made a point, a big point, of broadcasting that the money was always in the safe and *never* on her. I didn't ever want anyone waiting for her, thinking she had money, hurting her—"

I went for shock tactics. "Killing her."

"Yes," he said, his voice miserable. "You know, Kate, it's been hard for me to mourn this, to cry over her. It's not fair, I know, but I'm mad at her, not just for leaving me and Toby alone, but for the stupidity of leaving with the cash bag."

I wondered if it had been stupidity.

"For that she got herself killed."

Maybe, I thought; and maybe not.

"And I'm under suspicion. *She knew better than that, goddammit!*"

44

Yes. That was why it was so curious. The right questions were not being asked here.

He put his head in his hands. "It's hard to grieve when you're struggling to hold your head up, to pretend you don't see the suspicion in everyone's eyes, to pretend everything's okay. I'm not being fair to her, to her memory, her death, but I can't help it. Goddamn. The porch light's on but nobody's home. Goddamn, I'm tired."

His voice was exhausted and dead. He poured more wine.

"I'm sorry," I said. It was the best I could do. "I'm *really* sorry," I added, making it clear I had a way with words as well as a sense of compassion.

He didn't say anything. Me, either. My way with words had temporarily deserted me.

He sloshed wine around in his glass. "Just bar talk? Middle of the night, shades pulled, defenses down, wine talk?"

"Not just bar talk." Investigator talk.

Another silence.

"Would you like to go on a picnic with me and Toby tomorrow?"

A picnic? In the (probably) rain? With a man the whole town figures is a murderer? "Sure."

"Good."

I pushed my glass back and we both stood up.

"Where are you staying?"

"The Sleepy Niner Motel for now."

"They're good folks there. I'll walk you to your car."

"It's okay. I think I'll walk back, not drive. I've had a lot to drink; I'll pick up my car in the morning."

"No," he said. "You won't walk. After the shooting I don't take chances."

I swallowed my reply. I remembered my heart-pounding, adreneline-racing nightmares. This was his nightmare, and as real as mine. He put our glasses in the sink and picked up the keys off the back bar.

"Wait for me at the front door while I set the alarm. I'll drive you." I didn't say anything. His hand touched my arm. "Kate, he's still loose, still out there, and it's two-thirty."

Yes. Good point. "Okay," I said, croaked really. I was a tough guy, for sure. Two points for me.

Ten minutes later, we pulled up in front of the motel. "Would you like me to see you in?"

"I'm okay."

"Is eleven-thirty tomorrow all right?"

"Yes."

"We'll pick you up." He held out his hand. "Nice to know you, Kate."

"Same here."

We shook on it. He thought about kissing me, I could tell.

I woke up at nine-thirty to the steady beat of rain. Kat had nightmares, Kate slept like a baby. I let a hot shower pound some of the hangover out of me, gulped down painkillers, and headed for the coffee shop. Coffee and toast, and I didn't fill up, just in case. Then I went back to my room at the Sleepy Niner, as a walk in the rain to pick up my car was not an appealing thought. Instead I read more of Deidre's romance novel.

> **His lips caressed her, her mouth, her neck, her breasts. She felt helpless with a passion she had never known, never even imagined. He trailed kisses across her breasts and down, down across her belly, down into the secret essence of her womanhood. Into the sweet softness of her very being, his tongue sought and found her.**

The phone rang. I jumped. Eleven-thirty. I'd lost track of time and place, was lost too in wondering about Deidre Durkin, and about her world and what was real and what wasn't.

Matt's voice was warm and cheerful, the opposite of the rain. "Wake you up?"

I laughed. "I'm tougher than that."

"Good. Grab your slicker and meet us out front in twenty minutes."

No slicker, just my leather jacket. I watched for them, ran for Matt's truck, making fast tracks. It was a stellar dash except for the puddle I hadn't noticed in time. So it goes. I hauled open the door and climbed in.

"That was a *really* big splash!" A solemn little face greeted me from a car seat buckled into the middle belt. Matt's arm across the back of the seat gripped my shoulder briefly.

I grinned at the kid. "Hey, I bet you're Toby."

He nodded, still solemn. "You've got mud on your face." There was an almost scared note there.

"Ooops. Help me, okay?" I leaned forward.

46

He hesitated briefly. "Okay." A little hand reached out and tentatively rubbed my cheek.

"Thank you." That got a half-smile from him. "I'm Kate. Hi." I held out a hand.

He hesitated again, then squeezed it. "Hi." He pulled his hand away quickly, still not sure, and leaned back in his seat toward Dad.

"Hi, Kate."

"Hi, Matt."

The truck roared into life and we took off into the rain. It was like driving in a waterfall.

"Four-wheel drive, I hope."

He laughed. "We won't need it, but I've got it."

We drove for about fifteen minutes. I paid attention at first but then gave up. The waterfall obscured local landmarks: trees, houses, stop signs, roads. Toby and I played peek-a-boo and then I taught him patty-cake. He took to both with great enthusiasm. I could see his interest was going to outlast mine, but only by five or six hours. No big deal.

We pulled into what seemed to be a driveway and slowed. By squinting I could see a large gray blur. Aha. Either a small and sudden hill, or a house. The truck crept forward into a carport. Toby stopped playing patty-cake to sing.

"We're home, we're home, we're ho-o-o-ome."

We piled out and dashed for the door. It was unlocked. I skidded on the flagstone floor of the entry and bumped up against a wall and Toby's giggles. The heat from the free-standing stove in the living room was definite and welcome.

"Look!"

Toby pulled at my hand as I shrugged out of my jacket and tossed it on the coat rack. I looked.

"Isn't it neat?!"

It was. Truly. A blue-and-white checked tablecloth was spread out on the floor. Paper plates, napkins, and a little antique glass vase of dried flowers were carefully set upon it.

"I helped! I helped!" Toby was jumping up and down.

"Wow!" I said with my usual impressive command of the English language.

Matt grinned. "Hungry?"

Suddenly I was. "Starved."

They wouldn't let me do anything as they loaded up the tablecloth with bread, cheese, cold cuts, potato salad, apple and orange slices, cookies, and sparkling cider. It was a feast and we did it justice. There wasn't a dainty or picky eater among us. Thank God.

Afterward I lay on the floor between the fire and the food (good move, Kate!) with Toby next to me.

"You're nice. I like you. Will you come again?"

I felt suddenly shy and didn't know what to say. I was, after all, an investigator, and this was a job. But not *just* a job. Not anymore.

"Will you?"

"Yes, if you ask me." So I got over it. Too fast, too—

"We will, huh, Dad?"

"I reckon." He smiled down at me.

"That means yes," Toby translated gravely, and I nodded. "You're pretty. My mommy was pretty. She's never coming back again but it's not because she doesn't love me. She does." He looked at me and waited.

"Yes, I'm sure she does."

"She *does*. Lots. Very much, very very very *very* much. Daddy said so and God does too only now she loves me from Heaven. I know that she's happy in Heaven but I miss her. I want her here. I don't want her to go away. Not ever."

The tears weren't in Toby's eyes, they were in mine.

Childlike, he pushed his grief into another compartment. "After lunch I always take my nap. I sleep with Bear and Daddy kisses me. Will you kiss me too? Bear cries at night if nobody loves him and kisses him. I wake up sometimes and he's crying."

"Do you hold him then and kiss him?" I asked.

"Yes." His dark head bobbed up and down. "And Daddy does too. He lets us come and get in bed with him and then Bear doesn't wake up lonely and afraid anymore."

"I'm glad you have such a nice daddy."

"Yes, me too." He thought it over. "But I want my mommy back. God doesn't need her as much as I do."

I was still lying on my stomach on the floor when Matt sat down next to me, Toby and Bear having been tucked in for their naps and kissed by both of us.

"Kate?"

"My little sister died," I said in a choked voice, "when she was just three. My mother was a drunk and let it happen." I could hear the judgment in my voice. "My sister slept with me—to keep the nightmares away."

Nightmares. I put my head down on my arms. Matt leaned over me and patted the top of my head the same way he had patted Bear. Hank was right. I was too wounded, too vulnerable, still in trouble.

Matt let me be for a while, then he moved to stoke the fire. "You've been through it. You understand what it's like for us then." His voice was oddly impassive. I listened for sorrow but didn't hear it. *It?* I wondered why he never said his wife's name aloud. "Kate, help me. You're smart. And you're new in town with a fresh view on things. I need that. You can see what I'm too wrapped up in to notice. I need that too. I need help with this."

I took a deep breath. So far I'd been a real big help. Right. When in doubt, ask a professional.

"Help me find her killer, the truth. Help me and Toby start again. There's been too much talk—I don't want to go through life with Bobbie and others like him thinking I did it. Help me figure it out. You're right here. You could keep your eyes open, be more than a bartender."

He handed it to me: permission to poke around. It seemed too easy. Again.

"Okay," I said at last.

"Good."

"The truth can be tough, *real* tough, Matt."

"Yes."

"If we go for it, we go for it."

"Yes."

It was a dangerous path we were on. Matt thought he understood, but he didn't, he couldn't. He hadn't done this before.

I did. I had.

And I felt a shiver of fear.

7

He looked at her with come-hither eyes and spoke in a sexy, low-pitched drawl.

"May I help you?" she asked in her best schoolmarm voice, a little stern, a little disapproving.

"I hope so." He smiled at her.

She melted like a chocolate bar on a hot day.

....

"Tell me about Deidre."

"What do you mean?"

"What kind of a person was she? What were her hopes and dreams? Her fears? What made her happy or sad? Did she have problems, enemies—"

"Jesus Christ! You're getting pretty damn personal, aren't you?"

"You asked for my help, Matt," I said reasonably.

"Help, yes, that's not the same as a third degree!"

"If we figure out why she died, maybe we can figure out who is responsible for it." An FBI principle, but I didn't bother bringing that up. "Was it random violence, a crime of passion, murder by someone who would gain financially, a crime committed in a rage—"

"Enough. You've made your point."

Not quite. "In order to determine why a crime was committed you need to know as much as possible about the victim. There is no privacy and there are no secrets in a homicide case." It was time to get down to business. This was the help he had asked me for.

Matt looked at his wristwatch. "It's getting late. I shouldn't be taking up your whole afternoon like this."

Yeah, I thought, *there's a lot of fun stuff I want to do in the rain.*

"Let me check with Elsa next door and see if she can watch Toby while I run you back."

He got up, pulled on his slicker, and walked out. It was like having a door slammed in my face, maybe on a couple of fingers too. I picked up food and utensils, threw away the paper plates, shook out the tablecloth over the sink, then folded it. While Rome burned and Nero fiddled, housewives were doing dishes, folding laundry, and baking cookies. I would bet on it.

"Kate, this is my neighbor, Elsa."

I looked up and smiled at a slim, frail-looking, small-boned grandmotherly woman. She smiled too, but there was a little reserve, maybe hostility there. I filed it away under Later.

"Be right back, Elsa," he told her. He didn't look at me. Maybe he regretted what he'd done, the help he'd asked for.

The rain had slowed and this time I paid attention to landmarks and detail, committing them to memory. With no chitchat to distract me it wasn't tough. I did try conversation, but only once.

"Lovely weather we're having."

The sarcasm was a little flat, but it's tough talking to someone who's doing a credible imitation of a totem pole driving.

He shook his head. "Don't bother."

So I didn't. It was a good thing I was getting paid for this. Not enough though. I should charge Tobias double for this kind of stuff, harassment pay.

Matt pulled the truck up in front of the motel. "You'll be working with Charlene tonight. She knows the setup and can answer just about any question you might have. I'll be in later to close. I—I don't like a woman to close alone now."

Gosh, I felt so cherished. "Thanks for lunch."

He nodded but kept his eyes on the newly repaired windshield. I opened the door and was almost out, almost home free. Almost doesn't cut it.

"You said you appreciated my honesty, Matt. You asked for my help and because I attempted that I'm getting the cold shoulder. I'm trying to write it off to shock and grief, but it's tough."

I got out and slammed the door. Hard.

And hoped I still had a job. Debatable.

I swung my hair back and marched off with all the nonchalance and dignity I could muster but it was a waste. The truck immediately laid rubber across the parking lot and down the road. Not headed for home, I noticed. I thought, with superiority, how immature it was to lay rubber in a parking lot. A calico cat watched me from under a rain-drenched bush, her eyes unwinking and clear. My sense of superiority didn't even last to the motel room.

"Aren't you an ace investigator," I said, mumbled actually, to myself. If talking to yourself is a bad sign, mumbling is worse. "Such a sense of professional balance. Love the way you maintain a distance, don't get personally or emotionally involved, and *especially* the way you don't do or say anything to jeopardize the progress of the case."

Phooey. I was fed up with my thoughts, with this case, and with one-sided conversations. If I totaled up now, I'd probably owe Tobias money. More fed up. Damn.

The message light on my phone was blinking. "Charlene called," the desk told me, drawling the name, "and left this number." I wrote it down, took a few deep breaths, tried to calm down, chill out, before calling.

She answered on the first ring. "Hi! Matt said to call and remind you you come on at five."

Had he? He had told me himself. I wondered about that. I wondered too how she knew where I was staying.

"Thanks. Charlene, what are you doing? Want to meet for lunch?" I groaned inwardly. I was *stuffed.* "Or coffee?" Much better idea. "Do you have time?"

"Hey, sure, yeah, that'd be fun. Actually," her voice hesitated, "actually, it's perfect. I'm glad you asked, 'cause there's something I kinda wanted to talk to you about. And away from work is easier too, you know?"

She had an agenda, I could hear it in her voice. No problem, I had one too. I agreed to meet her in Nevada City, where she lived, at Molly's, a breakfast-and-lunch place. Then I walked over to pick up the Bronco back at the Pioneer.

The place was easy to find; parking was the hard part. Still, I was there first. When Charlene came in, the waitress waved at her and greeted her by name.

The smell of freshly baked goods filled the room and almost made me hungry. The tables had cotton tablecloths and old-fashioned salt and pepper shakers. Bright café curtains hung at the windows, and watercolors and dried flowers and herbs tied with ribbons hung on the wall. I'd chosen an empty table near a window.

"Homemade pies," Charlene said, sitting down opposite me, "and worth every damn calorie." She pushed up the sleeves of her brightly colored sweater, tilted her head and jingled large metallic earrings at me. "Hi!"

We had pie, with herb tea to balance out the indulgence. And got right to the point.

"If I'm outta line, tell me." Charlene looked me full in the face. She didn't look like a vapid blonde anymore and nothing about her expression softened her comment.

"All right," I agreed.

"Well, and this *is* outta line, I know. I think it's because you look kinda like my older sister. She saved my butt all the time when we were growing up."

"And now you want to save mine?" I ventured.

She grinned suddenly. The earrings jingled again. "Yeah, something like that. In a way I guess I do. I liked you right off the bat, you know, the way you do or don't like people?"

I nodded. I knew.

"Matt liked you right off, too."

Yes, I knew that as well. "Is that bad?"

"I don't know." She wrinkled up her nose and became a pretty blond Norman Rockwell picture of puzzlement. "I mean no, because he's a nice guy, and yes, because his wife was killed recently and, if he had anything to do with it, he's not a nice guy. And mostly I don't know, and neither does anyone else. I even feel sort of like a shit for talking about it and him like this."

Time to cut to the chase, before she bogged down in guilt. "Do you think he did it?"

Charlene aligned the salt and pepper shakers carefully before she answered. "No," she said. "I don't. *Well*, I didn't at first. Nobody did. We were just sick about it, and real sorry for him and Toby. It's a horrible thing to have happen. We're not Sacramento, you know. People don't get murdered around here. They just don't."

We don't drop them like swatted flies in Sacramento either, but I let it pass.

"Something like this happens, the first thing is you feel bad, real bad," she said.

Yes, and when a woman is killed leaving a bar at two-thirty in the morning with a bundle of cash and not much common sense, you don't automatically suspect the husband. In fact, he'd be way down on the cops' list—after an assailant with or without robbery on his mind, known or unknown to the victim, after someone who might have been in the bar that night watching the holiday money flow and deciding to wait for her to leave, and so on. The big question then: Why was Matt so sure everyone suspected him?

"First thing is *not* that you suspect a guy like Matt, especially in a scene like this where it looks like someone wanted the money and then killed her, maybe so she couldn't identify him. It happens all the time, right?"

"Right." And for a whole lot less than twelve hundred dollars.

The waitress came by to pick up our dessert plates and refill our teapots.

"And people aren't suspicious for no reason." She thought that one over. "Well, we're not up here. In the city—" She shrugged off city morals and belief systems. "And I don't mean that theirs was a perfect marriage or anything. It wasn't."

"But what is?" I said, helping her out.

"Yes. Exactly. I mean, we even heard them fighting, especially at the end. Hey, Grass Valley's a small town. To a certain extent we all know each other's business."

Charlene was up to speed, rushing on. I'd have to come back to the fighting later. She paused to dump a packet of Sweet'n Low in her tea, another dubious attempt to counteract dessert calories.

"We're nosy and we talk about each other, but we're *not* suspicious for *no* reason, especially about people we've known for all our lives."

I waited patiently for the reasons. We were closing in on them now. She stirred her tea so hard it slopped over the rim of her cup. Her movements were jerky and anxious, or maybe angry.

"And there were reasons?" I prodded gently.

"Oh, yes."

She splashed tea around until there was more in the saucer than in the cup.

"They owned a good-sized piece of unimproved land. Matt wanted to sell it, or part of it, and do something, other investments—" She waved vaguely at them, big city stuff, I guess, and out of her scope. "Land prices here, everywhere I imagine, have been going crazy. We've been 'discovered.' Worse luck! Anyway, Deidre didn't want to sell. They'd been duking it out for months."

"Duking it out?"

"Well, not *really*. I don't mean *hitting* each other, just arguing. Matt would never *hurt* her."

Maybe kill her, I thought, but never hurt her. Still I knew what she meant, sort of.

"The day after the funeral he sold a land parcel."

Number one.

"A couple of weeks later he bought a boat. Deidre didn't like boats. She couldn't swim, you know?"

Number two.

"And then some girl, he *said* she was an out-of-town relative, came and stayed for the weekend. She didn't *act* like a relative," Charlene said darkly. " 'Less maybe a kissing cousin."

Number three.

"And now you. He hired you just because he liked you."

Uh-oh. I was number four.

"I just thought you should know."

She plunked some money down on the table and I followed suit.

"There's nothing wrong with any of it. Nothing. Everyone really wants Matt to be happy. And Toby, too. Especially that, the poor little kid. Everyone does. But—" She looked at me and I watched her face freeze up.

"It's the timing," I said.

"Yes," she agreed, "the timing. Exactly. Couldn't he wait? Out of respect, if nuthin' else. Couldn't he?"

"He could have."

"Yeah, but he didn't. People got suspicious, then the talk started. And I don't mean about you. There's nothing wrong with hiring someone just because you take a fancy to 'em, as my aunt used to say. Heck, I've dated guys on less than that." She sidetracked for a moment, mentally reviewed guys, and shook her blond head. "Unfortunately."

Charlene poured the slop-over in her saucer back into the cup.

"You should know, that's all. This is a small town. If you want to live and work here you should know, that's all."

"Thank you."

"Okay, sure." She rearranged the coins on the table, but didn't meet my eyes.

"How did you find me?"

She shrugged, still looking at the tablecloth. "Small town."

It sounded good, but it didn't tell me anything. Charlene looked poised to move, go, fly. I dropped her with a question.

"What was Deidre like, Charlene?"

She looked at me then. Her face was stricken. I wondered if she was going to cry, and felt myself tense.

"If I'm out of line, just say so." I said it softly.

She smiled at me, at the mimicry.

"Deidre's dead, but she seems very real, almost alive still in people's minds," I added.

"Yeah, she had that about her," Charlene said softly. "You know, when she was alive she didn't seem to take up much space." She frowned. "I guess I mean she was quiet. Well, not quiet exactly, but—hey, I'm really not sure what I mean."

I thought she was doing an okay job. Deidre was becoming more of a person to me, less of an unknown, or a grainy black-and-white autopsy photo. "Go on," I encouraged her.

"A lot it seemed like she was in her own world and she never told you about it nor invited you in. And that world sometimes seemed like it was more important than the real world. Or maybe it seemed like that world of hers *was* the real world, at least to her. Goofy, huh?"

We sipped our tea in silence. I didn't think goofy was the right word.

"She changed around a lot too. Like she'd go from one world to another and be different, her clothes, her hair, her way of talking, you know?"

"No," I said. Not yet, not quite. But almost.

"Well, like one time she just wore long-sleeved, high-necked lacy blouses with long, maybe three-quarter-length skirts in little flowery prints, boots. She wore pearls and a cameo pin and pulled her hair up on her head with loose curls all around. And a shawl. She looked like the girlfriend in 'Butch Cassidy,' remember?"

I nodded.

"And she talked real sweet and low. That one lasted quite a while. Then she started wearing only straight tight black pants and vampy blouses. Her hair was pulled back on one side with a comb, and fell in a wave over her eye on the other. She'd wear bright red lipstick and nail polish and sometimes she'd stand around with a cigarette in the corner of her mouth like someone in a Humphrey Bogart movie, only she didn't smoke.

"Or she'd go western with tight faded jeans, cowboy boots, silver earrings shaped like little spurs and a belt with a big old silver buckle. You know?"

I knew.

"Or city sophisticate, or business woman or . . . well, shit, you name it."

The photos at Tobias's hadn't shown me these particular Deidres, but had prepared me for them.

"It was just Deidre, just the way she was. It wasn't like she was pretending to be something she wasn't, there were just a lot of different sides to her, different parts to her."

"Which one was she really?"

She shook her head. "Shoot, I don't know. It was hard to tell and I didn't really know her all that good. She worked at the Pioneer and was easy to work with, get along with. I liked her, liked her a lot, but I don't think I knew her. Hey, I gotta go."

We walked out into the rain.

"Charlene, did you and Matt have something going?"

"Ouch! Darn door!" She snatched her hand away from the door and sucked a finger. "Almost broke that nail, too."

"Charlene?"

"You're coming on at five. Me, too. See ya soon, then." She waved and darted off, running into the rain and taking my unanswered question with her.

I dashed back to my car and drove to the library to look up back issues of the local paper. I was betting the murder would have been covered pretty thoroughly.

I won that bet.

But I didn't learn anything new.

Out of curiosity I looked up something else. Deidre was an Irish Gaelic name, preferred spelling Deirdre. Someone had taken the "dear" sound out of Deidre's name.

I left the library with a heavy heart.

"Has anyone ever told you how beautiful you are?"

"Oh!" She laughed. "What an old line that is!"

"Only it's not a line, it's the truth." His eyes caressed her. She felt naked before that look. Naked and alive.

....

The bar was almost full although the tables were still pretty empty when I walked in at five of five wearing worn Wranglers, somewhat worn sneakers, a good shirt, and a smile. New bartender.

On the jukebox Vern Gosdin sang "That Just About Does It, Don't It." I hoped not. The smoke draped itself around me like a shroud. My stomach was tight and jumpy. It had been three years, and more, since I'd been behind a bar.

The day bartender looked like a sleazoid—little, ferrety, and sly— someone who should have been selling tickets at a porno film. His eyes slipped and slimed over things, his hands moved fast and seemed, suspiciously, to be out of sight a lot. On his bald head thin strands of hair were carefully spread out and sprayed down. No wonder Matt hired me without knowing my name, without knowing anything about me. I would have hired me too. *Anyone* would have. The fact that I could make drinks was a bonus.

"Hi, Kate."

Charlene chirped from behind me. She was carrying a tray filled with faux-cheese snacks in chipped wooden bowls and wearing a T-shirt that showed a rattlesnake coiled around a bottle of tequila. The snake had huge fangs that dripped poison and blood. Made me want a shot, for sure.

"Kate, you met Morty yet?"

I said hi to Morty from way back so the question of shaking hands wouldn't come up. My palms prickled at the thought.

"Wow-eeee," he drawled out. "Ain't you something?"

"Kate, the new night bartender," I said, editing out my initial response.

A guy at the end of the bar laughed. "Knock it off, Warty. You know better than to pick on ones with gumption."

Morty/Warty scowled briefly, then cleared it off with a smile. "Well, c'mon back, we'll show you the ropes."

He made it sound dirty, made it sound like more than ropes. I kept my face blank, flipped up the pass-through and walked behind the bar. I don't appreciate men like this. Appreciate doesn't cover it.

"Beer cooler and wines over there, backup juices, half-and-half, cut-up fruit—"

He stood in one place and pointed. I opened coolers and cabinets, checking the stock. Morty slimed up behind me, standing too close and smelling of cheap after-shave and three-day-old sweat. He fluttered a hand in my direction, brushing my rear, and I stepped back on his foot. Hard.

"Hey!"

"Oh. Sorry." I sounded sorry but someone snickered. I didn't sound *real* sorry.

"Huh. Ice machine around the corner, beer boxes back here, charge slips—"

He was hurrying right along, scamper, scamper. Slime, slime. "Computer cash register, you punch in the drink, not the price. Here's your well drinks, here's your call and premium; your beers, domestic and import; this here's for coffee and soft drinks—" He was edging closer, almost touching my thigh. "Here's your price list."

"Can we get a couple Buds down here?" a friendly voice called.

"Draft or bottle?" I asked and stepped sideways. Same foot and harder this time. There's a choreography to two bartenders working one bar. I had it; I wasn't using it.

"Jeez!"

"Oh. Excuse me."

He hopped, limped, and glared. I blinked innocently.

"Bottle, and make one a Bud Light."

"I'm outta here." Morty scowled at me.

I nodded and reached for the beers, popped the caps off and walked down the bar.

"Hey, bartender." Same friendly voice.

"Hi, I'm Kate."

I looked at a round face with pink cheeks, a curly beard, and a smile and then met Clancy, Jeff, Eddie, Tucker and Rideout (Ride out? What kind of name was that?) and we were all pleased to meet each other. Or so we said.

"Scenery sure has improved." Jeff, or maybe Eddie, tossed out the remark casual as yesterday's lunch. He grinned at me and I sort of smiled. "Don't be minding Warty. He means well."

"Naw, he don't."

General laughter and agreement. Patsy Cline was singing "Walking After Midnight." I thought of Deidre and shivered. Patsy had died in a small plane, slammed and crashed and spilled all over a mountain; Deidre had crashed into a bad guy and a bullet. Had they seen it coming?

"Kate, can we get a round down here?"

I crashed out of reverie. "Sure. Both beers out of this, Clancy?" I indicated the twenty on the bar in front of him.

"Yeah, I'll buy their round, and a beer for Jimmie, too."

"What are you drinking, guys?"

"Gin tonic, cuba libre, screwdriver."

I looked at the bottles in the speed rack. Left to right. Good. There was a shot glass but I free-pour. Back in the saddle again. It was good, it was fun. I carried the drinks down the bar and tossed out napkins. Cool. I hadn't lost it.

"Thanks, sweetheart."

"Kate," I said, but I smiled.

"Oh, yeah, okay. Kate."

So we got that straight. In bars you do this right away, marking rules and territory like dogs, I thought wryly.

"Order."

Charlene's section was filling up as we swung into Happy Hour with Elvis singing "Jailhouse Rock."

"Two manhattans, one up, one over, Scotch rocks, bourbon coke, gin tonic, whiskey sour, margie, keoki, rose, Bud, Coors, Lite, one with. Oops—add on vodka collins. How you doing? Okay so far? The guys at the bar are nice guys but you got to draw the line for 'em sometimes. You read Morty right, I saw."

Her hazel eyes were wide with fun and appreciation as she pulled drinks off the pour pad and onto her tray.

"He's a skunk, always got a stink on him. Matt wants to get rid of him but can't find anyone to take the job. Worse luck."

"Hey, Charlene," someone hollered, "how's about a couple of shooters?"

"How's about a please," she hollered right back.

"Puh-*leeeze,*" the voice mocked her.

"Tequila?" I asked.

"Worse. Schnapps." We both shuddered. "You're fast." She flashed a smile at me out of the side of her mouth like the quick flick of a turn signal, off/on/gone. Someone hollered a "hey there" and Charlene turned around, her tray on one hand and up in the air. "Well, look at that. Hot damn." She whistled under her breath. I looked but it didn't mean anything to me.

A couple had entered. She was pretty in a quiet way with long brown hair streaked with blond and done in a French braid. Her figure was round, full, womanly, not heavy at all, and she was wearing the kind of attractive and distinctive clothing that makes a "statement": a long skirt of hand-woven Guatemalan-type material over boots, crocheted sweater, suede jacket, a silk scarf matching the colors in her skirt. Dangling gold earrings framed a quiet face set with dark eyes and a flawless complexion.

At five ten or eleven the man with her was six inches taller and dressed more conventionally in jeans and a heavy jacket. He had a stocky build and construction worker muscles, dark hair, mustache, and skin roughened by outdoor work.

Neither was smiling.

"Chivogny and Stu," Charlene said. "She's Deidre's sister. To be continued—" Winking at me, she pushed off the bar.

Bob Seeger sang "Old Time Rock 'n Roll" but nobody's soul looked soothed. I sang along with him. So did Jimmie. I sang under my breath. That made one of us.

Chivogny saw me and visibly started. She took several steps toward the bar, then abruptly turned and walked across the room to a corner table.

Why was she startled and what was the problem? I didn't get it. I did wonder but it was the last thing I wondered about for a while. Things were smoking and I was making drinks and running.

When there was a pause in the action I learned some new stuff: names, faces, and the regulars' drinks; that Betty had a boy; Rod had tipped a dozer on Wednesday clearing his back slope; the place to eat in town for Mexican. And that it was Chivogny's birthday. Deidre's sister was thirty-one and getting sloshed. It doesn't take long on vodka gimlets, either.

I didn't speak to her then. She didn't come to the bar and I didn't leave it. I was too busy. It was later, after dinner, that she made her way over. Her husband wasn't in sight.

"So you're the new bartender."

I didn't answer. It was obvious I was. Drunks prattle the obvious as though it were a brand-new insight. She was pretty high. That was obvious too.

"It's my birthday."

Maybe there were tears in her eyes. Maybe not.

"Happy birthday."

"Happy?" Her fingers tightened on the glass she'd brought to the bar with her. She wore a plain gold wedding band, like the one Deidre had worn. Then she tossed the rest of the drink to the back of her throat and swallowed. "Down the hatch," she said brightly and shoved the glass across the bar at me. It tipped over but there was nothing in it to spill.

"Another?" I asked, giving her a chance to think it over, smarten up, change her mind. Drunks rarely do that; I didn't really think Chivogny would. Stu came out of the restaurant and stopped at a table to talk to a couple of guys. She heard his voice behind her and an odd look flickered across her face.

"Oh, yes, please. To celebrate my birthday. Do you know what he gave me?"

He? "Your husband?"

"Yes."

A Fredrick's of Hollywood outfit? A Sears riding lawn mower? A partridge in a pear tree? "No." In fact I couldn't even guess. I'm not good at that kind of stuff.

"Chivvy, I'm going to stop over to Orville's place, check out a job. You okay here or you want me to run you on home first?" He crossed the room as he spoke and leaned on the bar with an easy, intensely male grace. It wafted over to me but seemed to leave Chivogny (Chivvy?) unaffected. "Hi," he said to me. "Stu Beckering. You're Kathy, right?"

"Kate."

"Good to meet you." He transferred a dark-chocolate goo gaze from me to Chivogny. "Well, baby doll."

His wife winced at the term. And who could blame her? "I'll stay here." Her voice had gone a little flat, like open beer on a warm day.

"Sure. Back soon. Won't be but ten. Run me a tab, will you?" he asked me as he gooed me with chocolate eyes, smiled and left.

"He said that to hurt me and it won't be ten minutes, it'll be an hour. Easy. Happy birthday, Chivogny."

She spoke softly and clinked her empty glass on the bar. She sounded okay, more or less sober, but it was a drunken logic, thoughts strung together on an emotional line like lights on a Christmas wire. And some of the bulbs were out. Surprise.

"Could I get you some coffee?"

"Oh, yes, please, with brandy in it and whipped cream."

I made it for her. Charlene waved at me from across the room where she was sitting at a table with customers. It was ten-thirty. The juke played softly; the place, for now, was quiet, dead even. Chivogny sighed over the drink I rang up on Stu's tab.

"Would you say something to hurt a person on her birthday?"

A no-win question for sure. I tried to remember the phrase Hank had used to describe me. *World of hurt,* that was it. And this one was no stranger to that world, that hurt.

"Would you?"

No good answer to that question. "He seemed very nice," I said, dodging it, trying to stay out of the quicksand, the mud and the emotional traps.

"Yes, he does seem nice, doesn't he?" There was a faint emphasis on *seem.* "This is what he gave me." She hooked her thumb under a gold chain around her neck. A sizable and expensive chunk of gold studded with pearls and diamonds dangled from it. It was beautiful and still tasteful, though it flirted with gaudy.

"I hate it." She let it fall to her chest. "We've been married for six years. He knows what I like. He knows what I don't like. My sister would like this, but I don't. Would have liked," she corrected smoothly.

"He smiled when he gave it to me but he was thinking about something else, not about me."

She was doing it again, stringing unconnected thoughts on an emo-

63

tional wire. These weren't burned-out thoughts; they were alive with hatred. Deliberately, delicately, she stirred the whipped cream into her coffee drink.

"How does a person feel on her birthday?" she asked.

More quicksand. "Older? Wiser? Thankful for another year?"

She dismissed that with a small shake of her head. "Oh, no. That's how you're supposed to feel maybe, but how do you—does *one*—" she corrected politely and sipped at her drink, "feel? *Really* feel?"

The jukebox made busy sounds as Charlene fed a customer's dollar bill into its mechanical maw. The music doesn't sound the same played with dollar bills, which is odd, but fitting. I love the sound of quarters thunking into the juke; I love leaning there, arms braced and feet apart, reading song names and punching buttons, feeling the bass notes pulse in your arms as the music plays. Jukeboxes and bars, drinks and drunks.

Home again. Home away from home. Home sweet home?

"Hey Chivogny, hey birthday girl, whaddya wanna hear?" someone called.

"Happy bi-i-rthday to *me*," Chivogny sang under her breath and out of tune.

"What?"

"B-eleven."

It was a song about a lady all broken up, brokenhearted, broken into little pieces and stomped on, tromped on, spit on. Heck of a song. Perked my spirits right up.

Chivogny sang every word and drank on the instrumental breaks. The next song was sung by a woman with a voice that was wild and high and sounded as though it led her and not the other way around. She'd rolled up the rug, dusted off her walking shoes and left her man eating dirt. Only, only who knows?

Was there no hope for us? For us or love? Would someone please punch an upbeat tune for godssakes?

"Would you put more brandy in this?"

I would. I did. It was her hangover and she wasn't driving.

"Whatever they are, they're not supposed to be about hate."

George Jones was singing "Bartender's Blues." It's a song bartenders relate to. I did. I was. It is not upbeat.

"What?"

"Birthdays. They shouldn't be about hating your present. And your life. And your job. And maybe your husband. And maybe your sister, even though she's dead. Dead as a doornail. Dead as a cockroach. Dead through and through."

She looked at me and waited for an answer, demanded one. *Cockroach?* I thought.

"I think birthdays are supposed to be fun."

"What a concept." She laughed.

The door busted open. Customers. Good. Jerry Lewis danced on the jukebox piano keys and sang "Great Balls of Fire." Someone in an alternate reality had stocked this jukebox. I was sure of it.

"I want another drink," Chivogny said, "and I didn't mean it. She was my sister and I loved her. She couldn't help it that she had what I didn't . . . that I couldn't . . . that she . . . Oh, and it was wrong of me to hate her for that. I know it was, but I couldn't help it. She was so good, so kind. She was *always* there for me, always helped me *so* much. I loved her. I hated her," she whispered. "I loved her, I hated her, I loved her, I . . ."

I thought of the daisies we picked as kids, picked and pulled apart. *He loves me . . . he loves me not . . . he loves me . . . he loves me not.* The end of the litany came with the end of the petals. Chivogny hadn't run out of petals yet, but she was working on it.

"Another drink. Please?"

Hers, theirs.

Charlene and I swung into action. The bar was filling up the way bars do, suddenly and with no apparent reason. Somewhere the gods were laughing and spinning lost souls around and into the bars for comfort.

Only comfort is not what is handed out in bars. I handed out what I had.

Another round.

9

"I think I have the wrong office."

She looked up from the computer screen at his six-foot-four-inch frame, brown hair, green eyes, and smile.

"No," she said, her heart beating wildly, "you don't."

"You don't know what I'm looking for," he said in a sexy teasing irresistible voice that sent shivers through her.

"No," she replied smiling, "but I will."

. . . .

Chivogny was docile when Stu returned to collect her. And right: It had been over an hour. He returned without apology or explanation and she asked for none. They seemed to be used to it. A married routine, I guess. Stu spoke briefly to a couple more good old boys—it was early spring and their necks were red already, that kind of good old boy—and Chivogny whispered to me once more.

"Come to my store and visit."

And.

"We could be friends, couldn't we?"

Her voice was bitter and angry. Hatred filled up in her eyes and spilled over and down her cheeks like dry tears. And she spoke of friendship? I trembled inside. I couldn't help it, though I tried. She reached up, put her hand on the gold chain around her neck, and yanked. It took two tries. She dumped the broken chain and pendant on the bar and pushed them toward me.

"Your tip."

The hatred was like acid, etching furrows and wrinkles into her beautiful skin and flawless complexion. I picked up the crumpled golden pile and dropped it into her open purse.

She smiled weakly and clicked her purse shut. "Tomorrow then. Always tomorrow."

Stu tossed a twenty on the bar for a ten-fifty bar tab and escorted Chivogny out. His face was smooth and unreadable.

I hoped I never had a birthday like that.

"It used to be worse." Charlene dumped her tray at her work station. "When Deidre was here and they'd come in."

"How?" I said, but I guess I meant what. As in: What happened and how could it be worse?

"Oh, most times Stu would start it. I don't think he even realized what he was doing. He couldn't help himself anyway. Deidre was flashes of light and sparkle, it was *something* to see her. She loved being behind the bar, played it out to the max. She was the star and everyone else was the audience."

I was stocking beer as she spoke.

"When you see a picture of her, it doesn't do her justice. It doesn't catch it, that light and sparkle. In a picture she doesn't even look all that pretty, but she was. She was the kind of girl a guy would kill for, maybe without understanding it. Oh, my God!"

She put her hand over her mouth. I stocked beer and we both ignored her last comment long enough for her to recover and continue.

"And Stu, other guys too, couldn't help but watch her. Deidre acted like she didn't notice, like she didn't pay it any mind. But she did, and Chivogny did too. You better believe it. For sure."

I believed it.

"And when it *really* got to her she would say things that sounded polite but were mean."

She. Who? Deidre? Chivogny?

"Who?"

"Huh? Oh, Chivogny, of course."

Of course. "Was Deidre mean back?"

I finished stocking the beer and wine, wondered if it was too early to start breaking down the well.

"Oh, no. She was a very sweet person and mostly she let it go by. She wasn't so much for fighting. Every once in a while though . . ."

She paused so long that I prompted with a question, a speculation. "She got angry?"

"No. I never saw Deidre angry, not really. She wouldn't get angry mostly. She'd just go into her own world where she said—just joking around but not *really*, you know—she could make the story come out however she wanted."

Except that you can't ever do that. Not really. I looked at the clock: eleven forty-five. "Is it too early to break down the well?"

"Go for it. Leave a pot of coffee though. Matt likes a cup when he comes in."

Matt.

"If she didn't get mad, what?"

"Hmmmm?" Charlene was counting her bank. "Hey, cool, I did great, better than I thought, even!"

"About Deidre, Charlene?"

"Oh, yeah. This is for you." She put a stack of bills on the bar, tipping out generously.

"Thanks."

This is one of the great parts about being a bartender, walking out with wads of cash money in your pocket.

"Sure. Deidre. Well, it almost seemed like she could look into your heart. She could see the hurt and the bad but she didn't say that. She'd look hard till she could find something good and say that instead. Like when Chivogny was mean, Deidre would just smile sadly and say something like: 'You don't mean it. I *know* you don't. Your sadness is getting to you. I'm so sorry for that.' "

Charlene fussed with fruit in the fruit tray, threw out some pathetic olives and dried-out limes. I waited in silence, not wanting to break into the memory.

"You see, Chivogny wanted a baby more than anything, more almost than life itself. She and Stu had—have—been trying for years, I guess. At first, when she still thought it would just happen, she fixed up a room in their place for the baby. That was five years ago, at least. She never opens the door to that room now. Never talks about it. I hear the doctor says that probably she can't ever have a baby, even after two operations."

So that was Chivogny's world of hurt.

"She almost had a breakdown when Deidre—right away, mind you—

68

got pregnant with Toby. And it's her, too; Chivogny, not Stu. Deidre was wonderful, always understanding and kind. It helps, I guess. I mean, I'm sure it does, but it doesn't take away the pain, the wanting something you can't have."

Our eyes met in silence, in brief understanding, in sympathy with Chivogny's pain. Then the door swung open and three guys walked in. That's life in a bar. It can be quiet, dead for hours, but the minute you decide to close up, customers walk in.

Charlene and I both sighed like a couple of disappointed little kids. Poor sports and lousy losers was more like it.

She took the order, then took the drinks out and came back to the bar. They drank the first round before the ice had even settled.

"How about another?" A tall lanky guy with a clean smile and dirty eyes stood at the bar slightly too close to Charlene. "Okay," she said, as she moved away from him. I made the drinks.

"What are a couple of pretty gals like you doing in a place like this?"

Hoo boy, that was a new line. Charlene and I didn't meet each other's eyes. We would have lost it.

I put the drinks on the bar in front of him. "Five seventy-five."

He leaned on the bar. "Couple of cute gals like you two must get a lot of calls, eh?"

He was looking at me. He was pissing me off. I smiled. Bad sign. And answered. "Yeah, we do."

"Probably like to get a call from ole Max here, eh?"

Oh, sure, talk about making my day. Strike one. And I can't stand people who talk about themselves in the third person. Strike two.

"Hey there, no need to be shy. Go on and give ole Max your phone number."

"No," I said, not shy like he thought.

"C'mon now. Course nothing a man likes better than a challenge."

"Five seventy-five."

He took out a five and a single. "C'mon now." He winked.

I smiled and gave him a quarter in change and a number.

He winked again and walked off with the drinks, leaving the quarter for me. A big tipper. I was impressed.

"Kate!" Charlene snarled under her breath. "You *didn't* give him your number!"

"No," I agreed. "I didn't."

"What was it then?"

"Dial-A-Prayer."

So that was when we lost it.

"Hey," one of the guys called. "Could we get a couple of olives over here, sweetie?"

Charlene sighed, put two olives on a napkin, walked over to the table. I leaned on the bar, looked out the window and mentally urged the clock on. "Only the Lonely" was playing on the juke and Roy Orbison was tearing off pieces of my heart. Charlene let out a yip and then a yelp. I turned around. One of Max's buddies had a meaty hand clamped on the back of her thigh. Charlene was struggling to get away. Max was laughing.

I got out on the floor. Fast. This was strike three and they were out.

"Let go of her." My voice sounded real hard, real mean, even to me.

The guy with the meaty hand looked up, startled. The hand dropped. Charlene scuttled away. There were tears in her eyes.

"Hey," he said, "no sweat, no problem. Maybe you'd like a little action?"

"There's a problem."

"Yeah?"

But he wasn't really interested, I could tell. He was looking at my tits. And grinning.

"You." His grin faded. "But it's not a big problem because you're leaving."

"Hey."

"*Now.*" My voice got dangerous.

"Hey!"

I looked at Max. "Get him out of here before I get *really* mad."

Max sat and looked at me with a goofy grin.

"Charlene, get the guys in the kitchen," I said. Only there weren't any guys in the kitchen. They'd left. I was bluffing. "And if they've left, call the cops."

Max started moving. "Yeah, it's late, let's go." He pounded his drink, got to his feet, and winked at me. "See you." He hauled his buddy off, the third guy trotting docilely along behind them.

I locked the door, the place empty now, looked over at Charlene, then walked behind the bar.

"You okay?"

"I wish I could handle it better," she said miserably. "I wish—aw, shit! Thanks, Kate."

"Sure, that's what bartenders are for."

"Don't tell Matt, okay?"

"Okay. Why?"

"He gets mad at me, thinks I should—"

She was picking over the fruit again. Her eyes flickered. She tossed out a few cherries that looked okay to me.

"So, tomorrow I get my nails done. *Look* at this." She held up her hands for my inspection. *"Trashed."* They looked fine to me. "That's the only problem with this job, it trashes your hands."

And your mind? How did we get from tonight to nails?

"So what are you doing tomorrow? I do your nails, you do mine?"

We looked at my hands and laughed simultaneously; it would be a bigger job for her than for me. There was a draft at my back. Her eyes flickered again.

Okay, I got it.

10

"You think that you can just walk in here and I'll be yours, but you're wrong!"

He smiled.

"You think you can just snap your fingers. Hah!"

He inclined his head.

"It's not so."

He snapped his fingers.

. . . .

"Busy night?"

"Hey, Matt. Yeah. Wow. Everybody came in to see the new bartender and stayed to drink too much. It was wall-to-wall for a while. Kate did great."

Charlene threw away some more okay cherries, her nails dipping in and out of the fruit like sharp nervous little birds, her voice too bright and cheerful.

"Kate." Matt nodded a formal hello.

"Hi, Matt."

"It go okay?"

"I had fun." I grinned. And it was true, except for the last fifteen minutes. "This is a great place. The bar setup is super and the people are nice, real nice. Who stocked the jukebox?"

"My wife." He turned his back on me.

Okay.

I put away what was left of the fruit before Charlene could throw it all away. Matt relaxed a little. On a tension scale of one to ten, he was now a nine. It was a start.

He came behind the bar, poured a cup of coffee and took the cash drawer. "We're closed. Have a drink, you two." Headed out again. I looked at Charlene, who nodded.

"Top Shelf, rocks, easy salt." I made two. It sounded good.

"Charlene."

"Hmmm?" She licked the salt off her glass and then licked her lips.

"My motel room is done in olive and baby-poop green; the bedspread has four-inch fringe; it's ninety-eight percent plastic, and there's a picture of Bambi with dinner-plate-sized eyes on the wall, the *green* wall. Help!"

She laughed and licked her lips again.

"It's depressing beyond belief." I took a shot at pathetic dinner plate eyes myself. Not like Bambi, not that good, but not bad. I was angling. "Can you help me find an apartment or a room, even something temporary, while I look around? Something homey," I said, a desperate edge to my voice, "and *not* green."

"I'll think about it, see what I can come up with."

"Thanks."

We sat in semidark silence for a while.

"Why did Deidre work here?"

"I don't know, though I asked her once. I mean it helped the business and all, but she didn't *have* to. She said, kinda kidding but kinda not, that she worked here so Prince Charming could find her. One day he was going to ride into town and take her away from all this."

"Prince Charming?"

"Yeah, for sure, isn't that something? She said she couldn't count on him finding her, a housewife you know, at home, so she came here. Where he would find her."

"And she was right. Only it wasn't Prince Charming."

"No kidding. Hey, who believes in him anyway? He's a flake."

Our voices were low, intimate. It was after-hours bar time, secret-telling time again. A door shut somewhere in the back, then a latch clicked.

"You still got my number?" Charlene asked.

I nodded a yes as Matt walked in.

"I gotta go." Charlene finished the last of her drink and stood, winking at me.

"Me, too." I left half of mine and headed for my purse and jacket.

"Kate, I'd like to talk to you for a moment."

Uh-oh.

"Bye." Charlene smiled at us, mostly me. "See ya tomorrow."

Matt walked her to her car and came back. I sat glumly on my stool, drinking faster than before and doing it with a noticeable lack of enthusiasm or interest.

He stood behind the bar. It's a psychological thing: height, distance, and power. And it works, but not necessarily on me because I know it, I do it too. So, I sat and drank. It was his agenda. He was clearly uncomfortable and I didn't help him out.

"I owe you an apology."

Yeah. He did. I thought so, too, but I had the wits not to say it. A nice change for me.

"When you get stuck, sometimes you have the sense to ask for help but not the sense to listen."

"Or you're not ready to hear it yet." Discretion is a short-lived thing with me.

"Whatever." He moved his shoulders the way a fighter might, testing, flexing. "Anyway, I asked, you answered, and I came down hard on you. I'm sorry."

"Okay. Sure."

"Could we try again?"

He made it a question but his voice said he was sure we could. It made me contrary. I danced away, teasing, tempting, like a bright silk kite flying high, a fish running strong and hard downstream, a P.I. playing hard to please and sure of the player.

"It might be simpler to stick to the job description: owner, bartender. I need this job, Matt. I can't afford to jeopardize it."

His eye caught a glimpse of that bright silk, untethered and flying free; a silver gleam flashing briefly downstream and then gone. I thought he looked startled, maybe scared, but it was gone before I could analyze it.

"Fair enough." He leaned across the bar, arms spread wide, palms down. "I give you my word that nothing that happens between us on a personal basis will affect your job in any way."

"Is your word good?" Be a jerk, Kat, go for it.

He threw back his head and laughed. "It is, yeah."

"Okay, we're on."

"A word of advice?"

I looked at him cautiously, warily, but nodded.

"Put together some capital or get a backer, get your own place. You'll do a lot better working for yourself than for someone else. Diplomacy is not your strong point."

Boy, was that the truth.

"Okay, so after I got over being mad—"

"Anything left of your tires?"

He grinned. "And peeling rubber, I got to thinking on your questions: What did she want out of life? What were her dreams? What kind of person was she? I was married to her for six years. I should know, right?"

"Not necessarily. I never knew my mother and I lived with her for seventeen years. I could tell you what she liked for breakfast but not what her dreams were."

"Deidre talked about her dreams. She wanted to be a writer. That's what she said." The emphasis was on *said.*

"But not what she did?"

"I don't know. Well, yes and no. Hard to say, I guess."

The phone rang, drilled its way into the conversation. Matt made no move to answer it.

"Want me to get that?"

"No. It's someone wants to know if we're open. We're not, but if I answer it they'll be on over here anyway pounding on the door."

It rang about twenty times. Stopped. Started again. My mind went on hold while it rang. It always does. The ringing stopped. Finally. My brain felt slightly shredded.

Matt continued. "She wrote stuff down but it wasn't like a book. Short stories, maybe, or thoughts. She didn't like to show it to me so I never asked or pried. I respected her privacy. I'm not even sure where it is now. Funny."

I flushed slightly, but fortunately in the dim light he couldn't tell. He might not know where it was but I sure did, on the bedside table of Sleepy Niner room 23.

"What did she write?"

He shrugged, an almost fatalistic gesture, not an I-don't-care one. "You're asking me?"

I was. Why not? He was there, he was handy, he was talking.

"Romance, I think. That's what she talked about, romance, true love, your *one* true love." There was not only emphasis there but bitterness. "She wanted what she couldn't have and if, by chance, she got it, it lost its magic. It was only an imitation then, a copy, and not the real thing."

Like so much in our lives, I thought, the dream was more appealing than reality. I decided to cut to the chase, dump my brutal questions and thoughts on the table. As Matt pointed out, tact was not my strong suit.

"Like you?"

"Yeah," he said and cracked his knuckles. "Like me."

"How did it go?"

"I met her because I was dating her sister."

"Chivogny?" Of course, dummy, I snapped at myself, who else? My mind was playing for time, running on full-tilt boogie, running, not scoring. "You and Chivogny were serious?"

"I was interested; she was too."

"And Deidre?"

"She . . ." He spread his hands out, palms up. "She was irresistible." He thought it over and added a footnote. "When she wanted to be." Bitterness again. And anger. "And for as long as she wanted to be."

"Were you happy?"

"I thought so then, for a while anyway." He poured more coffee into his mug. "Did you know that intermittent reinforcement of behavior is more effective than a consistent reward policy?"

I shook my head; I hadn't known that. It was a rhetorical question. Matt wasn't looking at me, didn't care if I knew or not.

"Reward a dog now and then for a given behavior and you have him panting and slavering at your heels, hoping, begging for that next pat, biscuit, or word of praise."

He looked at me for the first time since he had poured his still untouched coffee, eyes like open wounds.

"She was the reward; I was the dog."

II

"Hello."

His voice was soft and sexy. And masculine, oh, yes. Very!

"Hi."

"How nice to see you."

Yes, she thought. Oh, God, yes! More than nice. Much more.

"Do you have time for a cup of coffee?"

She nodded dumbly. Yes. Oh, yes, yes. Coffee and cocktails and dinner and dancing and love and forever.

She had time.

....

My phone rang early and long. I caught it only by risking my life scrambling out of the shower and doing a maneuver worthy of an insane teenage gymnast skateboard artist.

I slid across a slippery linoleum floor, hooked my foot in the bedspread fringe (I've always hated fringe!) which sent me flying and sprawling across a virulent green expanse of carpet and bedspread, where I barely maintained as I knocked the phone off the stand, thumped naked onto the bed, and almost sobbed a hello into the receiver (10, 8.3, 9, 9.1, 10—if you're wondering). For future reference I silently noted that grabbing a phone call was not worth chancing your health in this fashion.

"Hey, I didn't wake you, did I? C'mon, the bacon's going, the eggs ready to fry, and the toast—oh, boy, can I burn toast."

"I was in the shower." I went for understatement.

"No wonder it took you so long. Look, Kate, I've been thinking. My roommate's gone for a month, out of town. You could stay with me until you found a permanent place. It's not luxury, but it's really nice."

Her voice was hesitant. She didn't give me time to answer.

"You know, all the time I worked with Deidre, she never would of backed me up like you did last night."

"No?"

"No. No way. She would of gotten a little mad at me, like it was my fault, like I shouldn't have let it happen, maybe even made me apologize to those creeps for the sake of business and stuff."

I made a sympathetic noise.

"So, anyway—" Very hesitant now. "Anyway, I thought you'd be a nice person to get to know, to have as a roommate and stuff. Or whatever. Or, just breakfast?"

"Breakfast sounds great, Charlene."

"Cool! So throw your clothes on and come on over."

"I'm on my way."

I thought about Charlene as I dressed. No, not about Charlene, but about the proposal I had angled for. The disadvantages to rooming with her were one: lack of privacy. I would always have to be in character, in costume, with my guard up; always Kate, never Kat.

The advantages were many: I had an instant friendly local connection and would be accepted in a way that could take me months to earn on my own, and I didn't have months. Accepted and welcomed. This good-time girl would haul me along to parties, outings, the works, I could tell. And she would know the inside story. More importantly, if the past was an indication, she would readily tell me what she knew.

Rooming with Charlene would also insulate me from Matt and an unwanted intimacy. I seemed available but I wasn't: I had a job, a life, and, in best-case scenario oh-tell-me-it's-so, a boyfriend in a somewhere-else alternate reality. Matt needed help, love, comfort, a roll in the hay, and who knows what else, but not things I had to offer him. Never mind the issue of my job, my presumed impartiality, and the fact that he *could* be the killer I was hired to find, not roll in the hay with.

How many reasons was that? Three? Number four was the same as the disadvantage. Since I didn't like living in my life, my world, right now, I might as well live in Kate's. Kat was a drag anyway, worrying, brooding, having nightmares, torments, and heartaches. Last night's dream played again in my mind: the shots, the screaming, the blood, the tears.

Hey, Charlene, where do I sign on?

I roared around a corner, up Broad Street, through downtown Nevada City (so much for that thirty seconds) and turned on a quiet residential street not far from the historic Catholic cemetery. There were restored Victorians, quaint country cottages, and ramshackle shacky houses within spitting, or tea-sipping, distance of each other on narrow, tree-lined streets.

I love Nevada City.

I parked in front of a little and cute (cute is okay, cute *plays*, in Nevada City) house that needed a paint job, but not too badly, and had climbing vines twining around and over a beautifully wrought iron fence and promising wonderful roses and other things unspecified for spring.

I was wearing a smile. I was Kate, not Kat. I knocked on the door and said good-bye to Kat's nightmare albatross.

"Kate," Charlene called, "c'mon in. I'm in the kitchen."

I walked through a pleasant but small living room with an overstuffed couch, doilies, and a ceramic shepherdess in a place of honor on the mantel. There was more but that was all I had time for. Doilies, a shepherdess, and Charlene? Live and learn.

"How do you like your eggs?" Charlene gave me a little hug with one arm and waved a spatula hello with the other. She was wearing jeans with rips in the knees and a faded T-shirt.

"Sunny-side up."

"Mmmmm, me too. See. We'd be perfect as roommates."

I thought eggs were too small an issue to generalize from but I was reckless and game. "Why not?"

She grinned and slapped bacon, perfect eggs, and toast, all done at the same time (how did she do that?) on warmed plates. I was impressed and said so.

She dimpled. "I used to be a fry cook. Dive in while it's hot." We ate before we talked.

"Well?" she asked, after eggs and toast.

I let it hang in the air for a while before I answered. "Well what?"

"You and Matt have fun?"

I made a face.

She laughed and dropped her voice: " 'Kate, stay, will you? I'd like to talk to you.' " Her voice was gruff as well as low, surprisingly like Matt's. "Hey, he likes you."

"Yeah, no shit, Sherlock."

She dimpled.

"What am I going to do?" I asked.

"What do you want to do?"

"I want to keep my job and stay out of trouble. I don't want anyone in my life right now and if I did it wouldn't be a guy whose wife was just murdered, who's still all screwed up about it, and is my boss besides."

She nodded in agreement.

"No matter how good looking and sexy he is."

She giggled; we both did. I hadn't giggled in years. Of course it wasn't *me* giggling, it was Kate. I had just started to wonder about that, to wonder if I should worry about it actually, when Charlene intercepted my half-born/half-baked thought. That's life with a roommate.

"He is, isn't he, and it's not just looks, he—" She turned abruptly and began stacking up the dishes, then piled them in the sink. "So, what color you want your nails?"

"I never do my nails." But Kate might, I thought.

"Never? Well, shoot, it's time for a change."

"Okay, what color do you think?" I listened to the words coming out of my mouth with surprise. This Kate had a mind and life of her own.

"Coral? I got a nice pinky coral. Let's try that."

So we did, and Kate loved it, Charlene loved it, and I liked it okay too. We were practically unanimous.

"You know, we ought to do something about your hair. It's too thick and heavy around your face. We ought to layer it a little, streak it maybe. It'd be a world of difference."

I must have looked nervous. I should have. I *was*.

"Don't worry. I used to be a hair stylist."

"Hair stylist, hash cook, cocktail waitress. What else?"

"Beekeeper, produce sorter, bookkeeper—that was only for two weeks. I was rotten at it. I'm *great* at hair, though. What do you think?"

"All right." Where were these words coming from?

An hour and a half later I stared at myself in the bathroom mirror. My face was framed with fluffy, layered curly brown hair abundantly streaked with blond.

"Wow!" Charlene picked up a pink twistie and made an off-center topknot ponytail, then clipped on neon pink earrings. "You look *great!*"

I did. Or Kate did. We did. Something. I sure as hell looked different.

"C'mon, let's go shopping, maybe grab a bite of lunch."

No, I almost said, *I loathe shopping.* But Kate might not, I remembered in time. I bought some new stuff in colors and fabrics I never wear, then we had a house key made for me and I checked out of the motel. It was three-thirty. Charlene took off and I just had time to stop by Chivogny's store before work. I wasn't at all sure that she would remember asking me to come by her store, to be her friend. And, if she remembered, would she still feel the same way? Probably not.

I tossed back blond curls with coral-tipped fingers. What the hell. Kate was in a reckless mood.

The store was tiny, tucked in between an old-fashioned hardware store and a restaurant, and cute. Too cute, even for Nevada City. It was brimming over with "udderly" delightful cows, cats (meow-wow!) that were overgrown kittens, lace, bows, and enough country cotton to tent over a good chunk of Cleveland. There were horehound drops, root beer suckers, and licorice whips in glass jars on the counter. A cowbell clonked as I entered.

Terminally cute. Part of me longed for a hand grenade to put it out of its misery; the other part remembered that much of the world adored terminally cute. Coral fingernails and blond streaks flashed before my eyes and inspired a more temperate, tolerant mood. I looked around for a path through this jangle/jungle of cuteness. It was hard not to choke on the overpowering smell of potpourri.

"May I help you?" Chivogny's smile was automatic, her eyes wandering unhappily in another world, not really looking at me. There were circles under those eyes. There should have been after last night. Alcoholic justice.

"Hi."

I found the path and started to tread lightly, gently through the ribbons, lace, and ceramics. What did people who like this call it? Not cute, surely. Country? Quaint? I would have to ask.

"Hi," Chivogny said and let her eyes come halfway back from the other world to look in my direction. Do I know you? they asked, not caring if they did or didn't, but only if it would help make a sale.

"It's Kate," I said as I made it to the counter with an inner sigh of relief. It had been touch and go but I hadn't destroyed anything, hadn't stepped on anything. "We met last night. I'm the new bartender at—"

"Oh."

I recognized that oh. It was the I-had-too-much-to-drink-and-said-things-I-shouldn't-have oh. The kind of oh that remembered that while she was drunk I had been sober, and although she might have forgotten what transpired I wouldn't have. I had to get it out of the way, neutralized immediately, or kiss off this conversation.

"Hey, I didn't get a chance to talk to you all *that* much last night, but from what you said—" She blanched slightly. "—your store sounded *great* and I couldn't wait to come by."

"Oh?"

Good. That was a maybe-it's-not-as-bad-as-I-remembered oh. We were doing fine. "Would you help me pick out a present?" More intemperate cash flow. Sorry, Tobias. "I'm terrible at presents."

"Oh!" Home free. "Well, sure, what do you need?"

"Charlene's letting me stay with her until I find my own place. I'd like a thank-you present, nothing too fancy or excessive," (a stretch in here) "but not cheap either, naturally," I added hastily. "Something"—I took a deep breath and looked around me—"something cute maybe, cute but *tasteful.*" Another stretch.

"Of *course.* How about something like this?"

She bounced around the store and I followed, not bouncing, treading softly, carefully, a potential bull in this china shop. We looked at a cut glass bowl of potpourri, a mat that said WELCOME! and had kittens batting a ball of blue yarn about on it, a ceramic goose with cotton balls coming out of its arched back, and a copper basket with hollow painted eggs in it.

I knew I couldn't live, even for a day, with any of that. It was all I could do not to throw up right there. Maybe the eggs. Maybe not. They looked pretty fragile.

"What are those?"

"Oh! Aren't they adorable? Too precious for words! They're salt 'n pepper shakers."

I stared at them, positive that precious wasn't the right word. They were four-inch cows, white dappled with black, sitting on their haunches, front hooves on their "knees" with extended udders and hot-pink teats to dispense a ration of salt, a dash of pepper. They were smiling, even though cows don't smile. I *know* this. I know cows. Real cows.

I liked them anyway. I could live with them, too, which was more to the point. They weren't cute, they weren't tasteful; they were borderline raunchy. How had they survived in here? It was a wonder to me that they hadn't been mugged by enraged droves of little kitties and duckies.

"I'll take them."

She scooped them up.

"Do you have a gift bag?"

She scooped that up.

I paid in cash, then lingered, putting my money away. "This sure is a nice town."

"Are you new in town, or just new at—" She tripped over her tongue, or syllables, or thoughts. "—at the Pioneer?"

"Both. I've been up here quite a bit. I'm from Sacramento, but—shoot, I'm still an outsider, not a local. So help—tell me what I need to know."

I grinned as coral-tipped fingers flicked streaked brown hair over my shoulders and I remembered a movie I'd seen years ago—or had I made it up in my mind? No, I can't think up such weird stuff on my own.

In the movie, aliens took over the body of the hero's sister. Surprise, surprise. She looked and acted the same but something was off in the way she talked: *How* are *you?* she said. *Want* a Coke? she asked. Let's go down*town,* she suggested. So he knew, the hero did. That's what heroes are for, to know just like that. So he killed her. Just like that. Like all good heroes, he was a tough guy who didn't let feelings and sentiment stand in his way. Or have nightmares.

Of course primal certainty is a lot easier in movies than in real life. I made a quick sideways and surreptitious sweep for tough guys. None. So far, all clear. That was good. So far.

"Oh, Kate." Chivogny laughed and it sounded like the clonk of the cowbell on her door. "You'll be fine." Clonka-clonka-clonka, she laughed. "You probably fit in *anywhere.*" The emphasis sounded suspicious. I looked at her quickly, the alien sister still on my mind.

"I don't know about fit in. I just try to land on my feet."

Chivogny looked at her watch. "Oh, goody, break time."

I jumped on it. "How about a cup of coffee?"

"Sure."

Over coffee it got down and dirty. About time. I started it. Surprise. I brought up Deidre. Surprise, surprise.

"I said a lot last night. I—I don't feel good about it," Chivogny stammered.

"Don't ever apologize for what you say when you're drinking."

She shrugged, still embarrassed.

"I don't."

"Oh?" A she-understands-and-does-it-too-and-I'm-okay kind of oh.

"But I'm sorry your birthday wasn't more fun."

She looked out the window, so I did too. A beat-up panel truck with a *Make Love Not War* sticker (Where would you even find them these days, supposing—a big suppose—you wanted to, of course?) on it was fighting a Honda Accord for a parking place. The van won.

A degenerate bearded-hippy tattooed-biker type wearing a muscle shirt with ripped-out sleeves—it was fifty-eight degrees outside!—climbed out of the van and flipped off the Accord. Actions speak louder than bumper stickers. Peaceful biker type was probably an oxymoron anyway. Like liberal fascist, old news, militant peace, or—

"Yeah. Me, too."

Me too what? I yanked my mind back. Birthdays, that's what. "And I'm sorry about your sister. I didn't know." Okay, so I was lying through my teeth. I did know. At least the sorry part was true. "I didn't understand until—"

"Yes. Thank you. That's been hard." She was formal, reserved.

The biker type lowered his finger and waddled off down the street. He had fat thighs and walked like a two-year-old with a load in his diapers. Cute on a two-year-old, it didn't do much for him.

"She was special, Deidre, my sister, and I miss her, yet I don't."

"Oh?"

"She was already gone. Isn't that sad?"

"Huh?"

"Ooops." She looked at her watch. "Time's up. Look, I wouldn't mention it, but you asked."

I had, I agreed. Actually I'd asked a lot of things. Which one was she referring to?

"I'm only saying this for your own good."

Now, that was original. I thought this, I didn't say it. What I did do was nod in pensive appreciation and get ready for a load of spite. I could be wrong. I had been before, many times, but never about this.

She smiled sweetly, so I knew I was right. "It's Matt. It's obvious he likes you."

How? Matt hadn't even been there when she was.

She read my expression. "News travels fast in a small town, Kate. But take it for what it's worth. Charlene told you, didn't she?" Chivogny stood up. "No?"

I shrugged. She'd lost me.

"They had an affair. He was *fucking* her."

Could you have an affair without fucking? I wondered. Probably, but it didn't sound like as much fun as with.

"He was married." The words hissed out from between clenched teeth and lips whose lipstick had been half chewed off. Her face was pale, a pulse jumping in the hollow of her neck.

She picked up her purse and walked.

Without paying for her coffee and sweet roll.

Son of a bitch.

12

She reached out longingly for her dream. He was tall, dark, handsome, and mysterious. In her mind she could only see his silhouette. She couldn't see a clear picture of him, but he was there. She knew it. He was there and he was hers and he was coming.

....

"Don't judge her too harshly."

A young woman who looked like a slim, purple, poetically inclined elf with large gray eyes and surprise-shaped eyebrows slipped into the chair Chivogny had just vacated, pushed the dirty coffee cup aside distastefully and signaled for the waitress.

"Why?"

It was the obvious question, but what the heck? The newcomer didn't answer it either. What the heck.

"I don't mean to get personal but . . ."

Here we go again. People who say *I'm only saying this for your own good* aren't. People who say *I don't mean to get personal* do. And I hadn't even *met* this person yet. I braced myself.

"Did you know your aura's all out of adjustment?" Her earrings were yin/yang symbols and they swung slightly in rhythm with her words or inner harmony or whatever.

Coral fingernails, streaked hair, malicious storytellers, and now my aura was out of adjustment. What a day.

"Yes?" The waitress.

"Chamomile tea, please," the aura reader said prettily.

"No chamomile. We have lemon, peppermint, or Sleepy-Time?"

My companion wrinkled her nose. "Lemon. Oh, and a muffin, please. Bran."

Bran. Of course. Naturally. It was probably better for your aura.

"Who are you?"

"Oh, *must* we?" A sweet, unreadable smile played around her lips but wouldn't settle. "Couldn't we just *be* in the essence of *All?*"

We could, of course. "An introduction doesn't seem greatly out of place with tea, a muffin, and talk about others."

"Oh. Well, my name is Luna. Like the moon," she added.

Or like lunatic, I thought. "Why shouldn't I judge her harshly? And who is 'her'? Deidre? Chivogny?"

"Would you want another to judge you so?"

Begging the question and she had brought it up. I picked up my check and started to rise.

"No. Wait, please."

I sat back down, but kept the check in my hand, poised, ready.

"You haven't even told me your name yet."

"Kate."

"Your aura tells me you have suffered great pain recently, Kate, perhaps even that death has touched you."

Hey! What happened to aura privacy? Her eyes flicked over to mine, the smile flitting around her mouth, still not settling.

"You play at being cool and aloof, but underneath that cool hard surface is pain."

A world of hurt. And playacting. A world of that too. Not just Deidre's. Mine, Matt's, Chivogny's, and Luna's, I thought. Her gray eyes met mine and this time held. Luna had mastered the art of the dramatic pause, no question.

"I agree with you."

Satisfaction flitted across her face like a quick filmstrip. "Ah, yes, thank you. The truth, you know, can be read anywhere: in the aura, the palm, the stars—"

"I think you are being very personal, and surely you did not sit down just to fine-tune my ethical judgment and my aura?" My voice sounded mildly irritated, yet curious. And that was it. I was.

Curiosity kills the cat, Kate.

Another filmstrip flitted across her face, this one against a flushed background. "I wanted to warn you."

I thought over what she had said. "And have you done that?" I didn't think so but it was apparent that Luna and I did not operate within the same frame of reference.

"No."

"Well?"

"You *are* blunt, aren't you?"

"Not blunt enough to walk up to a stranger and comment on her aura."

"Ah." Her gaze held mine. She might look like a shy purple elf but she didn't act or sound like one. "I wish to warn you of evil."

How sweet. And service right at my doorstep, so to speak, just like the Avon lady or a Jehovah's Witness.

"Warn away."

She frowned at me. "Do *not* take evil lightly."

I didn't, I don't, not at all. We were in perfect agreement on that one. I just wasn't sure we were in the same frame of reference yet.

"I was a friend of Deidre's."

She sipped delicately at her tea, a pinky extended as I imagined an English lady would, or a nineteenth-century Boston Brahmin, not that I knew much about either.

"There was evil around her. At the restaurant. In the bar. I urged her to stop work there, but she would not. She was convinced that she would meet her destiny there."

And she had. "Destiny?"

"The meaning of her life, the completion of her being, the yang for her yin."

I must have looked a little blank. "Could you be more specific?" I asked when she showed no intention of elaborating.

"True Love."

Oh, right, *that* kind of destiny. "But Deidre was married."

She tossed a pitying look my way. First I hadn't understood the ways of the universe and now I didn't get it about true love. Sad.

"Married, yes. It was her destiny to meet Matt, to marry, to get with child by him."

Get with child? It sounded awfully biblical for the late twentieth century.

"But that was not True Love." Pity in her eyes again.

I was beginning to feel like Dumbo, but without ears to hide behind. Worse luck.

"That was not her Ultimate Destiny."

"Oh." I didn't have a lot to say on this topic so I figured I'd just throw in the usual ums, ohs, and ahs, keep the conversational ball rolling.

"She was convinced that she must meet her destiny, her True Love, out in the World and so she kept working there. I tried to guide her to meet him on a spiritual plane but she refused. She was very stubborn about it."

I thought Deidre had something there, and that it would be easier to get a date in a bar than on a spiritual plane. Unless, maybe, it was a 747. I almost laughed out loud at my own cleverness, but managed to choke it back to a smirk. I hadn't seen any indication that Luna had a sense of humor.

"And she thought that she could control the evil, that she could make herself a pure spiritual prism of light and keep it at bay, alas."

"She couldn't?"

"She wouldn't. She didn't. She died there, as I'm sure you've heard. The Force of Evil is very strong."

Yes. Especially when armed with a .22. "What was this force of evil?"

"I don't know. I tried to find out, to help protect her but, alas, evil is often impenetrable."

"Yes." She'd finally said something I could relate to. "How did you know it was there?"

She looked at me as a teacher looks at a dim and unpromising pupil. "I could *see* it. I could *feel* it."

Oh, of course.

"I *knew* it."

Naturally.

"If you need help, call me. Any time of day or night." She placed a business card on the table. The name, Luna, was centered on the card and beneath that, *Spiritual Consultant* and a local phone number.

"The evil is there still, at the Pioneer. I know it. I see it. Be *very* careful."

My skin prickled. My aura probably slipped further out of adjustment.

"Good-bye."

Had she accented her words correctly? Was she an alien? She slipped quickly out the door.

Without paying.

Son of a bitch.

"Are you getting that, too?" the waitress asked.

I nodded glumly. I was for now. Tobias was in the long run.

The waitress put her hands on her hips and pursed her lips. "She's slick, that one. Hardly ever pays anywhere."

"Maybe pure spiritual prisms of light don't pay?"

She snorted with laughter. "Maybe."

I left her a ridiculously large tip. She was wholesome and likeable and she wasn't an alien. Like Luna, I just *knew* it.

"Hey, Charlene." The door banged behind me.

"Yo."

She was in the bathroom in bikini panties and a lace bra, using a curling iron on her hair. I put the present bag on the kitchen table and stood in the hall.

"I was in Molly's Café having coffee and reading the paper when Chivogny came in, said hello and sat down."

A slight variation on the truth. Oh well, *I* didn't claim to be a pure spiritual prism of light.

"If that's your idea of fun"—Charlene flicked a curl back—"shoot, you got things to learn."

"She spoke about you."

"Yeah." Not quite a question, not quite a comment.

"She said you and Matt had an affair."

Charlene put down the curling iron, lifted an arm, and looked at her armpit. "Shoot, better shave these suckers." She looked around for a razor. "Anybody notice your hair?"

"No, but nobody knows me well enough to see the difference. It's great though. I really like it."

Maybe instead of coping with things on the inside I could just keep changing stuff on the outside, until finally I was a different person in a different world, the world of hurt, the blood, a dim memory behind me. Charlene finished shaving her underarms and doing her makeup and then carefully pulled a sweatshirt over her head and climbed into jeans. So far we were both practicing avoidance.

"Yeah. We did. Yesterday's news." Her voice was flat and hard. She would hide the pain by getting hard. I couldn't relate to that, of course. She started for the kitchen. "You want a Pepsi?"

"Okay."

She thunked a couple of cans on the kitchen table. "Hey, what's this?"

"A present."

"Cool!"

I love it when people don't say *Aw, you shouldn't have.* Charlene pulled the cows out of tissue paper and started giggling, then set them on the table and rummaged in the cupboards for salt and pepper.

"Here." She handed me the salt and the S cow and we filled them up.

"They're terrific! Thanks, Kate."

"You're welcome."

"I should have known better, of course." Her eyes got bright and shiny.

Yeah. We all should. That's the thing about love. We should. We do. But we don't.

"We didn't plan it. It just happened the way these things do. Not that we tried very hard to stop it. We didn't, either of us. You know how it is closing the bar together."

I know how it is.

"First we'd just have a drink and talk at the bar. One night Matt drove me home because my car had a dead battery. He came up for a drink and . . ."

Yes. And . . .

"And I got in over my head." She picked up a cow and played with it, shook some salt in her hand, and then licked a fingertip and dipped it in the salt. With just the tip of her tongue showing she licked her finger.

"It was my fault. Matt was really straight with me."

Her voice was bitter. I knew what was coming. There's a way some guys have. They say *Don't fall for me, I have nothing to offer you.* And then they do everything they can to make you fall. When you do, when you want more, they say *I'm sorry, but I told you.* And walk off.

"He said it was only an affair for him. Oh, he cared for me, yeah, but he would never love me, never leave his wife and baby. And he didn't."

No. And he was the boss screwing around with an employee, which didn't speak well for him.

"Did he do that a lot, have affairs?"

"No. He said not and I believe him. I never ever heard talk either, not until after Deidre died. He was desperate, I think, lonely and desperate. Deidre was often off in her own world and it hardly ever seemed to include him. She had her child and her friends, her writing and her dreaming."

Charlene took a deep breath. "Deidre hadn't slept with Matt since Toby was born. Can you *imagine?* A good-looking, sexy guy like Matt. I don't get it."

But good-looking and sexy didn't have anything to do with it. Those weren't the issues, the stakes. I thought of the story fragments Tobias had entrusted to me. "Was Deidre having an affair?"

"I don't think so." She sprinkled some salt on the table, then pepper, and started making black and white designs. "In fact, I'm sure she wasn't, except in her mind. She was looking and wanting and waiting for some big romance—that was her thing. It was almost as if she'd left Matt behind long ago. She treated him as a partner but not as a husband, not really. Oh, she was nice and friendly enough, but businesslike."

"And Matt?"

"He was waiting too, waiting and hoping she would come back to him, have another child, get over her dreaming and be real, be his again. He didn't really want an affair with me. He wanted his wife back. He just settled for me and an affair out of loneliness and desperation."

All the layers of hurt, one after another. That was what this job was about, that was what I did. I sifted through layers of hurt. People came to me with simple requests: Find this person. Untangle this business deal. Discover the facts in an unsolved death.

And sometimes I could do that. But what they really meant, really wanted, was different, was unspoken. It was: This hurts. I'm hurt. Fix it. Take away the pain and bring me happiness. And I couldn't do that. Not even for myself.

You can't outrun sorrow.

"Deidre was very beautiful in her way. Men would turn to look at her, but after a while I think they would lose interest. Part of it was that she was too caught up in her own world, but a lot of it was that she wasn't sexy. I don't think that she liked or cared about sex much at all. She wanted romance. She acted like she couldn't even, couldn't ever understand why people would get all hot and excited, covered with sweat and come and love . . ."

I shivered.

"Yes," she said, "exactly."

The first time I saw Charlene I wrote her off, wrongly, as an airhead—

that shrewd professional P.I. instinct, I guess. On maybe I was on the wrong plane. I'd have to ask Luna.

"What happened?"

"With me and Matt?"

"Yes."

"It ended kinda bad, but kinda okay. I knew it'd blow over in time. It was over before Christmas, before Deidre died. I wondered if after . . . if once he got over her death a little he'd . . . But he hasn't."

"He's not over it yet."

"No, but he's not looking in my direction, he's looking in yours."

"I'm not looking."

"And I don't care. I'm over it, over him." She swept the salt and pepper off the table onto the floor. Maybe she believed that. I didn't. "Hey, we got to get ready for work."

I yawned and stretched. It had been a long day and it was only half over. Rats.

"Charlene, do you know a woman named Luna?"

"Sure, yeah."

"What do you think?"

"She's spacey, but not nearly as much as she makes out. I don't think she is what she seems. Do you like these earrings? Do they go with this top?"

I nodded.

"But then, who is?"

That was the question, all right. And not just about Luna.

13

"Never!" she cried. "I would rather scour floors, scrub clothes, and wash dishes until my hands were raw and bleeding than let you lay a finger on me!"

"We'll see!"

His eyes were blazing as he advanced on her.

....

It was nine-thirty or ten when he came in, sat down at the bar and ordered a Black Label on the rocks. He wore black jeans, a black western shirt with pearl snaps, black hat, black belt, and black cowboy boots and he'd obviously watched too many B-grade movies.

He stared at me too directly, too much, and too long. A warning flag went up. Bartenders, like cops, develop a sixth sense for trouble. Not that I needed a sixth sense in an obvious case like this.

"Dancing in here?"

"We have live music on the weekends."

"Not tonight?"

It was a Thursday. "Not tonight," I agreed.

"You're new, aren't you?"

"Yes."

"Pretty as the gal who worked here before." I didn't take it as a compliment. It wasn't. An observation, perhaps. "What was her name, Deedee?"

"Deidre."

"Yeah. Play you for a drink?" He pointed to the dice cups on the back bar.

"We don't do that here."

"What *do* you do here?" It was almost a snarl. I walked away.

He was halfway through his drink before he got up to play the jukebox. At six one or two with wide shoulders, narrow hips, and muscular thighs, he fancied himself; he thought he was something. I did too, but not the same kind of something. *Beauty is only skin deep. Handsome is as handsome does.* That kind of something. My grandmother, Alma, is fond of saying things like that. And she is generally right—another thing she is fond of saying.

The jukebox started playing "Honky Tonk Angel."

"What's with Mr. Attitude?" Charlene asked.

"I don't know. He walked in like that."

"He's the kind of guy who only looks good till he opens his mouth."

"Yes."

There are a lot of people like that, men and women, and a lot of them go to bars, don't have the sense that God gave gravel, and don't keep their mouths shut. It's too bad but it goes with the territory.

"Nice place to have a bar, too bad you can't get a drink around here." He banged his empty glass down hard. An ice cube bounced out.

"Aw, shit." Charlene looked at me nervously, not quite sure of me or the situation. "Want backup?"

"Not yet."

I walked down the bar, crossed my arms and stared at him the way he stared at me, insolent, hard, challenging.

"We're kind of old-fashioned around here. We go out for a drink and a nice time. We say please and thank you. If you're looking for trouble, look someplace else."

"No trouble, ma'am." He put his hands up as though I had a gun on him. "Please, may I *please* have a drink, ma'am, thank you."

He paid for the drink with a hundred and left the change on the bar. He made that drink last and didn't buy another one, said nothing else to me, to me or anyone. All he did was watch me and play the Police singing "Every Move You Make" over and over. It was creepy. It was meant to be.

After I served him I didn't pay him much mind. There were drinks to make and a lot of regulars there. I had enough to do. When I wasn't busy I spoke with Charlene, with the guys, or cleaned behind the bar. I was pushing my way slowly through a cupboard that had last been cleaned out sometime in the Roosevelt administration (Teddy, not Franklin) looking for clean bar towels when I heard a quiet voice behind me.

"When you have a chance?"

"Sure."

I looked up into a friendly grin on a teddy bear face and bounced up to a standing position, kicking the cupboard door shut behind me and tossing a napkin on the bar in front of him.

"What can I get you?"

"Draft would be fine."

We exchanged drinks, money, and pleasantries. "Every Move You Make" came on for probably the fifth time, the second or third since the teddy bear guy, whose name was Barry, had arrived.

He looked the question at me. "What's the deal?" I looked back, my face a blank, and he laughed. "My guess is as good as yours?"

"You got it," I agreed. We grinned at each other.

He pulled a couple of dollars off the pile on the bar in front of him and headed for the juke. He was about five ten and wide, solid muscle in a plaid shirt and jeans. He didn't strut when he walked; he didn't have to. He was easygoing and confident and nobody in their right mind would mess with him.

The black snarl didn't even look up. Two bucks buys a lot of plays on the jukebox. Barry hit them all, all except the Police.

"Can I get another, please?" He slid back onto his stool and put his empty mug on the bar in front of him. "Can I buy you one?"

"Thanks, I don't drink while I work."

"Maybe another time, a rain check?"

I smiled in a noncommittal fashion and left to get his draft and make drinks for Charlene. He was too savvy and polite to pursue it, but he'd made his point. I had, too.

"Ordering," Charlene said. "Vodka tonic, bourbon water, three drafts, a Coors—no with, white wine, coffee back. That was cool."

"What?"

"The way you handled The Jerk."

"Thanks. Have you ever seen him before?"

"I don't think so. Definitely not in here and I don't even think around town."

She pulled her drinks and took off. He'd been in before though, he remembered Deidre. I looked at the clock. Ten-thirty. I sighed louder than I meant to.

"Long day?"

"Long day," I agreed.

"I know you from somewhere."

My heart sank. "*Hey*, everybody says that. You can come up with a better line."

"If it was a line, I could. You're not from around here, are you?"

My heart sank some more. It was stomach level and dropping fast, heading for my knees, maybe my shoes. "Sacramento mostly. Fresno, Stockton, Bay Area too." It was like making stockpot soup—I threw in whatever was handy. "Lodi, Modesto—"

"What do you do?"

"I'm a bartender."

I made my voice soft and patient. Out of the corner of my eye I could see Black Label Rocks. He was casual, relaxed, and obviously not paying attention, so I knew he was listening to every word. He'd been tense and taut all evening; I was now watching "A Study in Nonchalant Eavesdropping." *Damn!*

"Sure, I'm sorry, I didn't mean it that way. Just—what else have you done?"

"Gone to school a lot. I keep trying to finish up but then I change my mind. I started off in Social Science and then I—"

"Law enforcement? You ever take any classes in that or work in security?"

Aw, shit. Black Label stared with patent disinterest at the ceiling. If he could have angled his ears he would have. "No." I said it with, I hoped, shy sincerity and then zipped on to a lie. "Just a self-defense course at the Y, but that was all women."

Barry looked at me intently and shook his head. "The hair's different, but the eyes, I could have sworn . . . Don't see green eyes like yours often." Silently I blessed Charlene's make-over of me.

"Ordering!"

I blessed her again and walked off. I looked at the clock. Ten-forty. Rats. The night was getting longer by the minute.

"I could *swear*—" he said later.

So I looked him straight in the eye. "Maybe it was in the movies, I was big in Hollywood for a while; or on the society pages; or the sports pages when I was a tennis star. Gimme a break, okay? The world's a big place. I wish I were someone fancy and famous but I'm not. I'm a bartender. I'm just getting by like everyone else."

"Okay, sorry, I'll drop it and have another beer, if I may?"

"Sure."

So he dropped it but he didn't stop looking at me, or my eyes, and neither did Black Label. Like I said, it was a long night, and the later it got, the longer it got. Barry finished his draft beer, left me a good tip, said good-night-see-you-soon in a nice way, and left.

One down, one to go.

Black Label didn't leave until I gave last call.

"Hey," said Charlene, checking out the bar and watching him walk. Well, strut or saunter. Amble arrogantly. Something more than walk. "He stiffed you."

I finished making her drinks. "What a surprise!"

We both laughed.

"What is?" Matt was behind me, close, reaching past me into the well for ice. "Coke, please." The soda gun was near my hand. I splashed some into his glass.

"Tell Matt." I shook my head slightly. So Charlene told him. "Macho, Jerk, Creep." She wound it up in capital letters.

"Kate?"

"Yeah, he was, but it's nothing I can't handle, not yet, so no big deal."

Yet. That was the key word and we were all thinking of Deidre. Nothing like murder to make you paranoid. We finished up quickly that evening, no banter, no drinking, not much talking. We saw Charlene to her car and then Matt walked me to the Bronco. We both checked it out as I opened the door and the interior light came on.

"Lock your door." He thumped the roof of the car and walked to his truck.

I kept my eye on the rearview mirror as I drove off, saw it right away.

The vehicle, truck I thought, pulled out behind me about three quarters of a block from where I was parked. After a couple of blocks he snapped on his lights. If I hadn't been watching I would have thought he'd come on the road there, not back at the restaurant.

I didn't drive home. I detoured. This had happened to me before as a bartender, guys hiding out in their cars, waiting for me, hoping to get lucky or make their own luck. No way I wanted this clown knowing where I lived. He detoured too. Wasn't this fun? Midnight tag and I was IT.

I made a couple more turns, then got on Highway 49 North to Nevada City. My shadow, a black pickup truck I could see now, followed. He hung back, not going for obvious yet. Why he? I speculated. She? It? Aliens?

I tried to remember how Black Label had spoken, where the emphasis had been. How off was he? No help there, no telling. He was probably so far off in the big stuff that the little stuff didn't matter. Nice thought. Comforting.

The pickup was closing the distance between us now. We were almost to Nevada City. I got off at Broad Street, swung onto the off ramp, onto the on ramp, hit the freeway screaming and floored it. No big deal, of course. My vision didn't blur, my pulse didn't race, my adrenaline was calm. Flooring it in a Bronco isn't exactly signing on for whiplash or jet lag.

He was still behind me, the distance closing again—nothing like a V-8—Grass Valley getting close again. It was beginning to feel like a low-budget bad movie except low-budget bad movies aren't scary.

This was.

I got off at the Colfax exit in Grass Valley taking it a little too fast, laying down a little Goodyear and wasting a batch of perfectly good brake pad, turning right and then hanging an immediate left onto Main and then another quick left onto Stewart.

I burned through lights and stops—who was counting? not me—horn blaring (where was a cop when you needed one?) sailed past City Hall and skidded into the parking lot of the Grass Valley Police Department, narrowly missing a patrol car on the way out.

Son of a bitch.

I sat gripping the steering wheel and trying to breathe. I would remember how, it would come back to me, I was confident of it.

The cop was out of his car fast. Good reflexes. He was medium height with dark hair and probably seriously pissed off. I tumbled out of the Bronco. I could have hugged him, I *wanted* to, but I didn't. He was definitely pissed. Understandably. I pointed mutely at the pickup going down Stewart too fast. Gone. The plates were covered with mud. My hand, the one pointing, was shaking slightly.

"Do you know that truck, is it local?"

"Don't know it." Hard, unreadable eyes. Mean mouth.

My hand was still shaking; I stuck it back in my pocket.

"What's going on, miss?"

It was a good question, and one that I thought showed admirable restraint on his part since I'd nearly taken off his right front fender.

"He's been following me since I got off work about twelve-fifteen." I took a deep breath and told my story.

He listened attentively, without interrupting. "You're the bartender at the Pioneer?"

"Yes."

"That's where that gal was killed last Christmas."

"Yes."

He thought that one over. "You see the guy following you?"

"No." I stared at his name plate but couldn't quite make sense of the letters.

"Any idea who it was?"

I told him about Mr. Charm, the snarl in black, although all I knew about him was his drink, his favorite color, his favorite song, and the fact that he'd paid close attention to me tonight.

The pickup was black. Was that enough to link the two? *Get real, Kat. Get a job.* "I have no reason to think it was him, no reason to think it wasn't." No reason for any of this, actually.

"Anyone else in the bar tonight speak to this guy or recognize him?"

"No."

"You want to make a report?"

"Not much point in that, is there?"

"No. I'll put the word out though, have the patrol cars keep their eyes open. You okay to drive?"

He put his hand lightly on my arm, cocked an eyebrow. My hands were still in my pockets but I'd stopped shaking all over, was just trembling ever so slightly. That's how tough I am.

"Where do you live?"

I told him.

"Go on, take off. I'll follow you."

I didn't argue. I thanked him and got in the Bronco. He followed me, watched from the patrol car until I got into the house, then waved. I waved back, shot the lock and leaned against the door. I was still having trouble breathing right.

A world of hurt.

"What happened to you?"

Charlene's face was open, curious. I told her and watched it get closed over and afraid.

That was how I felt too. Maybe it was the Black Label snarl, or the guy who followed me—if they weren't the same. Maybe it was Luna's talk of the Force of Evil. Or aliens. Maybe all that. Or maybe it was someone who didn't want me looking into Deidre's death.

I didn't sleep well. It wasn't because of a blood-red nightmare.

Son of a bitch.

14

"For richer or poorer, in sickness and in health, in good times and bad, until death do us part."

They joined hands.

....

It was eight-thirty and I was caught in a lethargic state, stuck there as though it were a place down the hill, up the road a piece and over-the-river-and-through-the-woods-to-the-murderer's-house-we-go. I lay in my bed in Charlene's house and wondered what kind of person would decorate her room this way. It was country cozy with a kinky depraved slant. The curtains, comforter, and pillow slips all matched. It was a blue cotton print with tasteful accents of green, rose, and lemon, charming until the gag factor was reached, anything over twelve yards (and we were way over that) in a room this size, by my estimation.

A large wicker chair had cushions in a contrasting (but oh-so-adorable) print. The cushions had ruffles and bows. An old-fashioned metal bird cage on a stand was stationed in the corner. A little once-real, now stuffed bird had its beak open so that it could silently sing its heart out forever. A prettily contrived arrangement of silk flowers met its glassy ever-hopeful dead eyes. The cage door was open. Too little, too late for this birdie.

The walls were covered with pictures, some photos, some line drawings. The frames were beautiful—unusual and expensive—silver and gold filigree, cloth and lace, china, cloisonné, antique wood, and gold. The pictures in them were all erotic, some pornographic. I considered a naked, muscle-bulging thigh. No wonder I'd had bad dreams.

The phone tweeted, then stopped. There was a knock on the door and Charlene's tousled head popped in.

"Awake? Oh, good. Look, Kate, Matt's on the phone."

I made a face; she snickered.

"He wants one of us to baby-sit for Toby. His sitter stood him up. I don't want to. Shit. Yeah, like I might die if I didn't go shopping or eat lunch out or something. Yeah, right. But I might, though."

"I'll do it." No problem, in fact.

She wrinkled her forehead, suddenly serious. "You don't owe him. You weren't hired for this."

"It's all right. I don't mind." Another understatement. I picked up the receiver and said hello. Then I said I'd do it, but I made him ask twice, even rev up for three. Better that he looked eager than me.

There was relief in his voice. "Thanks. I got to meet with— Well, anyway. Elsa, my neighbor, you remember her?"

I did, barely. She had been a slim, half-smiling and all-graying blur as he hustled me out of the house and his life the day of the picnic.

"She'll take over this afternoon. She had to get her hair done or something." He said it in the scornful way men do when they can't imagine why a woman's life or plans might be more important to her than theirs. "You remember how to get here?"

"Tell me." He did and I had. "See you in an hour, Matt."

"An hour? Look, Kate—"

"An hour," I said firmly. "See you."

"Yeah. Okay." His assent was reluctant and impatient. Talk about looking a gift horse in the mouth! I yawned, stretched, and climbed out of bed and into the shower.

"So?" Charlene demanded when I appeared, damp still but clean, in the kitchen.

"I don't want to talk about it."

She laughed. "Are you just a really nice person, or a sucker?"

Neither. An investigator, I thought, and almost had the grace to blush.

"He would have taken either one of us; still he *really* wanted you."

"Sweet talker." But she was making me feel better about using him, less guilty. "It's okay, I don't mind. I like Toby. He's a neat kid."

"Yeah, he is. For a kid."

Well, true. There was that.

"I gotta run. I'll see you later." She finished her coffee and wiped her mouth on the back of her hand like a ten-year-old. "Have fun, and hey—" I looked up from the paper spread out on the table. "Keep your eye on your butt."

There was that, too. No kidding.

"I don't have time to go looking for another roommate."

Another roommate. After last night that comment was a bit too close to the truth to be funny, so we didn't laugh, either of us.

"Speaking of roommates . . ." I said, and Charlene raised an eyebrow. "What's yours like? Those pictures . . ."

Laughter. The kind that fills your heart and makes you smile. "Aren't they a *trip?* I mean, *really!* That's why she's gone."

"Because of the pictures?"

"Sort of. It's part of the whole thing anyway. She had a dream, a fantasy."

My mind shuddered, then backed off from the contemplation of her fantasies.

"So she finally decided to live it out." Her eyes were mischievous. "That's important, don't you think, to realize your dreams?"

"And—"

Charlene was playing this out; I was playing along. I aligned the cows so their smiling mugs and red teats were facing each other. I got up and poured another cup of coffee. "And?"

"She's a hooker at a brothel in Nevada. She loves it. I mean *this* girl has a calling for *this* job, plus she loves the money. So why not?"

Exactly. "Benefits too?"

She laughed. "Yup. Medical, dental, monthly checkups and condoms supplied by the management."

"And you don't have to babysit."

"Hey, for sure."

A quick wave, a slamming door, and she was gone. I sat in silence broken by the *uh-uh-uh* of a car outside, a battery that couldn't turn on a flashlight by the sound of it, never mind start a car. The *uh-uh-uh* became *uh . . . uh . . . uh . . .* and then that too stopped. I had one more quick cup of coffee while I thought things out.

"Hi-hi-hi-hi-hi-hi!" Toby was jumping up and down and glad to see me. Matt, on the other hand, was strictly low-key. If he was glad he hid it well and sure fooled me.

"There's lots of stuff for lunch and help yourself to anything."

Anything? But he wouldn't mean what I did by it, snooping through personal items, for instance.

"Emergency and medical numbers are posted here." He gestured to a board on the wall next to the phone. "A rough schedule here." He pointed to the counter and I saw a brief list with lunch, nap, and playtimes. His eyes got dark. "It's been easier for us since . . . it's been easier with a schedule."

"I understand."

"Dad said you'd read me a story before nap, will you, will you, will you?" Still excited. I didn't have to be an investigator to tell.

"You bet."

"Hey!"

"Anything else?"

They both spoke at the same time.

I responded to Matt. "No, you're out of here. See you later."

"Give me a kiss, little guy."

Matt squatted and Toby barreled into him, nearly knocking him over. He hung on to his dad's neck and held up his face for kisses, tucked his hard little body close into his father's arms for hugs. I didn't want it to be Matt, dammit. I hate my job sometimes.

"Be good, little guy."

"Okay." He jumped up and down. "But not *too* good."

Matt patted him affectionately on the bottom and stood up. "Kate, Stu called this morning, said he might be by to borrow some tools. It's all out in the garage and he's welcome. Thanks again."

He looked into my face for probably the first time that day and handed me a broken lopsided grin. Wow. He got over Deidre, he was going to break hearts. That was probably too bad, but that was that, that was certain. Not mine though.

"Kate, wanna see my trucks? I got a train too, wanna see?"

We waved at Daddy and then we got out the trucks and a wooden train with fourteen cars, not counting the engine and caboose. It had cattle and hog cars with livestock that could be loaded and unloaded—which we did —a flatbed with logs, another with cars, and more. Hands down it was my favorite toy.

In the next hour we had two wrecks, one almost-collision with a fire engine (*great* siren!) and one derailment. That was for starters. We lost three pigs and a cow in the derailment. Toby was sure of it; I argued the other way.

"See." I stood them up. "They're all right."

"No!" he shouted. "No, no! They're *dead*." He knocked them down emphatically and smashed them with his hands. "Dead, dead, dead. And now we have to bury them."

I took a deep breath. "All right. Do you know how?"

"Yes."

He got up and disappeared into the back of the house, then reappeared with a fistful of pink Kleenex. Carefully he wrapped each animal and laid it down. Then he arranged the pink bundles in a row and started pulling another tissue into bits.

"These are flowers." He picked the fragments up and flung them on the little wrapped pink bodies. "Now we pray." He put his hands together. "Like this." I did the same. "Please God take good care of these animals and take good care of my mommy. Amen."

"Amen," I said.

The knock on the door startled us both. It wasn't God or Mommy, it was Stu. We were disappointed.

"Huh?" he said and stared blankly at me as we all stood silently at the door.

"Hi, Uncle Stu." Toby was bouncing up and down again. I swear the kid had springs built into his feet somewhere. "This is Kate. She's my baby-sitter even though she's not really a baby-sitter. Say hi, Uncle Stu, say hi."

Stu's face cleared. "Hi, Kate. Hi, Toby." He reached down and roughed up Toby's hair. His eyes were on me. "Did we meet the other night? Are you Matt's new bartender?"

I agreed to both and asked him in.

"We're playing with trains. Do you wanna play, Uncle Stu?"

He didn't look like he did and that made two of us. After the funeral I didn't want to play trains either.

"We're going to make lunch now, Toby." *Funeral meats.* It ran through my head before I could stop it. "What would you like?"

"Peanut butter. Are you going to stay for lunch, Uncle Stu, like you did with me and Mommy?"

"Oh, I don't think—"

"Puhleeeze!"

"You're welcome to," I said warmly, telling myself I was just trying to provide a supportive environment for a saddened little boy, not investigate a murder. I don't fall for my own lies anymore though. Too bad.

"Well . . ." Stu looked at his watch. "It is lunchtime, isn't it?"

"Oh goody, goody." Toby was bouncing up and down again.

"Did Matt mention—?"

"About the tools? Yes. He said to help yourself. What would *you* like for lunch?"

"Peanut butter is fine," he echoed his nephew.

"Can I help you, can I?"

He asked Stu, not me, and they disappeared into the garage to do "men" stuff. I went to the kitchen to do "woman" stuff. Whoopee. Okay, I'm a good sport. I got over it. I did it.

I fixed (canned) soup and sandwiches with cut-up carrots and apples, and was reasonably sure I had all the food groups covered even though I couldn't actually remember them. There were cold cuts in the fridge but I couldn't get funeral meats out of my mind so I ignored them.

Lunch was a pleasant meal with Toby more or less the conversational center and the conversation more or less at a Sesame Street level. I was content to let it go like that and smile disarmingly and innocently at Stu. Ha. After lunch I announced the inevitable.

"Nap time, kid."

"Awwwwww!"

"Go pick out your story while I clear the table."

"Mind if I finish out in the garage, Kate? I didn't get much done . . ."

"Of course." He hadn't offered to do the dishes. Odd.

"Uncle Stu, come kiss me good night for my nap like you did before and sometimes you had a nap with Mommy while I had my nap, huh, Uncle Stu?"

There was an infinitesimal pause. I looked Stu right in the eye. He flinched.

"Uncle Stu!"

"Okay, I'm coming. Scoot along now." Toby scooted. Stu followed. I did the dishes and considered.

If Stu were smart he'd ignore that last (damning) remark. He couldn't do that, though, I'd bet on it. I waited until I heard Stu noises in the garage and then went back to the child's room. Toby was sitting up in bed clutching his teddy bear, grave-faced and subdued, almost teary-eyed.

"Uncle Stu said I was a bad boy and a liar, but I'm *not*, I didn't." His voice caught on a sob.

I held him. "You're a good boy and very sweet and fun to play with."

"I am?" He watched my face carefully, tense and unsmiling.

"Yes."

"Will you come play with me again?"

"If you invite me, yes." Dangerous territory, that. "Did you pick out a story?"

He handed me a book about a bunny rabbit who was sad and lonely and didn't have a mama but in the end it worked out. Thank goodness. I wasn't up to any more trauma today.

"That's a nice story, isn't it?" he asked sleepily as he fell back on his pillow. "I have a bunny, too, see?" He pointed to a worn, shabby bunny at the foot of his bed. "But I sleep with Bear. Night-night."

"Good night." I kissed him.

He was already almost half asleep as I watched, sad that we can't shelter our little ones from such sorrow.

> **She wanted so much to have his child, to tell the whole world of her love for this man. Then he would be hers and she would be his, and the child a symbol of this great love they had.**

Deidre had written that. Was it what she felt about Toby? Had she wanted a symbol or a child who had to be fed, cared for, held, loved and scolded? I kissed the little boy with the sad face again and walked out through the living room and into the kitchen.

"Kate?"

I was right. He couldn't let it be. I looked over at him inquiringly. I was mad that he'd bullied Toby but I stuffed it down. I didn't feel good then, stuffed full of lunch, righteousness, and mad.

"Kids will say anything, won't they?" He laughed but it was uneasy and forced, like roller skates on a gravel road. Uphill.

"No, I don't think so. I think they tell the truth, or what they think is the truth, what they see. Lying is something we learn as we get older, when the stakes get higher. Murder, for instance."

"Listen—"

I listened. I heard the birds outside and a car race by with the windows open and the stereo cranked up to earsplit. I listened for words but I didn't hear any. I started to leave the room, to call his bluff.

"Look—"

"Listen, look, and lies, Stu?" I baited him. "This isn't a child's primer, it's a different kind of story." Not a twice-told tale though; it had been told many more times than that.

"Fuck you! I don't owe you anything, lady."

I agreed, but why let on? I stared back at him, wordless and intimidating. He caved in.

"It's not what Toby made it sound like."

"Yeah. Right. Nice uncles have 'naps' with mommies, and pigs have wings."

He flushed. "Fuck you," he said, but he said it in a tired voice. "You never knew Deidre, so it's hard to explain. She was something it was almost impossible to walk away from."

Some*thing,* not some*one?*

"It was like she was a force field and when she turned it on that was it, the power was too much to resist. You were like a bug drawn to a bug zapper. Get too close and it's over."

"And you got too close."

"Yeah. Look, could we have some coffee or something?"

I put water on to boil and looked for the coffee, surprising myself at my dutiful housewifely response. Stu sat like a man used to having women wait on him.

"I would have done anything for her."

Or to her? I thought. I wanted to say it out loud but not that much, not as much as I wanted to stay out of trouble. I felt sorry for Chivogny, for his wife.

"Deidre didn't care about that." He punched his fist into the palm of his other hand. "Zap!"

I looked for a smushed bug but there wasn't one. He'd smashed a metaphor, not a bug.

15

"Do you love me?" she asked.

His face darkened. "I don't use that word."

"But you do *care* for me?"

He looked at her steadily.

"A *little?*" Her voice quavered.

He glanced at his watch. "We're late. Let's go."

. . . .

"Milk? Sugar?"

I was getting good at this, could probably be a waitress as well as a bartender. Or a housewife. There you go. Dazzling the way career opportunities open up like that.

No answer.

"Yo."

Stu twitched a little and shifted on the vinyl kitchen chair. "We used to sit here and talk for hours sometimes."

I guess that was a no. I didn't bother looking for the sugar and put away the milk.

"I built a deck and spa area onto the house for them. I was around a lot then. Too much." He sipped his coffee and made a face, then stood up and headed for the refrigerator, pulled out the carton of milk. "Damn, why am I boring you with this? Why am I telling you even?"

110

"I'm not bored." Not by a long shot. "Folks always talk to their bartenders." That and guilt should cover it, I thought.

"You heard it all, huh?"

"Oh, no." Thank goodness. But enough.

He poured milk in his coffee, sat down, stood up, sat down. I made
myself sit still and wait.

"I was married to her sister. There was no love lost between them but
still, shit, *sisters* for godssakes."

Another piece of news. Stu was turning out to be a walking, talking,
indiscreet-as-hell gold mine. I encouraged him.

"They weren't close?"

Stu gave me an odd look. "Close? They hated each other, would as
soon as spit as talk."

"Did they?"

"Spit?" He frowned down at his coffee. "Or talk?"

"Either."

"They talked. They could be social, like at Thanksgiving, a barbecue,
or a party, but they didn't visit, or talk their hearts, or share things. They
hated each other. It wasn't on-the-surface hate, it was old, cold hate, childhood hate."

"Why?"

"Maybelle favored Chivogny."

"Maybelle is their mother?"

"Was, yeah. She's dead now and good riddance. Her real name was
Mabel but it didn't sound fancy enough to suit her so she changed it to
Maybelle. Didn't change her personality any though, worse luck."

Another character playing a part.

"To say she favored Chivogny doesn't really explain it. It was much
worse and it was no favor, certainly not to Deidre, but not to Chivogny
either. I always thought it was a shame—the wall of hate between those two.
They wouldn't let it wear down either, kept it in good repair. Maybelle was a
help there."

I listened for birds, trees in the wind, something besides the sound of
hate. Nothing.

His hands were fists and he stared at them. "Why are people such
bastards to the ones they love?"

I was confused. I'd lost track of the characters. "What do you mean?"

"Chivogny loved me. I was her husband, we were trying to have a
baby. So what was I doing playing games with Deidre?"

"Was it a game?"

111

"Not for me," he said miserably.

"For Deidre?"

"I don't know. Well, yeah, in a way it was. Not to hurt me, but part of one of the games she was always playing in her head. Part of that stupid make-believe world of hers. And the thing was, the thing she couldn't understand, was that even though the game, the fantasy, might be over and played out for her, it might not be for the other guy."

He shrugged. "When she was done, she moved on. It never occurred to her that someone else might not be able to do that, might be hurt because of it. She wasn't mean, she just didn't get it. That was part of it." He stood up. "More coffee?"

"Thanks." I waited for the coffee and the other part.

"Deidre always wanted what she couldn't have."

"Like her sister's husband?"

Carefully he poured milk into his coffee, then spoke. "First Matt, then me. As a child Chivogny got whatever she wanted. Deidre got shit and had to say pretty please and thank you for it. As an adult Deidre turned that around. If she didn't have it and Chivogny did, it was a challenge, it became her heart's desire. She was desperate, wild for it. It was something to see Deidre desperate and wild. Something. It was hard to resist."

"And you didn't?"

"I tried, but no, I didn't, I couldn't. I hate myself for that."

"You had an affair?"

"Deidre had an affair, I really fell for her."

"That was when you were working on the deck here?"

"Yeah, and afterward. She was hot for me, wild for me then. I was still trying to stay out of it and she could hardly behave in front of the kid. She wanted me like that until I gave in, until I was hers for the asking. Then I was yesterday's news, good to wrap the garbage in maybe, but nothing else."

There is so much hurt in the world, so much pain, and so much of it in the name of love.

"I loved my wife but I was cheating on her. And the 'love' I felt for Deidre? It was craziness, even hatred sometimes when she wouldn't love me back. I was a man possessed and I hated myself for it."

His face was contorted and ugly, hate written in the lines around his face, in the shape of his mouth and in the depths of his eyes. Had he loved enough, and then hated enough, to kill?

"And you know what? You know what was funny? She wasn't even that good in bed, she didn't care much about sex. But it didn't change anything, didn't change the way I felt. I ran into her on the street once."

Heartbreak must breed non sequiturs.

"When it was over?"

"Over?" He laughed. "Yeah, when it was over. I loved her but she wouldn't listen to me. I never got to say anything to her then, anything real. It was 'Hi, how are you?' when inside I was shouting: *I want you. Love me, need me, live with me.*"

My heart felt heavy with pain. The birds still wouldn't sing. There was no radio outside, no dying car batteries to distract me, nothing but this horrible pain that wasn't even mine. I wasn't paid enough for this, not nearly.

" 'Fine, thanks. How are you?' That's what she said to me. I asked her if she had time for coffee, meaning *I miss you. I think about you all the time. Give me a chance to win your love, just a chance.*

" 'I'm late, gotta run.' That was all, that was it, that was what she said. And that's not love, not by a fucking long shot." He dragged his hand wearily across his face, grinding hate and anger in deeper. "Did Juliet say 'Late, gotta run,' to Romeo? I don't think so." He looked and sounded belligerent.

"Probably not."

"Yeah, probably not. You got it. Here's the kicker though."

He was silent. I waited for the kicker. In the flickering leaves of the tree outside I saw a guy walk up to the upended football, dance in place, shake his arms out, then stand silently in contemplation—or prayer?—before pulling his leg back, connecting with the ball, and watching it spiral end over end into the blue sky. Between the goalposts? A point? I watched, holding my breath—

"I made myself go as cold and hard as she was, on the outside anyway."

I saw it coming. It was a kicker. "And she was interested again?"

"Yeah."

"Did you—" How to say that?

"Fall for it?" He laughed a laugh that was a parody of good humor. "That's the question, huh?" He stood.

A question he wasn't going to answer apparently.

"Thanks for letting me blow off steam, Kate. See you."

He walked out the door to the garage pulling it shut behind him. I was still sitting—thinking how ugly vinyl kitchen chairs are, how hard it is to make love work out right, wondering when Elsa would be home and if I had time for a quick tour through Matt's stuff—when the door opened again.

"And lunch. Thanks for lunch, too. Next one's on me." Gone again.

Had Stu killed Deidre? Had Matt? The betrayal of love was enough to kill for. Idly I looked at the newspaper on the kitchen table.

> *A woman, 27, was viciously beaten then stabbed 14 times by her estranged husband. The oldest child, a girl, 4, was also beaten. A boy, 10 months, was unharmed. Neighbors said the victim, Kayla Merton, was terrified of her husband, George Merton, and had called police on numerous occasions.*
>
> *Officer John Bolt said that in 17 years in the department he had never seen such a savage attack. "There was blood all over. She had obviously tried to escape and had been slashed in the back as well as stabbed in the chest and arms," he said.*
>
> *The woman was taken to Sierra Nevada Memorial Hospital and is reported to be in critical condition. The children were treated and released to relatives.*

I folded the paper, feeling sick. I told myself that this was different. Deidre was not an abused and battered wife. It was different. I took a deep breath.

Make yourself at home, Matt had said. *Help yourself to anything,* he had urged.

So I did.

16

She trusted no one, not after he had betrayed her, trampled her heart into tears and sadness. And yet, could she tell him no? For she loved him, even now.

. . . .

Toby was asleep. His breathing was deep and peaceful, his body wrapped tightly around Bear. The innocence there was an unwelcome contrast to my next undertaking.

The den had file cabinets and a desk but was otherwise uninteresting, even ugly, in shades of mouse brown, retch green and boredom. The files were strictly routine: last year's taxes; a maintenance agreement for the new washer/dryer; car service and repair records; Toby's health and immunizations, and other also not so earth-shaking stuff. The desk had stationery, pencils, pens, highlighters, and a drawer of kid's craft materials at kid level.

A bust.

Feeling dumb I checked for false bottoms to drawers, for something taped underneath or behind a drawer. Another bust. Clichés in this business are just not what they're cracked up to be.

Dining room? Zip. Living room? A lot of books. If I had time later I'd flip through them. Bedroom? I was saving that for last, for best, I hoped. The bedroom is a private place, a place for intimate thoughts and acts, a place where you can be yourself, let yourself go and still remain hidden.

This bedroom had a stripped look to it. There were nails on the walls but no pictures, blankets on the bed but no spread. The bedstands held lonely and dusty lamps but nothing else, no books or ashtrays, not even a half-empty half-full glass of water. There was an alarm clock on the floor as though an irate swipe had landed it there. I could relate to that and to the clean, rectangular clock-shaped place trailing a smear in the dust on one table. Nothing under the bed but a man's sock and dust bunnies.

There were two bureaus in the room. One had Matt's clothes, one was empty. Nothing on the top of the empty one, not a hairbrush, a barrette, perfume, earrings, nail file or dead flowers. Nothing.

I was getting the picture.

The clothes in the walk-in closet were Matt's. The closet looked, felt, and smelled male. Something inside me cried out in sadness for Deidre. Five months gone and she was erased. Her things, her pictures, even her scent was gone.

The top of Matt's dresser was cluttered and messy. I went through the drawers first. No big surprises: socks, shorts, shirts, all neatly folded right out of the dryer. A pair of black shorts with red hearts was stashed at the bottom of the pile. They looked virgin, unworn, unseduced. Pity. Matt would look good in them.

Much of the collection on the dresser top was what you get when you empty your pockets out. Loose coins, gum wrappers, ticket stubs, a dollar-off coupon for pizza, lint. There was an abalone shell almost filled with pennies, a few stray keys, some hardly used men's cologne, a tie tack. I took all that in at a glance.

What caught me was the open letter. It was a business-size envelope with several sheets of paper in it. The handwriting was dramatic and slanted across the page in emerald green. The stamp had hearts and the word LOVE on it. It was very slightly scented with an herbal fragrance.

Only lowlifes and slime read other people's mail. I put it down. And private investigators. I picked it up.

Wed.

Oh, God, what happened, Matt? I care for you so much and I thought—you said you cared for me too. I was there for the hard

time, the bad time. I did it all, I helped you, and now what? Now
nothing? I don't understand. I don't get it. Please call or write,
just tell me. Anything is better than this.

I skipped through the rest of it quickly wondering what, exactly, she/
he/they had done. What was the hard time, the bad time, and how had the
writer helped? There was no signature, just a scrawled letter that could
have been an A, a C, a D, maybe a Q. Heartache screws up penmanship
something awful. No date other than Wed. and the date on the postmark was
smeared.

I had snooped. I was slime. And what had it gotten me? A return
address. It was something, but maybe not enough. Not enough for slime.

As it turned out, I had another forty minutes before I heard Elsa's car.
I went through everything I could think of and found almost nothing else.
Condoms in the bedside table nearest the alarm clock made Matt careful, or
hopeful, but not necessarily sexually active. And it didn't name names.

There was nothing in the bathroom that showed that a woman had ever
lived or even visited in the house. No prescription medicines and nothing
stronger than aspirin. The shampoo and soap were standard supermarket
brands, nothing fancy. Deodorant, toothpaste, assorted Band-Aids, ditto.
Deidre had been effectively erased there too.

With time to burn I snooped through the computer, finding nothing but
business files. All of Deidre's writing that I had seen so far had been
handwritten or typed so I wasn't surprised to see nothing of hers in the
computer files or in the selections I randomly pulled up. Handwritten was
more romantic, I guess. Or maybe just more convenient.

I heard a car door slam and went to the window. Elsa. She went inside
her house with a bag of groceries, a parcel, and a handful of mail. When,
five minutes later, she knocked on the door, I had long since turned off the
computer and was sitting on the couch flipping through *True Confessions*. It
was the only thing I had seen with Deidre's name on it. She was dead; her
subscription was alive and well.

My Love For Him Refuses To Die
Midnight Message
They Told Me We'd Live Happily Ever After

I didn't know if the stories were true, but they didn't sound romantic or
heartwarming. There was another light tap at the door. I put the magazine
down and answered it. Elsa smiled at me, her hair in tight new curls that
were ready for anything. She was about sixty-five, slim and frail-looking,

with coordinated polyester slacks and sweater in shades of pale blue and maroon. Yuck.

"Hi. Come in. Toby's asleep."

"Oh, good. Poor child, it's so hard on him sometimes. He's afraid to go to sleep now, afraid that when he wakes up something will be gone and not come back. You explained to him, didn't you"—she peered at me nearsightedly—"that you wouldn't be here, that—"

"Yes, it's all right. He knows."

"Good. I'm not saying it hasn't been hard on his father. Well, goodness knows it has. Still—" She shook her head disapprovingly. "Still, the child should come first, don't you think?"

"I guess I don't really understand the situation," I said carefully.

Her face set suddenly. It was quick and solid, like double-dose Jell-O, the kind you make so that you can cut it into cubes and use it for erasers, or paperweights, or nouveau art. Elsa was not nouveau anything and she thought I was judging her, perhaps reprimanding her for gossiping.

"Won't you sit down?" I asked gently. "In here or in the kitchen, wherever you will be the most comfortable? Why don't I make us tea? And perhaps, since you have obviously been such a good and kind neighbor, you will tell me what you think I should know for the times when I babysit?"

She sank gratefully and gracelessly onto a kitchen chair, the vinyl squeaking and whooshing in response. "There are those who would say I am a busybody and a meddler." She tipped her head up to look at me through bifocals.

"Why not just concerned?"

"Yes."

Ha. Right answer. She rewarded me with a big smile, confident and going-to-be-gabby now.

"All those comings and goings, it can't have been good for the child, now can it?" She sniffed, a little old lady sniff, not a cold sniff.

"Mmmmm."

That was my contribution as I barged and banged through cupboards looking for tea, honey, and maybe cookies or something. I did reasonably well in all those departments.

"Comings and goings?" I asked.

"*Oh,* my *dear,* doesn't this look charming!"

I was recklessly laying out Matt's goodies.

"Well, there was Stu, of course. He was around a good bit of the time, now wasn't he?" Elsa paused to tuck into the goodies with abandon, then delicately wiped her mouth. "They *said* it was because he was working on the deck."

She kept her voice even but looked at me, obviously wondering if I would be so impossibly pea-brained as to believe that.

"Oh?" I asked, with just the proper inflection.

"Exactly." She munched up another cookie. "And then there was that waitress person, the one who looks like a tramp with that hair and all, though Matt says she isn't. Why, she was *forever* coming by, but *only* when Deidre wasn't here. Goodness me, sometimes they wouldn't miss but by ten minutes. I swear, the girl must have had a lookout."

As indeed must Elsa.

"She stayed *quite* a while on those days when Deidre was gone all day. That was Fridays and sometimes Tuesdays. Not that I really *noticed,*" she added hastily, "not on a regular basis anyway, just here and there. Are there any more of those yummy little shortbread cookies, dear?"

"Did Chivogny ever come over with Stu?"

"Oh my, no. She came over once or twice but always alone and never to stay long. Arrived with a frown and left with a frown." She shook her head. "My goodness, it's just a wonder that girl's face didn't freeze."

I put more shortbread on the table.

"Thank you, dear. And then there was That Person after Deidre died."

"His cousin?" I asked innocently.

"Well, my goodness, that's *not* what we called it in *my* day. She stayed the weekend too."

"But perhaps in the guest room?" I suggested.

She snorted. "The light never went on in *that* room. Not *once,* though it stayed on late enough in the master bedroom. And music, too." She heard her words and blushed.

I pretended I hadn't caught the implication, or seen the blush. Some people watched TV; some watched their neighbors. I was glad, and not for the first time, that my house was situated on an acre of land.

"Not that I was paying close attention. Hmmm." She cleared her throat.

"More tea?" I got up to fetch the teapot and poured for us both.

"Why, *thank* you, dear. This *is* cozy, isn't it, drinking tea and chatting on a drizzly afternoon?"

Tea and cookies and venom. Cozy? It was a stretch. "Yes," I said. And wondered if lying put your aura out of adjustment. Lying and snooping and —aw, rats. If so, I was in deep shit. Did caring about a little boy help make up for it?

The phone rang before I had the answer. It startled me and made Elsa jump for the cookies. Different reflexes. She had wiped out the shortbread and was now working on the marbled ones. How did she stay so skinny? Spying must be a tough calling, one that burns up all those little cookie calories like crazy.

I said hello into the receiver, listened to a long silence, then a click. I hung up, not bothering to wait for a dial tone. Elsa's bright, slightly bulging eyes peered up at me again through bifocals.

"So?"

"Wrong number, I guess."

"Oh, my *dear.*" She shook her head meaningfully. It was obvious I had a great deal to learn. "You're *quite* the innocent, aren't you?"

I thought about how I'd tossed Matt's house less than an hour ago, read his mail, and was now stuffing his best cookies, $1.79 plus tax for a package of six, down Elsa's face so I could pump her for information and, on the whole, thought not. I said as much. Short version, of course: "Not really."

Elsa didn't reply immediately. She was too much of a lady to speak with her mouth full of Macadamia Nut Crunch Crispies. She swallowed hard and fast. "It was probably A Woman, and she heard your voice instead of Matt's and hung up." She sniffed in disapproval, not too much of a lady to judge her neighbor and find him wanting.

"Oh. Well, after all, Matt's a single and attractive guy. Why not?"

I'd had enough tea and et cetera. If there was more information to be had I didn't have the heart to go after it, not now, not until the poison level had dropped.

"Well, aren't you sweet," she said. Her mouth said that. Her eyes said: Aren't you a gullible dope.

I wondered when she had last been loved and held and if it made her frantic and wild to think that others had that and she didn't? Would cookies kill that sour taste in her mouth? I squinted to see if I could see her aura. No. Just steel-sprung gray curls.

"Elsa—" I looked at the clock.

"Oh, *poor* dear, I've kept you forever with my chatter. It's been *such* fun, though. Please come and visit me *any* time. *Don't* stand on ceremony.

And *don't*"—she stopped me from clearing the table—"bother with these. I'll take care of it." She looked hungrily at the last two cookies.

I thanked her, picked up my purse and the latest copy of *True Confessions.*

Maybe I'd learn something.

17

He pushed her hair back and off her face. She looked into eyes that were cold, hard, determined, and yet aflame with passion. His kisses fell on her neck and trailed across her face, leaving her skin hot, seared, blazing with desire.

"Yes!" she cried out.

His lips claimed hers.

. . . .

The postmark on Matt's love letter was Colfax, close by. I decided to give it a try before work and was rewarded with a cute little house on Luden Street.

It had a small, very well-kept yard and lots of tinkly irritating wind chimes. The house had just been painted and sparkled in pale yellow with dark green trim that looked like rickrack.

It was the one nice house on the block. The others looked like fixer-uppers in various stages of desperation. A lot of junker cars lived on this block; a lot of them would never leave. I walked by a clean white Toyota on my way to the house. The walkway was brick with a small-leaved ground cover stealing up between the bricks. There were two names on the mailbox: B. Harte and Q. Johannsen.

One doorbell. I pushed it.

A slim-figured woman of about twenty-five with pixyish blond hair answered the door. She tugged her sweatshirt down over worn blue jeans, pushed the sleeves up, put a single finger to her lip and then, in a voice only slightly above a whisper, said, "Yes?"

"Q. Johannsen?" I almost whispered back.

"B. Harte."

"Brette?"

"Bette." She flushed. "My parents were big fans of Bret Harte's. Quilla's outside if you want her. This way."

Quilla was on her knees in dirt setting out onions in a well-cultivated plot. Her knees, elbows, hands, and face were smudged with mud. Bette called out softly, "Quilla," then went back into the house without looking at me again.

"Hi."

A beautiful woman with long blond hair pulled back with combs, flushed cheeks, and a smile looked up and said hi back.

"Think you'll get away with it?" I gestured at the plants.

"Probably." She grinned. There was mud in her hair too. "Early May is pretty sure past frost danger. Almost. I could get nailed, of course. I guess wrong, I start over. I guess right, I have early vegetables. Who are you? What do you want?"

"I'm a staff writer for the *Auburn Journal*," I lied glibly. "We're doing a feature on local businesses with regional color and character, like the Pioneer Hotel. I understand you know the owner and I wonder if I could ask you a few questions?"

She flushed, bit her lip, was silent.

"Did you know both Deidre and Matt Durkin?" I pulled out a notebook and a pen, all ready to take down her answers.

"Regional color and character? You mean murder, don't you? Who are you really? And what do you really want?"

"Quilla—"

"Totally bogus. Tell me straight or you're out of here."

All right, she got points. Most people will go for bogus lines. Most people will tell you anything if you look personable, sound reasonable, and ask politely. Anything. It's scary. But Quilla Johannsen wasn't most people. Good for her.

"Kat Colorado. I'm a private investigator."

She looked at me with clear wide eyes, a fixed, though not yet hostile expression on her face. It could get hostile though. Fast. Easy.

"I was hired by a corporate investor who is interested in the Pioneer Hotel. He wants information on Matt Durkin's background, his financial stability, character, and general reliability. Your name came up as a friend and associate of Mr. Durkin's and I wondered if you would mind answering—"

"More bogus bullshit."

I didn't dignify that with an answer, mainly because I didn't have one.

"Matt's an open book with regard to character, background, and business. So it's murder, isn't it?"

I said nothing but I managed to look as though I agreed with her. And I did, especially on the "more bogus bullshit" part. She wanted to talk about Matt, I thought, and it made her vulnerable, less quick to question me on the bogus and the bullshit.

"Let's see your ID."

I showed it to her. "Do you mind talking about Mr.—"

"Call him Matt, for crying out loud. And no, I guess I don't mind. What exactly do you want to know?"

"What kind of a person is he?" My conscience was bothering me now.

"Matt? He's a good guy, a nice guy, fun and hard-working and straightforward. Mostly."

"Mostly?"

"Yeah. Well, look, I don't want to talk about all of it, okay?" She pushed her trowel into the ground. "It gets pretty personal, you know."

"What about the murder? Something like that could make it difficult for a person to manage a business, couldn't it?"

"Yes. A business, a life, a relationship, you name it." She looked at me and sighed. "That doesn't answer your question, does it? But I don't know about his business, only about us. We met too soon after her death and he couldn't get over the murder."

I murmured encouragingly. "Oh?"

"He felt guilty. I mean, there was no reason, he couldn't have done anything, or stopped it, but maybe that doesn't matter. Maybe you always feel that responsibility, that guilt.

"It takes so little to make a difference, doesn't it? I once missed being in a car accident, probably by a heartbeat, a second. Maybe five minutes would have made the difference for Deidre. Maybe ten, and then the guy would have been someplace else doing something else to someone else. But he wasn't. He was there and he blew her away. And it's too bad and that's that."

She was down-to-earth, sensible, and emotionally tough, that was obvious. Yet she had written a letter that was passionate and full of feeling, and she had referred to helping him. I filed both observations away.

"Matt's not over her, not by a long shot. In fact, he's screwed up pretty bad. Real bad, actually. Big time, actually. He's a decent guy. Hey, he's a great guy, but I wouldn't say he's a good bet right now, or that it would be a good business investment, not until he gets over it. Tell your client that. Now, I've got things to do." She went back to setting out the onions.

Garlic, too, I thought. "Don't put in your tomatoes yet."

"No." She smiled. "A little too soon, a little too risky. Just like love." She said that softly.

I felt bad again. "Good luck. I hope things work out for you."

"You mean that, don't you?"

"Yes, I do." I did. I liked her a lot, thought she'd be good for Matt.

"Thanks."

We both went back to digging in dirt. Hers was more appealing than mine. And it would eventually produce lettuce, radishes, onions, beans, sweet peas, tomatoes, hot peppers, whatever. Mine? Maybe nothing. Maybe mud and blood. Maybe an answer. Maybe a killer. Hard to tell.

It was four-thirty. I was back at the house and it was time to get ready for work. I was exhausted. Working three jobs—babysitter, private investigator (or snoop, depending), and bartender—was for the young and strong. Younger and stronger than Kate and Kat. Friday night, too. Slammed night. Live music night. Let's get drunk and party night.

I had a quick shower and got dressed: jeans and a Hawaiian shirt in hot pink, turquoise, and yellow, a turquoise belt, turquoise socks and white high-top Reeboks. We're talking fashion statement. Or something.

I looked into the mirror at blond-streaked brown curls and winked at Kate. Hot, no doubt about it. And I thought maybe I'd dress more like this when I went back to being Kat. I'd exchange old nightmares for a new look. It would be a good trade.

After tonight I was off until Tuesday. On that thought I headed for the phone in my bedroom and put a long-distance call onto my credit card. Approximately seventy-six, or maybe a hundred and twelve, calling card/ credit code/personal code/easy (sic) access numbers later I listened to the phone ring. It sounded like next door. I love that about long distance, and sometimes I hate it too, when someone sounds close and there, and is not, is miles away. Someone like Hank.

"Detective Bureau."

"Hank Parker, please."

"One moment, I'll see if *Sergeant* Parker is available." She snapped her gum in my ear and I winced. 1–0. "May I tell him who's calling?" Snap, snap, snap.

"Kat."

"Last name please, miss," she snotted, and snapped her gum again. 2–0.

She knows, of course. My name, my voice, probably my dog's name. Hank and I have been together for almost a year and a half and I call often enough. She despises me because she wants Hank and I have him. I used to be indifferent but now I can't stand her; she makes it impossible for me to reach him.

"Miss?"

"Ballou, Kat Ballou," I said. 2–1. She was probably too young to remember the movie.

There was a long silence and then she thunked the phone down on the desk, no dignified hold button for me. "Tom, is Hankie still here?"

Hankie? Give me a break. *No* one calls Hank that, certainly not Ms. Bubble Gum.

"I'm *so* sorry," she said a moment later, sounding triumphant. "He's out in the field."

"Tell him I called, please."

Yeah, right. They'd be serving dry martinis up—stirred, not shaken/extra olives—in Hell before that happened.

"Oh, and did you know?" I made my voice concerned. "There's a new study just out: Chewing gum causes tooth decay, overbite, pimples, and cancer of the larynx."

Shocked silence. 2–2.

"And," I lowered my voice and whispered into the phone, "a diminished sexual drive and capacity."

I hung up. 2–3. She brings out the petty in me, no question. And I hadn't gotten through to Hank and I didn't have a hot date this weekend.

Damn.

The bar was relatively quiet when I walked in. The Friday night Happy Hour crowd was still arriving, still getting revved up. That made a bunch of us.

"Hey!" Charlene hollered as I walked behind the bar. "How come cowboys make lousy lovers?"

There were at least ten pairs of cowboy boots in the place and all of the guys wearing them immediately starting looking cool.

"They think ten seconds is a long ride!"

A lot of laughter and the guys wearing the boots are still looking cool, but uneasy cool, not easy cool. The "cowboy" in black from last night wasn't there. I looked, I noticed. Too bad.

"Lemonade, please," Luna said in a soft, pretty voice. I hadn't noticed her.

"This is a bar, not a health food stand."

I was hostile. Hey, and why not? This was the woman who was into me for tea and a bran muffin *and* had messed around in my aura. I gave myself credit for hostile. It could have been worse. Considerably.

"SevenUp please, no cherry. Did you know that it takes your digestive system five days, at *least,* to digest a maraschino cherry?"

"Are you paying this time?" I kept the hostility out of my voice, kept it a simple question. And I made no move to get her 7UP.

"Ten days sometimes." She took a dollar out of her purse and put it on the bar. "Isn't it a *crime* the things we do to our bodies?"

Maybe, but what we did to others' bodies was a bigger crime. I shook away an image of Deidre's autopsy photos, put a 7UP on the bar in front of her and took her dollar.

She sipped delicately, poetic in purple again. "I can't stay long, but I needed to come. No, I *had* to come. Deidre asked me. I could *never* refuse *that* request."

Deidre? Dead Deidre? Twilight Zone music played briefly in my mind. Deidre. Okay.

"Ordering, Kate," Charlene called. "Gimme a Scotch rocks, bourbon seven, two Buds and a bottle of Cab. You got a wine opener I can borrow? I forgot mine."

"Don't Be Cruel" came on the jukebox. Luna whispered something at me when I finished Charlene's order. I stood across the bar from her but refused to lean forward to hear her whispers.

She raised her voice slightly. "It's still here. The Evil. I can *feel* it and I am afraid for you, Kate. You must protect yourself and be very careful. Deidre wants that too."

Then the bar filled up: the guys from last night, including Barry, the draft beer drinker who thought he recognized me, Stu, Chivogny, Matt, and a bunch more I couldn't yet put a name or a drink to.

"It's *here. Evil!*" Luna said. She slid off her stool and stared at me wide- and innocent-eyed. *"Evil. Be careful!"*

She left without finishing her 7UP but not without picking up her change. No tip. Why wasn't I surprised? I tried to be flip but her words bothered me. Evil. It bothered me.

"Kate! Order, please!"

Friday night and hopping. We swung into action.

At last call, Stu and Chivogny were still there, still drinking. They were the only ones left besides us. The band was gone too. Chivogny wasn't talking tonight. Stu was.

"Hey, Matt, you asked the girls, didn't you?"

Hostile and curious looks were directed Stu's way.

"To the Spring Blast-off?" he continued.

Chivogny and Matt were hostile, I was curious, Charlene was excited.

"Charlene, you're going, right?"

She shook her head. "I've heard of it, of course, but I've never been invited."

"Aw, hell, Matt, what's wrong with you?"

We'd stopped cleaning and stocking and were listening. Chivogny sipped on her vodka tonic, Matt glowered. Stu turned to us and spoke to me.

"It's an annual event, first good weekend in May. Tomorrow's supposed to be clear and sunny, maybe seventy. Folks come from all over, bring tents and sleeping bags and stay for the weekend. There's fishing, hiking, softball, badminton, all kinds of games. Saturday night we have a barbecue and a band."

"All right! And you're inviting us?"

Charlene was up on the notion, I could tell.

"Hell, yes, I am! Out to the old Ryder Ranch. You know where that is?"

"Yeah!"

"You coming?"

"Yeah, we are! You got that right," Charlene said.

We. Okay, good.

"Be a bunch of single guys there too," Stu continued, and Charlene grinned. "They come in from all over for the war games on Sunday."

War games? The kind with popguns and paint pellets and soldier-boy wannabes running around in camouflage and pseudotough-guy attitudes. Oh, boy. Fun stuff. My kind of game. My kind of guy.

"Sound like fun?"

"You bet!" That was Charlene.

"You girls coming?"

"You bet." Both of us answered. Charlene could play and cruise. Me, too, but cruising for different things, playing a different game.

"When you coming up, Matt?" Social Director Stu still at it.

"Don't know if I am." Matt's face was closed up, dark. "It's different this year. . . . Be tough with Toby."

"Naw, c'mon. The girls will be glad to help with the kid, huh, girls?"

Chivogny, Charlene, and I were the girls. None of us said a thing. Stu missed it, but Matt didn't.

"You got to get out more, Matt, and Toby too. Ain't no good in just sitting around wishing things were different. None at all."

Stu sounded almost cheerful. I gawked at him, amazed. Was this the guy who had gotten all choked up over Deidre and his smashed affair with her so recently? Grief had been dessert to that lunch, and yet he looked now as though he could hardly remember it.

"Stu's right, Matt. You should come." Chivogny's voice was quiet but insistent. "And there will be plenty of people to help out with Toby. There are always lots of kids there, too." Her voice broke a little. Liquor? Pain?

No easy answer.

Of course, I still wasn't sure what the question was.

18

"I couldn't live without you."

"Don't say that."

"But I *couldn't*. I would kill myself rather than face a single day alone."

"You don't mean that." He dismissed her words.

But she did.

....

The phone rang in the middle of the night—or maybe the end of it, as we'd gotten home in the late middle. I struggled out of sleep and a dream I couldn't quite remember, a dream that left me filled with a vague sense of unease. I looked at the clock: three.

Two sleepy voices, one of them mine, answered the ring.

"Kate?" He stumbled a little over the unfamiliar word.

"Hi!"

There was a silence and then the sound of a phone hanging up.

"Katy, you all right, everything okay?"

"Yes, fine, tough to talk though." I paused. "I'm too sleepy, I guess." I was wide awake now and sounded it.

He understood. "You called. I know it's late but I just wanted to get back to you in case—"

Yes. In case. I thought longingly of my now impossible plans for a hot date weekend. "Thanks, Hank. How did you know?" Bubble Gum hadn't told him, for sure.

"Tommy told me. Jewel"—Jewel is Bubble Gum's alias, a name directly indicative of parental lack of know-how and bad call—"was moping around all afternoon upset about something, something it turned out you said."

"Me?" Genuine feigned astonishment.

He laughed. "I love you, Katy. I'm still not happy that—"

"Hank, the nightmares are almost maybe gone. And I love you, too."

A heartbeat. And two. And three. "Good. When?"

"Maybe next weekend."

"All right. Call me when you know. Go back to sleep now."

I did. Fast.

No nightmares, just a dream about a little boy who walked around asking people if they would be his mommy. He had a bunny in one hand and a bear in the other and he was crying. In my dream I thought I was crying too. And maybe I was. Better to cry over a hurt little boy than a dead killer.

The next morning Charlene and I got up late, ate breakfast, drank too much coffee, and sat around with the weekend lazies speculating about the party at the Ryder Ranch.

"It'll be a blast! Good folks, good fun. A hundred or more people come, depending. I've wanted to go for ages!"

"Does it get rowdy, wild?"

"No, never. It's invitation only. Your name's not on the list at the gate, you don't get in. You mess up one year, you don't come back. There's something for everyone, but lots of kids, lots of family stuff. I've been trying to get on the list forever. This is totally cool!" She yawned and stretched. "You gonna wear jeans?"

What else? I nodded.

"Yeah, me too. Okay if I ride up with you?"

"Sure. I don't have definite plans or know when I'm coming back though."

"No sweat. I can catch a ride back easy, I'm sure I can. Leave in a couple of hours?" We agreed to it.

"Let's take sleeping bags, a toothbrush and stuff, and a change of clothes, just in case."

That again. Just in case. We agreed to that too.

It was late afternoon by the time we got up there and a lot of people had beat us. It wasn't crowded; there was more room than there were people on easy rolling hills and fields with new grass and spring flowers. Most folks were spread around comfortably at picnic tables, campsites, and trailers in a sizable open area ringed in the distance by trees. We parked and then we cruised.

Cruising was an art form with Charlene, and I tagged along docilely, happily, until a large guy in a lumberjack shirt charged by, tucked her under his arm like a rolled-up, unread newspaper, and charged off again. She squealed and kicked and waved good-bye. I waved back, then drifted about. A group of women sat at a picnic table and one of then waved. I didn't think I knew any of them but I walked over anyway.

It was Chivogny—flushed, beautiful, radiant. I stared. No wonder I hadn't recognized her. She was, almost literally, a different person. I was welcomed, introduced, and offered beer or lemonade. I opted for beer. A place was made for me at the table.

"You're just in time for the good news, Kate," Chivogny called. "The Announcement!"

I put a properly eager, expectant, and curious expression on my face. Not difficult; I was some of the above.

"I'm pregnant! I'm going to have a *baby!*"

There was a brief silence, and then cries of surprise and congratulations, exclamations of happiness, laughter, and even a few tears. Somebody raised a beer can in a toast and we all joined in, Chivogny with lemonade, I noticed. An off-note nagged at me from the back of my mind, then disappeared when I paid attention. I sipped my beer.

"How long have you known?" "When is the baby due?" "A boy or a girl?" The questions played around our table like squealing monkeys.

"Yesterday. Not forever. Either, who cares?" More laughter.

Yesterday, that was it. She had known yesterday, she must have, and yet she sat all night in the bar drinking steadily and heavily.

The shouts started far away but traveled toward us quickly, like water in relay buckets to a fire, getting closer, sharper. We all stopped talking. Something was wrong. I thought I'd heard shots earlier but I'd discounted it. Wrongly?

The tension that dread builds had begun; it was a given that the news was bad. You don't shout like that with a twisted ankle, a scrape, or a bee sting. Not even when the hot dog buns don't match up with the wienies and the pickle relish runs low. Or the ice cream melts. Not even then. Only when it's an emergency, when it could be life or death. In the silence we could hear the unspoken questions: What? How? and finally, Who?

Search on. Missing child. Meet at the firepit.

Every adult in the area was moving. Teams were mobilized, areas divided up and assigned. And the missing child identified.

Toby.

I saw Matt looking frantic and tried to get over to him but was put on a team with four guys. Okay, Toby came first. The largest guy, with major muscle groups, assumed control. I tried, I lost. He spun us out in four directions and took a fifth.

"What about down there?" I pointed toward a steep and forbidding ravine on the other side of a livestock fence, a death trap for living things, four- or two-legged.

"Not likely." Our leader looked at me with disdain. "Women," he muttered under his breath. A major muscle group between his ears too. How helpful. "No one would be dumb enough to go down there. Besides, it's fenced off."

"I think it should be covered."

"Do it." He sneered and turned away, the others followed.

I trailed the fence, then scrambled underneath it, wishing Ranger were here. This called for dog expertise. *No one would be dumb enough to go there . . . to do that . . . to think this . . . to . . .* How many times had I heard that? Seen it proven wrong? How often does a child follow a ball into the street or a notion into absurdity?

I looked down the ravine, over a hundred feet deep in places and treacherous, slippery still with last month's heavy rains. A swiftly flowing spring stream ran at the bottom of the drop. Fifteen minutes to the Bronco and back, less if I ran. I debated it briefly, then ran. There was a sixty-foot length of high-tension nylon rope in the car. I hoped I wouldn't need it but it was better to have it than not. That was the second thing I called right. I swung the loops of rope over my head and across my chest, grateful that I didn't have muscle between my ears.

The slide marks down the ravine slope were the first tip-off, a damp downhill smear where the dry dirt on the surface had been scraped away. Then I saw a splash of red-and-yellow plaid. We don't have bushes like that out here.

"Toby?"

My voice sounded loud to me, but it wasn't. I didn't want to startle the child. The voices of the other searchers were faint in the background, sounds but not words. I would be the same to them if I shouted.

"He-e-elp!" His voice wavered and slipped.

"It's Kate and I'm coming. Don't move, don't be afraid. It'll be all right." I made my voice strong and confident.

"I'm afraid." He lost it on afraid and whimpered.

"Just a little bit more. I can't talk now, do you understand? Soon I'll be there and you'll be safe. Okay?"

"O——K."

The O and K belonged to two different octaves. I closed off the sympathy I felt. It was a luxury we didn't have time for.

The steep slope of the ravine was littered with rocks and bushes. I didn't trust the rocks. The bushes maybe, maybe not; the ground would be unstable so soon after the rainy season. I scouted the top of the bank, found what I was looking for: a tree almost ten feet back, twelve inches or so in diameter. I knotted the rope around it, tested it, knotted the rope around my waist, tested it. The tree wasn't directly over the spot where Toby went down but about six feet to the left. Perfect.

I went down right beneath the tree, playing out the rope as I walked backward down the slope and letting the tree take my weight, thankful for high-quality rope. I went slowly, carefully. It still didn't take me long.

"Kate."

"Don't move, honey. Don't talk." I said it in my best calm voice. "We're still not safe yet."

"Kate, you missed me." His voice was matter-of-fact but underneath it was afraid.

I looked down. He should be afraid. My stomach felt hollow, as though I hadn't eaten in days, and then it was filled up with fear. I hate heights. I fought back the fear and swallowed the nausea. Both were rancid, ugly. The red clay of the slope stared at me. I stared back.

"Kate?"

"I'm coming, Toby."

I looked at him and smiled. His eyes were wide and terrified, his hair and clothing mussed and stained with red-clay dirt. We were level now. He reached out a hand to me. My heart stopped.

"*Don't.* Don't move."

"Okay." He stopped. Frightened eyes.

I looked away from the child to assess the situation. He was hunched over in an indentation behind a little rock and clinging to a sturdy but small shrub. A couple of feet beneath him was a boulder that looked like it had been there since the last Ice Age, and was content and immovable until the next one. I hoped to God that was true.

"I'm going to come closer, but don't do *anything*. Don't move until I tell you, okay?"

"Okay," he whispered. It floated over to me like a scared little breeze.

I started inching his way, scrabbling sideways like a crab. "Not yet, Toby." I had decided that a steady stream of reassurance was good. I made my dentist talk like that to me and it worked. "You just hold still, okay?"

"Okay." The whisper was fainter.

I tested the boulder gently. Solid. Harder. Still solid. I jumped on it, one hundred and thirty pounds of stress. Ice Age. Taking a deep breath and willing myself *not* to look down, I untied the rope around my waist, then retied it with no slack. It only seemed to take four or five months, not too bad. After that I started to breathe again. Nice stuff, air. I had ten to twelve feet of leftover rope hanging off my waist. Perfect. I looked up at the child. The tear-stained smear of clay on his face looked like dried blood.

"I'm going to reach for you, Toby. Don't move, don't let go until I tell you."

"Okay."

I put my hands around his waist and hooked my thumbs into belt loops, my hands onto sturdy denim and little boy. "Now, when I say so I want you to let go of the bush, gently lean back and topple into my arms. Don't jump, just fall real carefully, okay?"

"Okay."

"All right. Now."

"All right," he said bravely, but it took him a moment to let go of the bush. I understood. It hadn't been fun untying the rope at my waist either.

"Don't look down, Toby, look at me." I kept my eyes on his. "C'mon," I encouraged.

His eyes were wide—empty of everything but fear and full of that. He was holding his breath and biting his lower lip, his body rigid, immobile and tense down to white-knuckled badly scraped fingers clutching the manzanita bush.

"C'mon, sweetie," I said softly. His eyes got wider. "Almost there." I smiled at him. He let out his breath with a whoosh, tumbled into my arms, and wrapped his legs around my waist and his arms around my neck. I held on just as tightly and kissed him.

"That was a real good job." He started to cry. "Hey!" I kissed him again. "If you cry, I can't help us as well." I made my voice very gentle. "No crying just now, okay?"

"Okay," he hiccupped. What a trouper!

"Hang on tight!"

It was a totally unnecessary admonition. Limpets didn't have a thing on Toby. I held him around the waist with one arm and grabbed a loop of the rope with the other, passed it across his back and over my right shoulder, picked it up at my waist on the left, wrapped it around his waist and my chest a couple of times, up over my left shoulder in an X, down to my waist again, and knotted it.

"How you doing, little guy? Pretty good?"

"Yah." His voice was tentative, his body glued to mine. "Pretty good."

"We're going to rest for a minute and then climb up the hill." Hill, boy was that an understatement. "We're safe now, the rope won't let us fall."

I willed my mind to ignore pictures of faulty, unraveling, snapping rope. He nodded, the top of his head bumping my chin, making my eyes tear with the sudden pain. I patted his bottom, rested, and psyched myself up for the climb. Climbing uphill with one hundred and seventy pounds was tougher than walking down with one thirty. No kidding.

"Okay, here we go. All you have to do is hang on and try not to wiggle. I'll do the rest."

"Okay."

I took a deep breath, flipped the rope over so that it was roughly under the tree, and walked sideways in red, sticky clay dirt. It was tough leaving the boulder. Real tough. Toby didn't notice, his eyes were squeezed tightly shut. Hand over hand I hauled us up on the rope, inching upward, trying to dig my feet into the slope as we climbed.

Once I slipped and lost a foot and a half. Toby cried out in my shirt and I cried out in my mind. My hands burned and stung, raw with rope burns. "We're okay," I said through sweat and tears in an effort to comfort us both, and started up again.

It was less than forty feet from the shrub up but it took us a long time, a week, maybe two. Thirty-five vertical feet is different from thirty-five horizontal feet. Believe me. As I clambered and scrambled up, hands raw, fear in my heart, heart in my throat, I tried to imagine rock-climbing for pleasure and couldn't.

We were almost to the top. Toby sensed it and straightened up to look around. My hands hurt like hell.

"Almost there, not quite," I panted.

I scraped my knuckles in the dirt and gravel on the edge of the bank. Six or eight inches caved in and showered down on us, into Toby's hair and my eyes. My hands felt bloody, I didn't dare look at them, and the muscles in my arms were knotted and cramped.

I know how to have a good time, you bet.

Toby whimpered. I would have too, but I was trying to set a good example. My feet scrabbled and lost their place on the bank. For a terrifying moment we hung by my hands only. My life started to pass before my eyes. I was tired, very tired. Toby cried softly. My feet dug into the bank again *thank goodness.*

"All together now, one-two-three-HEAVE!"

"HEAVE!" Toby echoed, cheering us on.

I heaved. I dug my hands into the bank and pulled and scraped and scrambled. Up. Over. I crawled then on my hands and knees, Toby a limpet papoose strapped to my chest, until we were far away from the edge and close to the tree.

And there we collapsed. I gasped for air and Toby cried softly. I could feel his little hands patting me on the back. "Good job!" He kissed my dirty chin. "*Good* job, Kate." Filthy and breathless, we clung to each other. Not far away there were shouts.

After a bit I caught my breath, and then I said: "I'm going to count one-two-three and we holler HERE! Okay?"

"Okay."

I counted. We croaked out a feeble *here* and giggled. "Again." The second time was louder. The third time we really hollered, then lay listening with satisfaction to crashes coming through the bushes toward us. They found us on our sides, wrapped around each other and tied up by and to the tree.

Heck of a photo opportunity.

At that point the shouting really started. Toby shut his eyes. Me, too. Someone untied us and pulled the child out of my arms; someone helped me up. Toby started crying again. I didn't blame the little guy. Chivogny was there and reached out for him. He cried harder and pulled away.

"Mommy, I want my mommeeeeeee!" He sobbed it out, then caught sight of me. "Kate, I want my Kateeeee," he sobbed to me. I held out my arms and scooped him up.

He clung to my neck, arms wrapped around me, his little chest heaving with sobs and rising panic. I held him as close as I could without

137

hurting him, patted his back (dear God, my hands hurt!) and kissed the damp cheek he held close to me. When his sobbing stopped, he whispered in my ear between deep, ragged breaths.

"Someone pushed me, Kate. They said *Go see your mommy* and *pushed me*."

The words were punctuated by gunshots.

19

He caught her in his arms, holding her tightly. He would satisfy her soft need with his hard desire.

"You're mine," he said harshly.

"I'm yours," she echoed faintly.

....

We were top bananas that night, no question. Everybody loved and appreciated us in that immediate, fervent way you do when you've almost lost what you too readily assumed would always be there. Toby and I took shameless advantage of it.

We had the best seat at the camp fire, a broken-down overstuffed chair someone had dragged out. Matt brought us dinner and drinks and toasted us marshmallows and made us so many s'mores we almost got sick. It was swell. Toby drifted off to sleep several times in my arms but wouldn't let Matt put him to bed. Star quality and the right instincts. Fear and nightmares. Something like that.

A little way off, the band started playing country and western tunes and most of the camp fire folks cleared out. Toby burped toasted marshmallows and s'mores and shifted in his sleep. I held him gently with my raw bandaged hands. The camp fire light went out as a big good-looking guy stood, then squatted in front of me.

"Put your little boy down and dance with me?"

Toby woke up and clung to me frantically. "I can't now, but maybe later." I smiled up at him.

He smiled back. "Okay, rain check," and sauntered off.

"I'm not your little boy, am I, Kate?" His soft, sad voice tugged at my heart, pulled it lopsided.

"No, Toby."

"I want to be your little boy, can I, can I *puhleeze?*"

"No." I kissed him. "But you can be my little friend."

"That's nice." His voice was soft and sleepy. "But not as nice as if I'm your little boy and you're my mommy. Will you be my mommy puhleeze, puhleeze, puh . . . puh . . ." The please died on a last soft puff of breath and his hard little body sagged heavily in my arms.

I smoothed his hair back, whispered words of love at him in my mind, and hoped he'd have another mommy sometime soon. He stirred in my arms and a hand clenched, then relaxed. His breath was warm and sweet and soft. I thought about the long, steep, rocky fall down the ravine and the swift flowing stream at the bottom. If the fall and rocks hadn't gotten him, the stream would have. And me. I hoped I wouldn't throw up my marshmallows and s'mores.

"Shall I take him, Kate?"

I looked up at Matt, his face shadowed in the flickering firelight, his arms outstretched, and nodded. I hadn't heard him approach and I wondered how long he'd been there. His hands and arms touched mine as I handed his son over.

I went to look for the guy who wanted to dance—bright lights, music, and laughter sounded like a swell plan—and found him watching the dancers with his arms crossed over his chest.

"Slightly handicapped," I said, holding up the neat white bundles of gauze that presently passed for my hands.

"We'll improvize." He grinned, put a hand in the small of my back, and followed me onto the dance floor—well, dance dirt pack. I danced the fast ones, too, and the swing, with my partner holding me by the elbows or wrists or anywhere but hands. And, yeah, sure, I looked silly, but nobody minded and I had fun.

Later Matt found me drinking a beer and catching my breath. "Dance, Kate?"

140

I chugged the rest of the beer and dumped the bottle. I wanted to dance, drink beer, laugh, and think how glad I was to be here instead of smashed up at the end of a steep ravine slide. Even nightmares, I thought suddenly, were better than that. Strange as it seems, that was a healing thought. Life is too short to waste in nightmare. Or fantasy.

"Is Toby in bed?" We walked toward the dance floor.

"Yes."

"Is—" I stopped. I'd been about to ask if he'd had a bath and a story and been tucked in with Bear and Bunny and if, for sure, someone was there in case of bad dreams, or worse. I'd been about to, but I stopped. Toby's dad would handle it. It had nothing to do with me.

"He's fine, yes. Kate, I haven't thanked you."

"You don't need to." The band was playing a slow song, a sad song. We danced with my wrists on Matt's arms, his hands around my waist holding me loosely. "I did what anyone would have, and gladly. Toby's a wonderful little boy."

"Who's had a lot more come his way lately than any kid should have."

"You can't help that, Matt."

"But I can thank you for your help, for tonight and the comfort you gave him. And me."

"Yes. You already did."

He raised his eyebrows.

"I've never had so many perfectly toasted marshmallows and s'mores in my life."

He smiled, swung me around to the music, pulled me back.

"He wants you to be his mommy, Kate."

"I know. He told me. We talked about it. I said I couldn't be his mommy, but I could be his friend. It's all right, Matt, we'll work it out."

"Kate—"

I looked him straight in the eye and shook my head.

"It's not just Toby, Kate. It's me too. We both want you in our lives."

"I am in your lives. We're friends."

"Toby needs more than friends, Kate. So do I."

"But I don't," I said gently. "I can't."

He scuffed his feet, looking suddenly like his three-year-old son. "So you won't go out with me?"

"I'll do things with you and Toby, but I won't date you." Say it, Kat. Use words he'll understand. "I won't sleep with you."

"But we can be . . . we are friends?"

141

Bingo. "Yes."

"Okay. But I'd—"

"Hey," I said, as I steered him around the dance floor.

"Kate, I'm the guy so I lead, remember?"

I ignored that. "Matt, look over my shoulder now. Do you see a guy in brown with a cowboy hat?"

"Yeah."

"Know him?"

"No. Why?"

"I need to check it out but I'm almost sure he's the guy with the attitude in the bar the other night. The one wearing black then."

"I don't know him but I'll keep an eye open."

"Matt, is Toby an observant child?"

He frowned, trying to follow me. "Yes. Why?"

"Does he make up stuff, tell stories as though they really happened when it was only in his mind?"

"No. Why?"

"He's pretty trustworthy?"

"Yes. What in God's name are you getting at, Kate?"

"He told me somebody pushed him today."

Matt's hands tightened on my waist.

"He said he was following a lizard but he didn't go too close to the edge because his mommy and daddy had told him not to and he was a good boy, he wouldn't, and besides it scared him to be on the edges of things and look down far far." I was running the words together the way Toby had.

"Yes." Matt expelled a breath over my shoulder. "It does. I wondered about that too."

"He said someone came up behind him and wouldn't let him turn around—he was grabbed by the shoulders, I think. The person said, 'Go see your mommy.' Then he, or she, pushed him. Very hard, Toby said. He went off the edge, he couldn't help it, and fell down the mountain. He was scared, very scared."

Matt's hands were so tight on my waist it hurt.

"He fell far, far—but managed to grab onto the bush and climb behind the rock where he waited. Matt, you're hurting me."

"Huh? Oh. I'm sorry, Kate." His hands loosened, then tightened on me again. *"Pushed* him, a *child!* Who? *Why?"*

"I asked him if he recognized the voice."

"And?"

"No such luck. I asked him to try to make a voice like that. He did. It was just a low-pitched whisper. He didn't know whether it was a man or a woman. And he's still real scared, too."

"*Pushed* him? A *child, my* child! Goddamn!"

Vice-grip hands, tight, hard, ugly voice. But it still could have been Matt. I knew that, though his response and outrage seemed genuine.

I wondered if Deidre's estate, or part of it, went to Toby rather than directly to Matt; that would be something to check out. If Matt could only supervise and not actually control, liquidate, etc., Deidre's assets, whatever they were, that could be an interesting factor—aw shoot, I didn't want to think like this. "You're hurting me, Matt."

He dropped his hands from my waist. "Damn. Goddamn!" Grabbing my elbow, he hauled me off the dance floor. "Stay here. I'm getting us a beer."

I watched the dancers and followed orders, lingering by the fire. Matt shoved a beer at me. I took it gingerly.

"I want to beat the shit out of whoever—" He shrugged helplessly. "Now what?"

"Watch Toby very carefully. Don't assume *anyone* is okay. Don't leave him at all, or do it with several people, a bunch of adults with a bunch of kids, that kind of thing. Or me, I'll help."

The firelight carved shadows on his face.

"Make it public, Matt. Get on the PA system—" I nodded toward the band, "and tell people what happened. Ask them to help you keep your boy safe. You'll have everybody watching him and everybody watching everybody else. That's your best insurance. Tell the cops, too. Somebody may have tried to murder Toby."

Said aloud, it was ugly. Matt killed his beer.

"Do you have any idea—"

"No. Dammit, do you think I'd just be *standing* here if I did?" He looked at my almost untouched beer. I handed it over. "Thanks. Look, I'm going to bed. I want to be with Toby, think this out. I—*shit,* I don't know." He chugged the beer, dumped the bottle, then put his hands on my shoulders.

"I've got more to thank you for than I realized." He kissed me on the mouth, hard, angry, almost violent, and walked off.

I sighed. I was going to be an all-over bruise by tomorrow. Maybe I'd go to bed too. There was a sleeping bag and a pillow in the Bronco with my name on them. I was tempted.

"Wanna dance?"

Temptation died. I wanted to talk to Stu more than I wanted to go to bed. We swung out on the dance floor, me holding my bandaged hands high. I waved one of them at Charlene, who slid by in lockstep with a good-looking partner.

On the edge of the dance floor I noticed a guy in a tight T-shirt, a beer belly, and a scowl. I wouldn't have noticed him—what was there to notice? —except that he was staring at me. He looked familiar but I couldn't place him. Aw, shucks.

The guy on my rescue team who had told me it was "stupid" to check the ravine? Yes, I thought so, and yes, boy, did he call that wrong. He was not the kind of guy to take that sort of thing well. He looked mean, stared at me with malevolence. Or maybe I was just being paranoid? I looked at him again. Maybe not. I took a wild guess and surmised that he was also the kind of guy who didn't like being shown up by a woman. Not a tough brain stretch on my part, for sure.

"Sorry about your hands."

I turned my attention back to Stu and shrugged. And I was tired of being a hero so I changed the subject. "I hear congratulations are in order."

"Huh?"

"The baby. That's great, Stu! I'm happy for you."

He frowned. Wait a minute. Didn't expectant fathers smile, beam, smirk, something but not, surely, frown?

"Yeah, well, thanks."

I had the cue but I didn't take it. "Is something the matter?" It was a tactless, overly personal question. He noticed and stiffened, but said nothing.

"I'm sorry, I didn't mean to—" I had, of course. Alas.

"No, it's great if—"

If?

"Well, I mean, it's early days still, to be sure and all. I just wish— Hey, to heck with it, okay? Let's just dance."

So we did. It was a full moon and I was a party animal. After Stu I danced with Barry, the draft beer drinker from the other night, and other guys whose names, or drinks, I didn't know. I looked for the guy in the brown and saw him several times but never close enough to be sure. Nobody that I asked knew his name. I wondered what he drove. A black truck?

I wondered if the same person who tried to hurt Toby—*Murder Toby, Kat, call a spade a spade*—killed Deidre. Two such different assaults.

Where was the common motif there? And, if they weren't connected, was Deidre's murderer here? I wondered some more. Too much wonder is not good for you. It's like vitamins: Small doses are a plus, but you can OD on megadoses.

I decided to go to bed and started back to the Bronco. Uh-oh. I wasn't wondering now. I *knew.* There was no way I could unbutton my shirt, unhook my bra, or undress myself on my own. It had been tough enough going to the bathroom, which is why I'd consumed relatively little beer. I headed back to the action looking for Charlene, Chivogny, or another friendly familiar female face. Not a one in sight. Just a lot of hungry male ones.

To hell with it. I slept in my clothes.

20

His hand brushed across her breast. She gasped. Under his touch her body came alive, her nipples hardened with the desire she denied to him, to herself. His mouth covered hers, sucking her breath, her protests away.

. . . .

"You're a peach."

Charlene laughed. I stood in the shower, eyes closed, water running down my face, hands stuck way out as she shampooed my hair. Together we managed to get my clothes on and make me presentable, even attractive, not counting my mitts.

They looked worse than they were, I hoped, I thought. My hands felt a lot better today. The retired nurse, AKA First Aid Station, confirmed it. She efficiently dressed them with an antiseptic, a light layer of gauze on the palms, and a bunch of Band-Aids. I flexed experimentally. Not great, but not bad. I felt like a person again.

The tackle to my knees almost took me down. Okay, I was a person, but not a tough one, not yet.

"Hi Kate, hi hi hi hi hi!" He was bouncing up and down on his little piston-sprung feet.

"Hi, sweetie." I squatted for hugs. Why not? After his tackle I was relatively close to the ground already. "Where's Daddy?" Security was on my mind.

"Right here." Reassuring Matt words. Good.

"We're having bacon and eggs *and* pancakes, isn't that special? Do you want some?" Bounce, bounce, bounce.

"Yes, please. Lots and lots. I'm starving."

"We've got lots and *lots*, huh, Dad?"

We had lots at the beginning but not at the end. Demolition Breakfast Derby. Toby admired the way his full tummy stuck out and tried to stick it out further. I tried to suck mine in. We all laughed. The sun was warm and strong for May in the foothills and it felt good to be alive. I lay back on the blanket and dozed. The thing about being a hero with bandages on your hands is that you don't have cooking or clean-up duty. Broke my heart.

Somebody tugged at my shirt and I opened my eyes. Toby tucked Bear into my arm, then leaned over to kiss me, little syrupy pancake kisses. "Nighty-night." I smiled and closed my eyes again, my arm around Bear, and slid into sleep—not into a steep rocky-sloped ravine of nightmare, but into release, rest, forgetfulness, the first dreamless sleep I'd known in a long time.

"Hey, Matt buddy, we need you."

I struggled to hold onto unconsciousness.

"No."

"C'mon, we're short a guy." Stu's voice. I'd lost the struggle but refused to open my eyes.

"No, I can't stand those games and you know it."

I opened my eyes and sat up, Bear tumbling down, Toby's little comfort blanket, carefully tucked around me, now bunching up in my lap. Stu smiled at me and winked. "Hi, beautiful, how's our top girl this morning?"

I smiled back. There were two guys with Stu. One was Mr. Black Label/Brown Snarl, looking fetching today in jeans and a sweatshirt with ripped-off sleeves; the other was the potbellied muscle-between-his-ears "rescue" expert of yesterday. A plethora of riches.

I thought it through quickly. Matt might not want to play with these boys. I might. Investigation instincts were on alert this A.M. I looked at the guys again. Then again, maybe not.

"What games?" The words were out of my mouth before I could stop them.

"War games. Paint ball games. Wanna play?"

I looked at the guys behind Stu, their lips lifted in scorn, contempt, and macho.

"C'mon, it's the most fun I ever had with my clothes on." Stu had a nice smile.

"Naw, you nuts, Stu, we don't want a *girl.*"

"What the—what good she gonna do us?" they chorused simultaneously, but not beautifully, not Mormon Tabernacle Choir material by a long shot.

I flexed my hands experimentally. Breakfast and a nap, they felt great. "Sure." Aw, nuts, where did those words come from? And when would I stop letting macho jerks—both frowning in extreme displeasure, I noted with considerable interest—push my buttons? Not this weekend, obviously. I hoped the fun of rumpling their Neanderthal fur would overcome the annoyance of playing war games, for crying out loud.

Games like this, like heights, are something I scrupulously avoid whenever possible. War is not a game. Shooting people is not a game. Neither of these things is fun. I don't like being tracked, or chased, or shot at, and I'm not an adrenaline-high junkie. It's not only not fun, it's too much like parts of my job. I sighed. Think first. Look before you leap. Live and learn.

But mostly: Work before play, and this game was work.

"Goddamn, Stu, goddamn wimmin can't shoot or nuthin."

"I can shoot." They looked at me. I can not only shoot, I can use correct grammar; I let that slide, though. "I'm pretty good, as a matter of fact." Pretty good? Read: Ace.

"Of course, I've never tried a paint ball gun. What do you use? Pellets powered by a CO-two cartridge?" They gaped at me. I've never tried it, boys, but guess what? I'm a damn fast learner. Stand back.

Stu laughed and reached down a hand to give me a wrist up. "Hey, I want you on my team, lady."

I smiled amiably. The guys looked dubious; maybe they weren't so easily fooled anymore. About time. Of course muscle-for-brains slows you down and muscle-bound-for-brains does so even more. They quickly recovered their versions of poise and debonair and snarled at me.

"When and where?" I stretched. The guys stared at my tits—now *that* was a surprise—and Stu answered.

"Half an hour. The course is laid out behind the corrals."

Way behind, I hoped. Poor horses.

"You know anything about the game, Kate?"

I shook my head. The guys sneered, one for the road, and took off.

"Well, a regulation or competitive game is a lot tighter, strict rules, a judge, the works. We play for fun, kinda loose, kinda informal." Stu was warming to the explanation. "There are different setups. One is on the flats with bunkers—you run, you hide, you dodge around and it goes to total elimination of a team. Another is the maze, that's my favorite, but obviously a maze takes a formal, more permanent setup. And finally a village-type scene."

Black and white stills of MyLai, of Vietnam, flashed through my mind click/click/click in rapid succession, the twisted bodies of villagers—old men, women, children—the blasted huts, the trenches, the GIs with impassive faces and quieted—but still hot?—guns, the . . .

"A village scene is attack and defend. One team in the village, one in the field."

Rice paddies, pigs, chickens, bundles thrown or blown aside in bloody dirt, spent shell casings, napalmed children . . .

"We run kind of an informal combination of bunker flat and village. Hey, Kate, you listening?"

I nodded. I was, but to too many channels and refrains: Stu's; a song of loss and lament, guilt and grief; and a cosmic hymn of query. God, I was sounding like Luna. I shook myself.

He misunderstood. "Don't worry, it's not complicated. The course is laid out with the old barn at the center. Each side has obstacles, bunkers, etc. Each team starts at the end of its territory. The object is to grab a flag in the barn . . ."

Old Glory; the Red, White and Blue; Stars and Stripes forever; Oh-Say-Can-You-See? snapping in the breeze, flying proudly, triumphantly. Proud, yet what was the triumph in the bloody dirt and ruins of . . .

"Once you have the flag, you run like hell, try to get into the safety of your own territory and team and get the flag back to the starting point marker without getting ambushed. Got it?"

"Got it."

"It sounds simple and it is. Of course, it's simpler in the telling than with shouting and turmoil and guns going off all around you."

Mortar shells exploding, cries of the wounded and damned, bombs bursting in air . . .

"Ready?"

"Ready."

"Got an old sweatshirt?" I nodded. I was pretty sure there was one in the Bronco. "Good. Meet you in fifteen minutes out by the barn."

Matt watched him walk off, then turned to look at me. "Are you crazy?"

I shook my head. Not crazy, no. An undercover investigator at work was, I thought, a preferable way to put it. But I didn't put it that way; I lied. "Just curious."

Matt shook his head in disbelief. I didn't blame him.

There were two teams, each with ten players. I was the only woman and Stu saw to it that we were on the same team. Muscle Mass and Snarl were on the other one and looked as though they could hardly wait to pelt my delicate little body with paint. A short balding guy almost as round as he was tall and dressed in full camouflage was running through the rules. He intoned them as though they were commandments from on high.

"One: The object of the game is to retrieve the flag from the barn and get it back to your team's home base.

"Two: No physical contact is allowed. You remove an opponent from the game by a hit and only a hit. Once hit you must immediately exit the field.

"Three: Certain areas in the barn have been marked or 'roped' off with red tape. These areas are unsafe and game participants are not allowed there. The barn is an old structure and parts of it are unsound. This is important!"

His voice droned on in a high-pitched whine like an insect trapped in a small, hot, enclosed space for too long.

"Okay, now equipment. Everyone's got goggles and face masks?" We all nodded. And boredom. I yawned. "We're a little hit-and-miss on guns today. In fact, we're short a pump action gun so I'm—" The *m* whined out in the air and sailed around for a while before it dropped dead. "—going to give my semiautomatic to our rookie girl player with the bad hands. Whad-dya say, guys, kinda even up the odds for the plucky little gal, eh?"

The guys said, okay, fine, swell, let's get on with it, and I smiled in a plucky, girlish way, whatever that is. And gloated. Semiautomatic? Nice idea, but maybe a bad call on their part. I am a good shot, damn good.

"Okay, pick up and load your weapons, then you've got ten minutes to reconnoiter the lay of the land, plan strategies, and get into place."

Everybody nodded. We didn't synchronize our watches though. Darn.

We did pick up and load our weapons. The guys watched me curiously but my IQ was equal to the task and I loaded up fine. Kind of a disappointment to a couple of them, though Stu looked proud of me.

Then we reconnoitered and they debated strategy and I tried to take it seriously, which was tough. I was assigned to stay in the back and cover my team with the semiautomatic as we advanced. Then, after a run at the barn, I was to dash up in a sacrifice play, grab the flag, and toss or pass it on to a teammate. At that point I could walk my presumably paint-spattered body off the course, a war game casualty.

Golly, didn't that sound like fun.

The warning call was sounded and we took up position. The guys were excited, intense, and pretty much wired up. You could almost smell the adrenaline in the air, taste it on your tongue. The joking and bantering (if you can call talk like *Let's go out and* kill *those mutherfuckas!* joking and bantering) died down into tense silence.

5 . . . 4 . . . 3 . . . 2 . . . 1

We took off, dodging across the field—crouched and running low, cradling our weapons to our bodies—scooting from one bunker or shelter to the next, closing in on the barn and starting to fan out. Out of the corner of my eye I saw an "enemy" approach. I slid to one knee, partially behind a wooden shelter, aimed, and dropped him—well, splashed him. My goggles slipped down my face, they were too big, and I pushed them up again and pushed off for more excitement. We had lost at least one player on our team and downed another "enemy."

I reckoned we were having some fun now.

One of the guys gave the charge signal and about three of them took off with me bringing up the rear. We blasted into the barn, took another "enemy" down, blazed (popped) away at a few more, and then, on cue, I made a dash for the flag.

Got the flag, got another fearless foe—would we never run out of them?—and started backing up.

"Kate, over here!" someone, on my team I hoped, shouted. I zigged, zagged, and passed off the flag. Score one for me, my team, and "plucky little gals." I was backing up, covering myself and almost out, almost clear when I saw it coming.

I couldn't stop, I was moving too fast. Momentum was first to my advantage and then to his.

A foot shot out . . . *No physical contact!* . . . from behind a stall-like enclosure neatly blocked out in red tape . . . *Stay away from taped areas!* . . . I was going to go down, no question, good momentum going, but I twisted to roll and take the fall on my side as well as on my (OUCH!) hands, and to see Mr. Good-Clean-Fun-Team-Player.

Silence draped around us like a miasma in a bad mood: no shots or shouts, no pounding footsteps. Everyone but us had, wisely, followed the flag.

I caught a glimpse of a paint-spattered shoulder . . . *Once hit you must leave the field immediately!* . . . maybe camouflage or dark green or— Something wrenched my goggles and mask, making it almost impossible for me to see, adding—no doubt—more color in the form of bruises to my already lovely multihued body.

Something? Somebody.

I hit the barn floor. The smell of horse, manure, and hay was still there although it was a long-ago desiccated memory. The flooring sagged and groaned, or maybe that was me. A huge—size sixteen EEEE minimum— combat boot flashed by my face and stomped into the floor next to me. The already weakened dry-rot-ridden wood lamented, then cracked and started to go . . .

"Little girls shouldn't play guys' games," someone hissed malevolently.

. . . and gave. A boot in the middle of my back shoved me through. Dust-filled black widow paradise blackness opened its scaly bat wings and welcomed me.

Score one for him.

21

"I will never have you!"

She screamed and pounded his powerful chest with her fists.

"You'll have me," he said calmly. "You'll have me now."

His power silenced her protests.

. . . .

It wasn't a long fall. Eight or nine feet onto dirt. And I wasn't hurt. Much. A few more bruises but, by now, who was counting? I'd left double digits in the bruise department behind me long ago.

I sat quietly, waiting for my eyes to adjust. What had been black started turning into shades of murkiness and gray. The hole above me was too far to jump for so I didn't waste any time on it. My hands weren't up for it, anyway. There were cobwebs in my hair and on my face and I brushed them away, trying to gauge how sticky they were, how strong. Black widows have strong, sticky webs. I swallowed hard, I swallowed dirt.

Fun game, this.

I blew the hair out of my face and tried to feel like a tough guy, or even a plucky little gal. When that failed I opted for survivor. I could do that. Piece of cake. I peered around into the murkiness willing it to give up some comfort. That failed too. Okay. Fine.

The thing is, you *cannot* grow up or spend time in rural California and not have black widows and rattlesnakes drummed into your soul. After years of this there's nothing you can do about it—it's genetically encoded. Little California babies probably imprint on this the way ducks do on their mothers.

Understand, I *like* snakes and spiders. They eat insects and rodents, which I don't like. But not black widows. Uh-uh. Not a chance. And I was in black widow country, no doubt about it. It wasn't as bad as a pit full of tarantulas or the leeches in *The African Queen*, but still— I shivered. Black widow country? Hey, try black widow *heaven.* I shivered again.

Little girls shouldn't play guys' games.

I hadn't had the leisure or the energy to get mad at that yet, but I would. I was looking forward to it. He'd half hissed, half whispered the words. Just like Toby's attacker.

Slugs and snails and puppy dog tails . . .

And spiders. I looked around me. There was old construction rubble, pieces of board, some with nails—rusty nails, I was as sure of that as I was of the black widows—chunks of heavily pebbled concrete. Old stuff. There would be a (latched?) crawl space somewhere. The barn was placed on a slight rise and I sat in the lowest foundation point. From where I was it climbed up to about a three-foot clearance and a faintly outlined square set in a wall.

I took a deep (spider-laden?) breath and started toward it, sheltering my face with my partially mitted hands and walking carefully through rubble and the unseen spider dens with riotous well-attended parties in full swing. A dull flash winked at me and I moved it with my toe. An antique Milk of Magnesia bottle in mint condition. I stuck it in my pocket, a smallish kind of silver lining but it would have to do.

When I had walked as far as I could, I gritted my teeth, got down on my knees, and crawled along on my knees and lower arms hoping I would squish the little devils before they chomped me. The door to the crawl space was locked. I was glum about it but not surprised. After all, most people went from outside in, not inside out.

I looked for latch hardware and saw none. Also not a surprise. It was probably a small block of wood nailed up and twisted across. I pushed. It squeaked. I leaned. Nothing. I sighed, gritted my teeth again—black widows are tough on teeth—and lay back, aiming my feet at the latched side.

One try and I busted out, stuck my feet and legs through and hauled myself out by my arms. I stood there blinking stupidly, happily, in the sunshine.

"*Hey,* where the hell have you been? Chicken out, huh?" The question was hard, the tone mean and nasty.

But not as nasty as me. I'd just done black widow time.

"Get everyone together, asshole."

"What the fuck you talking about?"

"Do it." Forget sugar and spice and everything nice. "Now!"

So he did it. Black widow mean is *mean.*

Five minutes later I looked at nineteen faces, most of them curious, or friendly, or neutral. "This guy"—I pointed him out—"just asked me where I was and accused me of chickening out. *Pond scum,*" I snarled at him. "Look at me." I was a mess, the word mess here being used loosely and charitably. "Do I look like I've been lounging on the sidelines eating chips, drinking margaritas?"

No answer, but I hadn't really expected one.

"I captured the flag in the barn and passed it off. That was our team plan." A couple of friendly faces nodded approvingly. I'd done a smooth job. "Someone tripped me up, shoved me in a red-taped area and stomped me through the floor." I looked around meeting eyes; I had to do it hard and heavy or they'd claim I'd fallen and made up a story; they'd talk me down for being a "girl."

"I didn't see his face." I watched for a sign of relief but couldn't see everyone, couldn't tell. "He was wearing a dark shirt, maybe camouflage, and paint-marked, so he was one of the early hits." I looked around again. Guys were shifting uneasily now, looking at each other and trying not to be obvious, not to get caught at it.

"*Chicken* out?" Pond Scum flushed. "It took me a while to pick myself up and crawl out. As he kicked me down Mr. Fun said, 'Little girls shouldn't play guys' games.' Pretty nice, huh?"

No answer.

"So I'm sure that a guy who's tough enough and man enough to beat up on a woman will have the guts to step forward and discuss it."

Nobody did. I was wrong. Surprise.

I got a lot of apologies and sympathy though. The guys were genuinely horrified. Except for one unspecified one who was pretending to be horrified. Someone retrieved my gun and I played two more games. Just because. After that I'd made my point and my black widow mean was gone.

Anyway, I hate it when I get macho.

Stu and I walked back to camp together. He had a camouflage shirt on, paint-spattered. Of course we all were by now. Prickles and suspicion crawled on me like spiders.

155

"Uh-oh." Stu stopped and pointed at my right breast.

I looked down but I knew already. Nothing moved, not me, not my breast—how could it? I'd stopped breathing—not the black widow with a dime-sized (DIME-sized!) body. Stu reached out and flicked it off with thumb and forefinger, then stomped it. I was trembling violently.

"Stu, check me out! Now! Look me over!" I dragged my sweatshirt off, shook it and flung it to the ground. "Please," I whimpered. I made him look twice. He did and he was real nice about it. Could he be that nice if he'd just stomped me through a floor? If . . .

Prickles all over: suspicion and spiders. I was still trembling.

"C'mon," he said firmly. "We need to find you a drink."

Wrong. We needed to find me a shower and clean clothes. I went looking for Charlene.

"Didn't we just do this?"

She was laughing at me as I stood in the shower with my eyes closed, my hands straight out and water and shampoo streaming down my face.

"Don't ask."

"You're not as smart as you look."

Boy, was that *ever* the truth.

22

"Look at me," he said, "really look at me." She yearned for that, but she was afraid, of his nakedness, his—

"Touch me," he said gently, and he guided her hand to the hardness of his body.

She gasped.

"Love me," he said, "and let me know you, let me love you."

. . . .

"Kate? That you? It doesn't look like you." His voice was puzzled, and no wonder.

"It's me, but dressed like Charlene."

I held a brief pose in black stretch pants, an oversized sweatshirt in neon colors, matching wild socks, earrings, and plastic bracelet. I was something, I wasn't sure what. Matt clearly wasn't either.

"I ran out of clean clothes after the black widows got my last outfit. Charlene came through with these."

"Black widows?"

"It's a long story, Matt." Black widows, aliens, P.I.'s, murder and mayhem—a very long story. I wasn't up to it yet.

"Kate, I need to talk to you."

Good. I was wondering when that would occur to him. "Where's Toby?"

"Playing with a bunch of kids. Several parents are supervising. That's what I need to talk about."

"Toby?"

"Yes."

Good. About time, even. We were walking around somewhat aimlessly.

"Here?" Matt indicated a yellow Ford pickup with the tailgate down. We sat there and watched people go by and things happen.

"Did you talk to Toby yet?"

"Yeah. He's scared, Kate. Still."

I nodded at that. I didn't blame the child. I thought Matt should be scared too.

"What does he say?" I asked.

"Just what he told you about following the lizard. He wouldn't tell me at first because he knows he's not supposed to go under that fence—he knew I'd be mad. But he said he was real careful and didn't go near the edge."

"Did he say he was pushed?"

"Yes. The same story he told you."

"And the words?"

"The same: *Go see your mommy.*"

"Would he make that up, Matt, so you wouldn't get mad at him? So that it would be an accident and not his fault?"

"I don't think so. I thought about it, of course. And I explained it to him, that I wasn't going to get mad—but, by God, we're going to have some new safety lessons," he digressed grimly. "Soon! Anyway, I said it was really important to tell the truth because, if it happened that way, then there was a bad person who would try to hurt little kids, and we had to find him.

"Kate, he promised me he was telling the truth. I believe him. And I don't think that he, or maybe any child that age, is capable of making something like that up. The line: 'Go see your mommy.' The nasty whispering voice. Do you think so?"

"I think from what I know of Toby, and what you've said, that it's highly unlikely."

"Was it an accident? Maybe someone was just trying to scare him and it went too far and they didn't . . ." His voice ran down.

"I don't think it was an accident."

"Or another kid, a mean kid?"

"Kids can be nasty, but they're usually more direct. My guess is that

Toby would have seen and heard a kid, would be able to identify him or her. And the words don't sound like kid words."

"No." Matt ran his hand roughly through his hair. It stood up like a little boy's, only with gray.

"Hey! Watch out!"

A Frisbee was sailing toward us. Matt was looking at his knuckles in case the secrets of the universe should happen to be revealed there. And scowling. I batted the Frisbee away with the back of my hand, smart enough —finally—not to try to catch it with bandaged hands. The kids dove for it and waved and hollered *Sorry, sorry!* and went sprinting off. Nice kids, not killer kids. Matt didn't notice any of it.

"So what does it mean?" His knuckles hadn't given him the answer. Too bad. "Someone is trying to harm Toby?"

Bingo.

"That's best-case scenerio." Hit 'em hard, hit 'em fast, Kat. Show no mercy. Take no emotional prisoners.

"What? *Best* case—? What the—?"

"Worst-case scenerio is murder. What do you think 'Go see your mommy' means?" Hit 'em again, Kat.

"Murder?" His voice was appalled. "A little boy?"

His voice was now outraged and appalled. He knew the words; he understood the concept; it was just that his mind had worked it out and found it totally unacceptable. Shock. Denial. It was understandable, no question. I waited for him to slug through it.

"Murder?" He was getting there.

"So far just attempted murder." *So far. Just.* Hit 'em yet again, Kat. Until he figures it out, in fact.

"So far?"

"Yes."

"It could happen again?"

"I think you have to assume that. There is no way of knowing whether it was a random act of violence by a deranged person, or whether somebody specifically wanted to get Toby."

"Get Toby?" He echoed me faithfully. "But *why?*"

That was the question all right. No good answer yet.

"Until we know, Toby's not safe, Matt."

"I'll keep him safe."

"You can't. No one could. You can't be with someone twenty-four hours a day. Tell everyone. Tell the cops."

"Goddamn." He sounded miserable, not angry. "I can't bear it, I really can't. We're just starting to get over her death and now this. *Shit.* I just want to live a normal—" He laughed, a hollow ugly kind of laughter "—normal. Yeah, sure.

"Kind of hard to do that with everyone staring, talking, wondering. We can't get over it, get beyond it, Kate. Not me, not Toby, when that happens. Then you live it every minute of every day. I can't keep doing that. *We* can't. Do you see?"

I did, yes. "Is there someplace safe you could send Toby, someplace out of the area?"

"Yeah. Sure. My sister. But I can't, Kate. Think about it. Right now we need each other. Bad. And if I send him away, he'll think he did something awful, that he's a bad little boy somehow instead of—"

"Rats."

"Yeah. Exactly."

"Another angle?" I asked.

He nodded.

"Try not to get mad."

"No." He sounded surprised. "No, of course not. I appreciate your help, your understanding."

That was a nice start. Probably downhill from there though. "Is there anyone who would benefit financially or in any other way, directly or indirectly, from Toby's death?"

"God*damn*, Kate. What the hell are you suggesting? Don't you—?"

He caught himself midsentence, and spread his hands out helplessly. I heard kids shouting in the background: happy, free, and safe kids. That's what it sounded like. Who knows what it was really?

"Sorry. It could come down to that, couldn't it?"

"Yes."

"Yeah. Let's start over. I know you're trying to help, and you are, it's just that—"

"It's hard, I understand."

"Damn hard."

He gazed blankly out over the field that had become a parking area. A starter motor coughed and caught, an engine roared to life. Those V-8's make a lot of noise. V-8. I looked up. A black pickup was moving out. It looked familiar but I couldn't see the driver.

"Matt, stop that truck." I said that because I wasn't sure it would stop for me.

"Huh? Where? Why?"

160

"Do it!"

Matt stood up and hollered. "Hey, buddy!" I faded a bit into his background until the truck braked. Matt looked at me. I tucked my bandaged mitt into his elbow.

"Let's go," I said. He shrugged. We sauntered over.

"Yeah?" the guy in the pickup said, looking at us without enthusiasm, or even mild interest.

Well, my, my. It was Mr. Black Label Snarl in his usual effusive mood.

"Yeah?" Matt said, also looking at me and squeezing my arm a little.

"Have you seen a little white poodle with a pink bow in—"

"Naw." He gunned the engine. Matt and I stood, ate dust, and looked at each other.

"That's him." So much for grammar.

"The one who followed you home."

"Yes."

"Mud on the back plate still. A poodle, Kate?"

So much for taste. "It was all that occurred to me. I'm not a great liar," I said, lying. "No mud on the front plate, though." I grinned. I had the tag, that's why. I said so.

"Son of a gun, Kate! You're in the wrong job."

Well, maybe not. "Matt, back to the question—"

"The answer is no. We had a joint will. We each left everything to the other. Toby doesn't inherit anything directly. "Well, he would now"—Matt made a face—"but let's hope that doesn't become an issue."

Let's hope indeed. Cross our fingers. Pray. Anything, everything.

"Nobody else inherited when she died. I gave away her stuff, clothing and jewelry, except for a few things I saved for Toby." His voice was choked and heavy.

"Oh, how nice."

He looked at me angrily, suspiciously.

"I wish someone had let me keep my sister's things. I still wish it."

His face softened.

"What did you keep?"

"A favorite shawl, her quilts, some scarves. Actually I gave him the scarves already. He uses them as blankets for Bear and Bunny. Her pearls and diamond eardrops and a pin, a ring that was her grandmother's, things like that. Things that maybe he could give to his wife someday."

If we could keep him alive long enough to grow up and get married, I thought, but didn't say.

"Toby's a lucky little boy, Matt."

"I sure as hell didn't try to kill him for his inheritance. Or her either."

"No." I meant it. At last. Either he was telling me the truth or he had me totally scammed. Still, why wouldn't he say Deidre's name? "Who did you give Deidre's belongings to?"

"I told Chivogny to take what she wanted. Was that stupid, trying to mend fences in death?"

"No."

"She and Luna came one day when we were gone. I wanted everything out of there. I thought it would be better. But they didn't take the memories, the reminders, or the guilt. Aw, hell!"

Time will, I thought, but didn't say. Again. Whoa, I was getting good at this restraint business. Anyway, it would be no consolation. Not yet. And I didn't want to get punched out for saying it. I had some sense. Not enough, maybe, but some. Guilt? What guilt? What guilt about what?

"What guilt?" I said it aloud. So much for restraint.

"There's always guilt." He dismissed the question with a shrug although I would have preferred to pursue that one for a bit.

"Do you walk under ladders, Matt?"

He wrinkled up his brow and looked puzzled, or like he thought I was losing it. One or the other. "Kate, there aren't any ladders out here."

"Or sleep on the thirteenth floor of a hotel, if they even have them, do they, do you know? Or get nervous when a black cat crosses your path or you spill salt or—"

He breathed out heavily in exasperation, a sound I recognized from my mother's long-ago repertoire. Not a good sign on the whole. "Just spit it out, Kate. I can take it."

"Do you believe in superstition, and are coincidences just a cosmic happenstance burp or a credible—"

"Kate!"

"Somebody just tried to kill Toby. Almost five months ago somebody *did* kill his mother."

"What are you saying?"

I didn't answer. I wasn't speaking an obscure Serbo-Croatian dialect and he'd heard me just fine. He looked at his knuckles. Me too. They were nice knuckles, sturdy and brown with little wrinkles like smile lines and no answers or insight into the question. Again.

"You're saying the two are connected?"

"I don't know. They could be."

"Or?"

"Or that it's one hell of a coincidence and a shit-deal-run-of-luck."

"Bad luck."

"Very bad luck."

A Frisbee sailed over in a crowd of shouts and landed at our feet. Again.

A coincidence?

"What was that?" I asked Matt as we walked back to camp. "Shots?"

He shrugged it off. "Didn't notice. Could have been. We're country, Kate."

Yes. I couldn't shrug it off though.

23

"What do you want?" she asked, and her voice trembled.

"You. To get to know you, that is," he corrected smoothly.

"I'm not sure that's what *I* want," she said almost firmly.

"I'd like a chance to convince you." He stepped closer to her.

Her heart did a flip-flop. It was either fear or excitement, she wasn't sure which.

....

That afternoon I was on my way back to civilization.

The balance had tipped. Toasted marshmallows, s'mores, dancing in the moonlight, hanging off cliffs and playing war games with black widows just didn't have the same wild appeal. How jaded one becomes. And so swiftly too.

Civilization, but not home, not even home away from home. I had errands. Two of them.

Tobias blinked when he saw me. I stood in the open door with the sun behind me, but that wasn't it, I was sure.

"Kat?"

My heart jumped. It was good to hear my name again. I liked being Kate, living her life, pretending, but maybe I was ready to stop running, to start facing . . .

"Kat?"

164

His voice was hesitant. His hand hovered uncertainly on the wheelchair arm, not sure whether to shake hands with an acquaintance, or shoo off a blond neon bombshell with lime green/hot pink/wild yellow plastic parrot barrettes.

"Hi, Tobias, it's my undercover look. What do you think?"

"Good. Very good." In a sudden switch, he looked pleased and approving. "I hardly recognized you." His hand clasped mine in a warm friendly grasp, then he backed up the wheelchair and waved me in. "I was just making some lemonade. Perhaps you would care for some?"

I accepted gratefully and we made small talk while he made lemonade. I like to get through the Hi-how-are-you? stuff before hauling out the big guns. Okay. Cannons. I shouldn't have worried. And I didn't have to do the hauling. He was.

"The investigation, Kat. What have you found out?"

Boom.

"You need to level with me, Tobias. There's more going on, a lot more, and I need to know it."

"What do you mean?" His eyes were hooded, guarded, and he looked like a mean old predatory bird peering down his nose at me and asking questions he knew the answer to.

"Do you ever watch soap operas?"

The eyes popped open, startled and alert. "Sometimes, but no, not often. I don't like them. The plots, the characters, they're just not realistic."

"No. I agree, and yet Deidre strikes me as a character right out of a soap opera. Not to mention Chivogny. And Mabel, their mother. Maybelle," I corrected myself. I was on shaky ground here, since I don't watch soap operas much either.

"It seems more like soap opera than real life, doesn't it? Or maybe it's that everyone is playing a part. Mabel becomes Maybelle, Deidre changes character at will, Chivogny is lost in her dream of motherhood. Stu and Matt—"

No, I wouldn't say it, that they slid between the sheets, between their roles as husbands and lovers. Not to Tobias, not yet.

"We have a whole cast of characters here, Tobias, changing with each act, each scene."

I thought how that kind of change is only a facade, a respite, and that it wears off, that it does nothing to address the deep discontent within, and I wondered if it could lead to murder. I thought so, thought it had, and didn't care for that thought.

"Even you, Tobias, are playing a part."

Even me. Blond-streaked hair, fingernail polish, new clothes, a new name . . .

"We can run, we can't hide," I said gently. I was coming to understand it.

He flushed. I'd never seen a mean, predatory old bird flush before. Maybe he wasn't really mean.

"I can't do a good job without information, Tobias."

"No." He exhaled the word on a long sighing breath. "No. It's not that I don't want you to have it, it's more that I don't want to rake it up, even to think on it. I wasn't sure, I'm still not, what this old stuff has to do with Deidre. With now. Maybe nuthin'."

"We need to consider it."

"All right."

When he sighed again it sounded as if his heart was stretching at the seams, cracking and in danger of breaking. And maybe so. I hardened my heart and waited for the story.

"I feel sorrowed by this." He addressed a point on the wall, a stain shaped like a dead fish. It didn't answer back and neither did I. "I was her godfather and yet I—" He communed with the wall and the stain some more. "I didn't do enough. It was not right."

There was a sugar bowl on the table and I sweetened my lemonade. Tobias had made it potent and tart and poured for us. A radio played in the background with a talk show blathering away.

"I saw what was going on but I didn't understand it, and I didn't know what to do. I don't understand you womenfolk so good." He sounded genuinely regretful and shook his head slowly back and forth, looked at me and my clothes, shook his head again. "It's a puzzler to me, always has been."

He was circling steadily in generalities but showing no signs of coming in for a landing on a specific. "Deidre?" I prompted.

He took a deep breath and then the plunge. I put more sugar in my lemonade, making it oversweet, as if the sugar could sweeten the words that I knew were coming, and the taste in my mouth I was sure they would leave.

"It would have been better for Mabel and Chivogny had that child never been born. She wasn't much wanted, she wasn't much loved. What she was was left out. Others tried to make it up to her, me and the wife, but, while it helps—it don't do the whole job. Your own mother, your own sister don't really appreciate you, you're in a pile a trouble, a heap a hurt, and there ain't a bit of doubt about it."

No. None at all.

"I think the child—well, she was a grown woman, of course, but I think of her often as that hurt little girl she was—and I think she never stopped looking for love. And when she found it—and she did, she married a good man—why, then she wouldn't trust in it. She even went on to spoil it. What's the sense in that?" he asked me, his voice cranky, querulous.

He didn't wait for an answer. "Well, there ain't no sense to it. You can't outrun sorrow, is what it is."

He reached for his lemonade and drank thirstily. I scrutinized the kitchen decked out in bright, clear colors and handmade accessories, in spices and knickknacks. Love had been said and shared and lived here.

And those who have known love don't understand that awful desperate longing of those who haven't. You wish for love, long for it, but if it comes to you, you throw it aside, trample it. Better to lose it that way than to come to depend on it, need it, and risk having it taken from you. Because then, if that happened, you would die inside. And it would happen, it always had. It always would.

"I don't understand it, do you?" he asked me.

I nodded, sorry that I did, and that I'd had a mother like Deidre's.

"Well, maybe you'll explain it to me."

"Maybe," I said, thinking that I wouldn't be able to any more than Deidre had.

"Damn that Mabel, anyway. A woman oughten to have children she can't care for, oughta have stopped with the one, with Chivogny."

Yes. true. But what ought to be so rarely is. I drank my too sweet lemonade; there was a bitter taste in my mouth still.

"And then Deidre, poor child, made the same mistake."

The sadness in his voice and heart seemed to dim the colors and love in the kitchen. I blinked, trying to make it right again.

"She had a child. But that don't work. A child needs love. It don't give it, not at first. This one, Toby, was luckier in his father than in his mother. He is a good man, is that man." His face darkened. "If he didn't kill Deidre, that is, and that's an if still.

"Them girls, they just about hated each other, you know. Chivogny had what Deidre wanted, what Deidre could never get, her mother's love. Deidre begrudged and hated her sister for that. She told the wife once that she must be a horrible child that her mother wouldn't love her like she did her sister. And cried."

The lemonade wasn't sweet enough for this. Nothing was. People called in P.I.'s to fix things that weren't fixable. Deidre had wanted a fairy-tale life, a happy-ever-after ending and hadn't gotten one. She had tried to write her own script and that hadn't worked either. Death had ended it, but not fixed it.

"Hatred. That's a pretty strong word."

"Yes. Hate is a strong thing, stronger than blood. Or love. Or life even."

"How much did Chivogny hate Deidre?"

"Enough to kill her? That's what you're asking me, isn't it?"

That's what I was asking. The silence answered for me.

"I don't know, but I don't reckon . . . I can't think the girl would kill anybody. But—"

Yes. But— And life was full of buts, though not ones that lead to violent death. Not necessarily. Not usually.

"But I don't think so, I don't. Except for Mabel playing favorites the girls woulda done all right together. Maybe they did finally. Mabel's been gone three years now almost. Maybe those girls was smart enough to get over it, or through it, or some damn thing."

Maybe.

"I like to think that."

Yes. I would too.

"Besides, the bad feeling, the bad blood, was running the other way. It was Deidre what had the hurt, not Chivogny. It was Deidre what was passed over for her sister, not Chivogny. If anyone had a hankering to kill, I think it'd rightly be Deidre."

Hankering. Hankering to kill? I got a hankering for peach pie, or to walk by the river, or to go downtown—but to kill? Surely it took more than a *hankering* to kill, even to think about killing. Surely. But this wasn't a business where things were sure. Even sure things.

"Chivogny's kind of quiet, not violent, not one to kill. Cross her off. Forget that. And that'd be a relief, that would. Surely would."

Surely would. If it's sure.

I digressed. "Tobias, did you get the information I asked you for?"

"Yes."

Good. I couldn't get it without breaking cover and he hadn't wanted me to do that.

"The coroner's report on Deidre. That was it, right?"

That was it. Right.

"Did you read it?" I asked.

"I—no." His face closed up again. "More lemonade, Kat?"

"I don't think so, thanks."

He poured for himself and spilled a little, then carefully wiped it up. "You see, look what we did. We done raked up and trucked out a whole load a muck and no good to come outta it."

"Too soon to tell, Tobias," I said, trying for a hearty note. And missing by about a car length. Or two.

"And you'll keep at it?"

Raking up the good, I hoped, not the muck. I would, I was. I was going to now. I said good-bye, the lemonade bitter in my mouth still, though not as bitter as the conversation that played in my mind. It would take more than sugar to sweeten that.

I had a map to Chivogny and Stu's house on the seat next to me. I couldn't have written a better ticket, but I hadn't had to. It had been handed to me. As had the house key. It was my next errand.

"Could you do me a favor?" I'd heard Stu ask a friend. "You're going back early, right? I need someone to stop off at my place. We're hoping to stay over until Monday." But the friend wasn't going back early. *Sorry*, he said.

I wasn't sorry and I made a quick decision. "I am. Can I help?"

Stu looked at me and brightened. "Chivogny got the store covered so she doesn't have to go in, but she forgot to get the key to Luna. Could you? If it wouldn't be too much out of the way? Shoot, I'd be real glad to pay for your time—"

"No way."

He looked a little crestfallen.

I grinned. "No way you pay me, but tell me where the key is. And where I deliver it." I wobbled as I spoke. Toby was playing ring-around-the-rosy on one of my legs.

"Thanks, Kate."

"You bet. My pleasure." That was an understatement. One of several. And he had told me. And given me the map.

"Just leave our house key on the kitchen table and latch the door behind you."

"Okay. You got a neighbor I should check in with, let them know I'm a good guy, not a bad guy?" A sort of good guy, I amended silently.

"Naw. We're somewhat isolated out there. Nothing to worry about."

So that was that, and here I was. I pulled into the driveway. Very isolated. Even better. I unlocked the front door and walked in.

A faint smell of bacon hung in the air and pushed briefly at my face

169

like a tired wrinkled balloon. The house was clean but cluttered. Newspapers, magazines, and videotapes were piled here and there. The furniture was new old-fashioned and the house was inundated with cute à la Chivogny's store.

I blinked. It was a lot to take in.

A ceramic elephant coyly offered to take my umbrella if I had one but, to my regret, I didn't. A kitty forever yawned and played the coquette at visitors from its place on the hearth. Ducks marched in disciplined fashion across the kitchen counter and country cotton rioted through the house. I blinked again. Our things—particularly our homes—speak for us in clear and definite voices.

As instructed, I put the key on the kitchen table, then headed for the key rack near the kitchen door to the garage where I found the shop key, neatly labeled and waiting to be stuck in my pocket.

One down.

I had permission, I had time, but there was no point in wasting either one. I started in the bedroom. A bedside table on each side of the bed, a gun in each. His and hers. How sweet. The hers was a .22, the his a .45. They were both fully loaded. I hoped the two of them always went to bed in a friendly mood.

I had settled on a quick toss and moved with some rapidity. Everything was clean and more or less neatly placed, so it was relatively easy. In the bathroom wastebasket I found crumpled and ripped packaging. I read the directions on the box: *Take as early as one day late! Easy to do and read. If the colorstick turns blue, you're pregnant; if it remains white, you're not pregnant.* And then I stared at it for a long time, asking for the answer that wasn't there.

Yes? No? Maybe so? Try again? Better luck next time?

The door next to the master bedroom was shut. I opened it onto a room flooded with sunshine, Pine Sol, hope and baby things. Cuteness, in a trendy juvenile version, had run amok here. The room was so stuffed with inanimate items there hardly seemed space for a child. The crib was covered with quilts, toys, and a doll. The Pine Sol and general sparkle spoke to recent cleanings. To renewal, hope, and planning. I felt like an intruder.

I was, that's why.

The spare bedroom was dusty and cool with the feel of the not used and not cared for. Pictures hung in cozy little groups on the wall. Old ones. Family ones. Both Chivogny and Deidre had been beautiful children, a beauty readily identifiable as their mother's, though Deidre would have been more beautiful had she smiled.

There were wedding pictures for both. Chivogny was striking, but Deidre was breathtaking, a heart-stopper. In her white-lace-over-some-thing-gorgeous-and-expensive-with-pearls wedding dress, she smiled brilliantly into the camera, her head slightly flung back and her hair a halo of almost moving light around her head. Her hands were tucked into the arms of her new husband and their best man. Matt and Stu were not looking at the camera, they were looking at her. In adoration. Both of them.

I saw her face again, pale and quiet, dull hair fanned out on the metal of the autopsy table. The difference between life and death was more than the pulse of blood and the breath of air. I looked at the wedding picture, saw the white of the dress and the full laughing, breathing breast splashed with red blood, red and spreading, pumping out with each beat. Each breath numbered. Hopes and dreams spilled forth, running out. Gone.

Blood. Red. Spreading. I put my head in my hands. This is what happened in my nightmares. I would see a person, alive, smiling, happy, and then the blood, the stain spreading wider and wider. Rivers of blood that I couldn't push away or run from. Death and blood.

I blinked and looked at Deidre again, the pristine white of the lace, of the wedding dress, the smile.

She had been trashed by a shot from a .22 like the one in the bedside table. I blinked away the blood and the autopsy photos as I had my nightmare. I couldn't do that with death.

I could get the hell out of there.

And I did.

24

"I despise you!" she cried out passionately.

"No," he said. "You don't."

"With all my heart and soul I do. I hate you." Her voice broke.

He pushed her roughly against the wall. She struggled briefly, then ceased and stared at him with blank eyes.

· ·

Luna answered the door in a purple silk shirt, purple suede skirt, matching (you guessed it) purple suede boots, a blue funk and a black eye. The latter two were a major fashion faux pas and made a mockery of her otherwise impeccable outfit. I noticed but I didn't comment. It took something; I was in a testy mood.

I was supposed to drop the key off at the Pioneer for Luna to pick up, but I'd decided to make a house call. Sweet of me. My hands hurt from driving and I had a headache and a longing for easy and simple. I tried to snap out of it.

"Hi, what happened to you?" I asked. Wow. That was snappy.

"I can't talk now. You should call first." She tried to close the door.

But that was tough; my foot was in it. "I'm sorry. Stu said it would be okay."

"Stu?"

Open sesame: the magic word. "I've got the shop key for you."

"Oh. Yes. All right, come in." She opened the door just enough for me to pass through. If I held my breath and sucked in my stomach. Talk about grudging.

"Where's the key?"

She held out her hand. So I guess grudging didn't cover it. Not quite. The key stayed in my pocket.

"Thanks for inviting me in. May I sit down? You said I could come around any time."

All right, I lied. She said I could *call* any time. Details. And pretty close. Close enough. I looked around. Her house wasn't purple, which was a relief. Big time. It was elegant and impersonal, like a suite at a good hotel, which was a surprise. Big time. I guess not paying for your tea and bran muffins adds up faster than I thought.

"May I?" I indicated a chair.

She started to shake her head.

"I need help."

Her pretty eyes, one rimmed with black and blue, looked at me with hostility.

"And so do you."

Her eyes filled up with tears, puddled over and spilled into the black and blue like dirty water in a midnight ditch, then rolled down across her cheeks in a zigzag pattern. How did she do that? She sank gracefully onto an elegant love seat and I followed suit, although not as gracefully. I noticed with interest, though not with surprise, that my neon outfit clashed hideously with the decor. It was a measure of her distraction that she didn't note it.

"What happened to you, Luna?"

She shook her head. More impeccable tears. I was impressed. I thought it was probably marketable.

"Your aura slipped? A low-flying crystal bonked you?" I was trying for a note of levity and was, so far, failing. "You walked into a door? Your boyfriend smacked you?"

She shook her head some more and cried. I wasn't batting a thousand.

"Luna?"

She looked up from her puddles of tears and her eyes were frightened. "What did Stu say?" she asked. The tears had stopped.

"Why did he hit you, Luna?"

"Who?"

She made her voice lighthearted. It didn't work. She could cry pretty tears and change her voice, but the fear was there. There, and stark, written high and wide in capital letters in the billboards of her eyes.

"Stu."

"Stu?" She echoed stupidly.

"Stu," I agreed.

"Oh."

The fear in her eyes looked for a place to hide, a bed to crawl under, a closet to dart into, and found none. Found me sitting and waiting. Like a patient in a dentist's office, I would be there until I'd gotten what I'd come for, or forever, whichever came first. Damn! I hate going to the dentist and I hate pushing around women who've been beaten up.

"It wasn't like that. I was sitting, he swung around, and suddenly his elbow—"

"Yeah," I said. "Yeah. Right. His elbow."

She burst into tears again.

"The elbow story is a pretty old one, Luna, pretty shopworn, ho-hum, and try-again thin." I didn't believe her tears; I did believe the fear.

"Stu came over to bring me the key, like you are." She gestured at me. "Only he left suddenly and forgot."

And lied, I thought. Interesting. He'd told me that Chivogny had forgotten to give Luna the key. Or Luna was lying. Also interesting.

"While he was here we got to talking. I invited him in for a cup of tea. Would you like tea?" The offer was half-hearted.

"No, thanks, but I'd love a couple of aspirin." Better yet, codeine or straight whiskey, I finished mentally.

"Aspirin?" she said in a shocked voice. "I wouldn't *dream* of having chemicals like *that* in the house."

Bummer. That being the case, I didn't bother with the rest of my list.

"Is it a headache? Come, I've got just the tea for that."

I followed her obediently into the kitchen wondering how we'd gotten stuck in a teapot and off Stu.

"Let's see." She pawed through a bunch of little paper sacks in the cupboard.

"One for headaches and another for a black eye?"

She flushed. "Yes. It does work, you know."

"Luna, about Stu—?"

"All things are connected. All things make Perfect Sense and Perfect Order, if only we could see It."

"Pretty big 'if', isn't it?"

She ignored that vile, rude, unenlightened interruption and kicked into turbo.

"All Being is a reflection of The Perfect One."

This was interesting news to someone with a headache. Or even with a black eye. Luna poured boiling water over herbal concoctions that instantly started smelling foul, loathsome, and repulsive. My already tenuous interest in tea slipped another notch, or ten.

All being is a reflection of the perfect one. Huh? Did she mean the perfect one had headaches and black eyes? In that case we weren't talking perfect here. Anyone who has ever had a headache knows that, and if I couldn't buy it with a mere headache, try telling it to someone with a hangover. Or perhaps she didn't mean me to take it that literally. What the hell did she mean? I *was* testy, no doubt about it.

"Deidre, for instance, and her death—"

I snapped to attention. And waited in silence. "Yes?" I inquired finally.

"Well, it's all connected, don't you see? It wasn't an accident that Stu came by. Not at all."

I agreed that it wasn't an accident but I didn't see all the connections yet.

"I was able to help him," she said with a patient plastic smile. "Quite a bit, I think."

I looked at her black eye. The plastic smile slid off her face into oblivion and the garbage dump of the unrecyclable and was replaced with a sudden flush. It was becoming, I thought, what with all her other shades of blue and purple. She ignored my unspoken implication. Still becoming, I guess, but what?

"Matt had asked Chivogny and me to clear out Deidre's things."

My, my, another different version: Matt said he had asked Chivogny, who had brought Luna along to help.

"Of course I was *happy* to be of help."

Of course.

"I was working on the closet while Chivogny did the bureau and jewelry box and I found a shoe box with some personal letters, uh, sort of involving, uh, whatever. I didn't say a *thing* to Chivogny because naturally I wouldn't want to *hurt* her."

"Why would it hurt her?"

"Well . . ."

She hadn't thought it through, didn't have a ready answer.

"Not would, but could," she said at last.

"How?"

"I don't know, just in case, I guess."

"I think you do know." A polite understatement on my part.

"Well, maybe I do, but I certainly couldn't tell *you*. They were *personal* after all, like I said."

"They were letters making it clear that Deidre and Stu had an affair, weren't they?"

Her eyes widened, even the black-and-blue one. "How did you— Well, never mind, it certainly doesn't matter now. The point is that *naturally* I would not want my friend to be hurt."

"Naturally."

She looked at me quickly. It was the sarcasm, I think.

"I just placed the tissue from the shoe box over them and then put some lavender pumps in the box and asked Chivogny if I could keep them. She knows how I feel about that color, about all shades of purple."

Only a blind person would not. "So she gave them to you?"

"Oh, yes."

"Without looking into the box?"

"Yes. Who would have thought that—?" She flushed again. "I was *only* trying to protect my *friend*. There's no need to make it sound *nasty* or something."

I lied and said I was sorry. "And Stu? How did he find out?"

"I mentioned it to him. Naturally I just wanted to put his mind at ease."

"Naturally."

"For some reason he got all upset."

"Oh? Why?"

"He took it wrong, I think."

"How did he take it?"

"I—I don't know." The words weren't foreign to her. Neither was the idea.

I gazed at her comfortable surroundings and wondered again what she'd done to afford them. "He took it badly enough to hit you?"

"He, uh, he was really upset, I guess. And well, it's too bad, but you know how men are. . . ."

"No, how?"

"Well, they take it out on a woman."

"Not the guys I know, like, and respect. They wouldn't take it out on a woman. Or a man. Not even a dog. Shoot, these are guys who wouldn't even smash beer cans on their foreheads to be tough."

"You're making fun of me." Her dark eyes drilled me. If she'd been Black and Decker electric and hit the on button I'd have been Swiss cheese. Easy call.

"No, I'm not, I'm making a point. There are men, too damn many of them in fact, who do that, but it's not across the board as you implied. And Stu doesn't strike me as one of them." That was a guess, though, and not an easy call.

She shrugged and pointed to her black eye, then pulled the sleeves of her loose shirt up to show me the bruises on her upper arms as if someone had held her there. Hard. See, her gesture said: evidence.

I thought it would take more than that to make Stu violent. Much more. I said so.

She shrugged again, a who-cares-what-you-think? shrug. Then her curiosity got the better of her. I almost liked Luna in spite of myself. "Like what?" she asked.

"Like extortion, Luna. Shall we try that one on for size?"

She flushed immediately, hotly. First guess and already the right size?

"No, no! I would never do that. *Never*. How can you even *think* that?"

"What then?" I asked. "He didn't just take it out on you."

"I don't know. I asked him for a favor, that's all. I mean, I was doing *him* a favor, wasn't I? And what goes around comes around, doesn't it? Well, of course it does. Naturally."

I filed the favor notion under Later. "You said in the beginning that this tied in with Deidre's death. How?"

"Some of Stu's letters were angry and threatening. *I* knew he was just upset and mad and didn't *mean* anything by it but somebody else might not."

"Somebody like the police?"

"Yes," she said simply.

I thought that her definition of a "favor" and my definition of extortion might be essentially the same thing.

"Why didn't the police find the letters, Luna? They looked, and they're good at this sort of thing."

"She had a secret place. I think I was the only one who knew. I just *happened* to see one time . . ."

"So you brought up the subject of the police and Stu slapped you?"

"Yes."

I had a hard time blaming him. Me. The one who never condones violence against women by men. "Where are the letters?"

"I have them."

"He left without them?"

She flushed. "I said I had to get them."

"I want them."

She shook her head.

"Now. Get them or I call the cops and nail you on withholding evidence and obstructing justice and more stuff that I can't remember but they will, or will think up."

She tried to stare me down. It didn't work. Her eyes hated me, the black-and-blue one especially.

It's a tough world out there.

Blackmail kicks it that direction.

25

He dropped kisses on her face like flower petals, soft and gentle and all over. She smiled and turned her face up to receive them. Then the kisses got hard and fast, rough and frightening.

"Stop!" she cried out. "You're hurting me."

He paid no attention to her plea.

....

The letters were handwritten, some in thick heavy black ink, some in pencil. They were all from Stu to Deidre. The writing was large and forceful, the lettering blocky and sturdy. Each letter began with one word, *Deidre,* and ended with another, *Stu.* Most were dated with only a day of the week. Postmarks on several envelopes placed the letters in the two-month period before Deidre died on a cold night behind the Pioneer.

The tone was at first passionate, full of avowal, love, laughter, and longing. This gradually became more temperate, modified perhaps by reality and everyday and more reasonable considerations. And then the planning for a future together started. And stopped. After that came the begging, the pleading. *Why don't you answer my letters, take my calls, come see me as arranged?* Finally there were threats. *I would die before I stopped seeing you. I would kill you before I let you—*

I looked up at Luna. "You read this?"

"Yes."

"What was the favor you asked of Stu?" The letters were heavy-duty, were trouble, big trouble. They would command a high price. I knew that. So did she. Stu would have known too.

"I— Well, nothing really."

"Come off it."

I made no attempt to hide the contempt I felt. If this was how it worked, if this was how her concept that "all things were connected and one" operated, then it and she both were worthy of my contempt and scorn. Nobody likes a blackmailer.

"Luna, I have no doubt that you put a high price on these. They were hot, and you felt they were worth it. What was that price?"

She sipped at her tea. "You don't like your tea?"

"No." I didn't like a lot about this. I wouldn't like the favor she was asking either, or the price. I'm not a betting person but I would have put money on it. And won. "Luna?"

She sighed. If I didn't know her better, I would have been moved. It was a sigh that sounded like a lot of little babies' hearts were being broken at the same time.

"You're very persistent, Kate. All right, I'll tell you. But let's talk about it another day when I feel better."

"No."

She sighed and more little babies' hearts broke somewhere. "I hate it here. I thought it would be a good place to live and work, but I was wrong. The people are too down-to-earth, too . . . too drab and commonsensical. I want to go to someplace like L.A., where my soul will be free, will be unfettered, where I can breathe deeply and fill my lungs with air and light and—"

"Hydrocarbons, not air."

"Hmmmm? Oh." She waved that away with a fretful gesture. "But it's *so* expensive to move and I just don't have the money." I looked around at her house and all the things that money can buy. She followed my glance. "This isn't mine, it belongs to a friend. I'm just staying here."

"So you wanted Stu to give you the money?"

"Give? Oh, no!"

She sounded shocked, but I wasn't buying.

"Just *lend,* and just until I'm on my feet again."

"How much?"

"I could make do with three, four would be better."

That sounded modest. "Hundred?"

"No." She blinked in surprise. "Thousand. Moving to L.A. is very expensive, first and last and— Look, you won't tell Stu, will you?"

"Tell him what?"

"About our conversation? That you—"

"That I know about this so there's no point in paying out hush money? Yeah. I will, actually. This kind of thing makes me sick."

She closed her eyes in pain until only the black-and-blue one stared owlishly, blankly at me.

I tossed the shop key on the table.

"Oh, *please.*" Her eyes popped open. "Please don't do that. How will I manage? What will I do? Oh, *please!*"

I dug in my pocket again and tossed a coin on the table next to the key.

"Here is a quarter, call someone who cares."

I made it to the door before Luna made it to the phone, but just barely.

That night again. You know how sorry I am that it happened, and if I could take it back, I would. But life isn't like that. I shouldn't have forced it, I know, but at the time I couldn't stop, couldn't not do it. Don't hold it against me. Tell me it is behind us. You must. I would die before I stopped seeing you. I would kill before I let you go. Or before I would let what is between us and private become public.

I was reading from Stu's letter. Whoa. If I were Stu I would empty my bank account to get a letter like that back. *You know how sorry I am that it happened.* What happened? Possibilities jumped around in my mind. Clearly Deidre had been deeply hurt by it, victimized. And Stu was the one who had hurt her. *You know how sorry I am* is not an apology, is not the same as: I am sorry. *Forced it.* It? Her? What? He was not asking for forgiveness, but demanding it. *Don't hold it against me. Tell me it is behind us. You must.* And then the threats. *I would die. I would kill.* No velvet glove there to cushion the blow.

How much was rhetoric, how much reality? Had Deidre refused to forgive, to forget, to continue the relationship? Had Stu gone down there to talk with her, to talk with the .22 from his wife's bedside table in his hand, rage in his heart and—

The cold jangle of the phone hit my mind and ricocheted wildly about

181

before it exploded, leaving me in an instant spent, exhausted, and afraid. The letters were spread out on the kitchen table before me, along with my notes, empty pop cans, the salt and pepper cows and fear. It was crowded. The phone shrilled again. Reluctantly I answered.

"Kate—" Charlene's voice blew through me like warm air and sunshine. "I just got to work. I goofed off with friends on the way back and didn't have the time to come home. Anyway, there's a note here to call you. Matt's not coming in tonight and he wants you to work his shift. He works the bar Sunday and Monday."

Aw, shoot. I was tired and feeling busted-up. I wanted to relax. I wanted to give my hands a chance to heal. "Can you call someone else?"

"There isn't anyone," she said in a small voice. "Just you."

Aw, shit. "Okay, I'll get ready and I'm on my way."

"Thanks, Kate. You're a peach."

And that made me laugh. Good thing.

It was Sunday, early evening and quiet, a few regulars at the bar, a couple of tables filled, one with a spring romance, another with two overweight guys in golf shirts and a semidrunken haze. I figured we'd just coast through the evening and close up early. I figured wrong.

I was staring out the window trying not to think. Charlene was taking drinks out to her scattered customers when the door opened. My draft beer drinker walked in with a swagger and a grin.

"*Hey*, I was hoping you'd be here. Could I get a beer?"

I smiled. I didn't feel like it but I was on the clock; I was getting paid to make drinks, smile, be nice. I was still getting the draft, my back to the bar, when I heard Charlene's tray slam down.

There are slams and slams, especially with Charlene. This one didn't bode well. I delivered the beer, took payment, and scooted down the bar to her station.

"What?"

"Assholes, *fucking* assholes, I've *had* it. They treat you like dirt, like *scum.*" There were tears in her eyes.

"What happened?"

"He pinched my butt and then he called me a cunt when I told him to knock it off."

"Who?"

"The Vodka Seven."

I slid out from behind the bar and walked over. Overweight, middle-aged guys in golf shirts aren't that tough, just rude. The Vodka Seven knew I was there; he took his time looking at me. A child's game, but he was pretty obviously a child in an adult body.

"Yeah?" he said. "You got a problem?" His voice was defiant.

"No." I smiled. "But you do. Mister, this ain't baseball, and you don't get three strikes." I had his attention now. "You call my cocktail waitress names, you're out." I picked up his drink. He looked non-plussed.

"Fuck!" said his friend.

"And you got company." I picked up his buddy's drink. They were full drinks, which added insult to injury. "You leave now, you can come back. You come back, you do it with an apology."

I walked off. Behind the bar again I dumped the drinks in the sink. Nobody was talking. The jukebox wasn't playing. I was the only show in this part of town and I was a headliner.

"Look—" They stood in front of me, but across the bar. "You better have friends—"

A stool scraped as someone pushed it back. The noise was loud. But not the voice; it was low, low and very definite.

"She's got friends."

"You go. We'll leave it at that," I said.

They left, but they didn't leave it at that. On the way out they kicked a couple of chairs and slammed a fist here and there to show us they were real men, tough guys who couldn't be pushed around by a woman. I was impressed, you bet. And I wondered why I had thought it would be fun to be behind the bar again.

"Have I had bad luck with customers lately, or what?" Charlene tried to make light of it but her voice was shaky.

I winked at her and pulled some tokens off the back bar. "Play the jukebox?" She nodded, took a deep breath and walked off. I waited for the music. One down. How many more to go?

"I remember now," the Draft Beer said. He didn't smile and his eyes met mine. "You testified in a case that sent a guy down on arson and insurance fraud. You're a private investigator."

I didn't say anything, thought I'd be silent, hang out with the fifth amendment for a while.

"I followed that case pretty close. The guy you helped send down was my cousin." He finished his beer, picked up his money, leaving a dollar for me, and walked out. Two down.

The music didn't lift our spirits much. That's a lot to ask of a jukebox. Charlene and I made an executive decision and closed up early. We were out of there by eleven.

"Kate, I'm going over to Steve's, have a few drinks, chill out. You come too. We'll end the evening on a nice note."

A concept I could get behind. Easy. But my way was a hot bath, a glass of wine, a good book and a quiet night. "Thanks, Charlene, I think I'll go home and collapse instead."

"Okay. Katy—Kate—" I smiled. Katy was fine coming from her. *"Thanks* for . . . for stuff lately. I'm so glad you work here. I *hate* it when guys do that, but I don't know how—I'm not good at—"

"You're welcome."

She hugged me. "I'll be home tomorrow morning. Want to go out for breakfast?"

"I'm counting on it."

"Cool!"

I watched her drive away. I watched the rearview mirror as I drove away. Everything was clear so far. Cool.

I hoped we had crackers, cheese, something to munch on at home—I'd had no dinner. I thought we did, but I was too tired to worry about it. Not too tired to worry about other stuff though.

My cover was blown. Barry might or might not talk, but I had to assume the former. For all practical purposes I was ID'd as an investigator and was no longer undercover. I could sing, tap dance, piss up a rope, lie up a storm and maybe get away with it. Or maybe not. That's how it stood now. Three down.

That was still just for openers.

Barry might be holding a grudge on his cousin's account. The dude was doing state time, not fun time, and I had been a part of putting him there. Luna hated my guts for blowing her blackmail scam and escape route. Stu wouldn't be overjoyed to hear that I was in on his dirty laundry, or that I was an investigator.

Four, five, and six down.

I wondered how long I had before Stu found out. Did he know now? Had Luna gotten to him already? And Tobias would be pissed, justifiably so, that the lid was off this can of worms. I was too. No kidding. I was closing in now. The timing was bad.

Seven, eight down.

Barry and his cousin. There was no way to predict that, to see it coming, to stop it happening. Shit happens.

What was the score now? Not in my favor.

And I wondered who else would be gunning for me.

26

Her eyes were bright blue and fearful as they looked up at him.

"I knocked," he said apologetically.

"I didn't hear."

God, he was handsome! She felt the fear diminish and a new, unfamiliar longing fill her.

"May I come in?"

She stepped aside helplessly, unable to deny him.

. . . .

I don't mind cracker crumbs in bed.

I do mind the sound of glass breaking somewhere in the back of the house where I am staying. I mind that a lot.

And, suddenly, I minded not having my dog, Ranger, sleeping on the rug next to my bed. Ranger doesn't take kindly to broken glass and strangers in the middle of the night.

This day, however awful, still wasn't over. Figured.

There was a phone by my bed. I used it; I was fresh out of heroics. Defying cliffs, black widows, and drunks had temporarily taken the starch out of me. The operator was irritatingly calm.

"Nine-one-one. What is your emergency, please?"

"Someone's breaking into my house, I heard the glass go." I gave my name and address. I urged them to hurry it up. I heard, with dismay, that my voice caught and broke. Then I said I was putting the phone down to defend myself.

I didn't have a plan, I just didn't feel like being a sitting duck. Not that I had a lot of options. I looked at my hands; I put my mind in gear. That was it, those were the options. I'd left my gun at home.

Guns were, for me now, part of the nightmare, the bloodbath, the reality of killing someone however much justified and later exonerated. After the shooting I'd gone out to the range to practice. My hands shook. They shook when I loaded, handled, or fired the gun. I'd put it away and gone home. I hadn't taken it out since.

So when I'd left home, I'd left my gun behind. It seemed like a good idea at the time. Now, of course, it seemed pretty stupid. Bullets killed. Hands didn't, not against guns, insanity, or superior strength. Not a chance.

I looked around for a weapon. Nothing but country chic and borderline pornographic pictures.

An escape route?

I was on the second floor. I am also athletic and much prefer leaping off short squat buildings to undefined, but no doubt ugly, alternatives. The windows were painted shut.

So much for that. I turned out the lights and stationed myself next to the closed door. In the background, and faintly, I could hear the 911 operator squawking away. I got ready to clobber the asshole. My poor hands.

The door slammed open, kicked in; the intruder stayed in the hall. A high-intensity, high-beam flashlight swung jauntily around the room. And found me. There was a gun next to the flashlight. It covered me. What fun.

The man holding the gun flipped the light on. I blinked, then started yelling.

"White male, five eleven, one-ninety, muscled build, black clothing, ski mask, armed, thirty-eight maybe—"

"Shut the *fuck* up!"

"Rude," I hollered. "No apparent accent, no visible scars or tattoos—"

He had caught sight of the phone and was moving toward it. I started out the door. He swung around to cover me.

"You said five minutes," I yelled at the phone. "Hurry *up!*"

Okay, so I lied about the five minutes. You would have too. He hung up the phone. We faced each other.

I broke the silence. "That was nine-one-one."

"*You* say."

"Yeah. I do. Turn around, walk out, call it a day. You're lucky, you're gone before they get here. You're unlucky," I shrugged, "it won't break my heart."

I heard sirens. He did, too. No telling where they were, or where they were going of course. And the cops wouldn't use sirens in a case like this anyway. Sirens were an easy warning. Details. I didn't bring them up.

"Bitch!"

Takes one to know one, I almost said, but I bit it back. It was the gun. And the knowledge. The blood. It cooled out the smart-ass in me.

"Who are you?" I asked, casual and unchallenging.

"Someone who's gonna teach you a lesson."

He started moving toward me. Tough guys don't blow words around like soap bubbles; they act. They don't wave guns around to establish ambiance; they use them. Mostly. Exceptions could be disconcerting, of course.

The sirens were getting closer. So was he. They stopped. He didn't. He chuckled and rippled his muscles.

Rats.

"Now," he said, as he stuck the gun under his belt in the small of his back, and his hands in the air, "get this straight. I do this because I like it. I like beating up on interfering scumbags like you."

"Wait a minute. Interfering? Okay. Scumbag? No way."

He ignored me. "I like teaching a lesson to a goddamn, pushy broad." He flexed his hands and arm muscles.

Uh-oh, this didn't look good. We weren't going to get along, I could tell. I guess we just didn't have enough in common. He leaned over, looked at the worn Oriental rug, hawked and spit. It gave me a second. That was a start.

I kicked him in the balls. A running kick and not that easy to do, but I pulled it off. Nothing worse than a touchy woman. I hate being called a pushy broad. He writhed on the floor, screaming. Hoo boy, some tough guy. I pulled the gun out of his belt. Plastic. Maybe a squirt gun. I tossed it aside in disgust. Then I ripped his ski mask off. I was riled.

A white face I didn't know, with freckles, a bland cherubic look, blond thinning hair, and watering eyes blinked at me. This was a guy who needed more tough guy lessons. A chain had slipped out of the neck of his black sweater. An amethyst amulet dangled from it.

I made a guess. "Did Luna give you that?"

He groaned. He hesitated. His eyes narrowed. "What the fuck you

188

talking about?" he asked and tried to get up. I waved my foot at his crotch area. He stopped. A *lot* more tough guy lessons. The $19.95 refresher course alone was not, in his case, going to do the trick. Someone pounded on the front door.

"Police. Open up!"

"Oh, don't get up. I'll get the door," I said politely.

He groaned. I didn't blame him. Then I ran downstairs and opened the door to two cops with drawn guns. I pointed. They thundered past. My kind of guys.

"You incapacitated and disarmed him?" one of the cops asked me quite a bit later after the guy who looked like an unkempt body-building cherub with freckles, but wasn't, left in handcuffs. Long before then I had jumped into jeans, a sweatshirt, and sneakers.

I nodded. "It was a toy."

"It looked real. You thought so?"

"Yes."

"Nice work."

"Thanks."

"You know him?"

I shook my head. "I've got an idea why he might be here, though." I grinned loopily. This was more like it. I was going to have some fun dropping a dime on Luna. Was that how *all things are connected* worked? I put some water on to boil for coffee. This could take a while.

The cop, Jim he said his name was, looked at the cow salt and pepper shakers sitting on the kitchen table next to his clipboard stacked up with report forms. And raised his eyebrows. This, mind you, was on top of the low whistle and then polite silence over the pornographic pictures in my bedroom.

"It's for low-salt diets. Takes away your appetite, I think." He chuckled. I pushed a cup of coffee his way, waved at the milk and sugar.

"What's your idea?"

"I'm the new bartender at the Pioneer. The owner's brother-in-law asked me to deliver the key to his wife's store to a woman named Luna. I don't know her last name."

There was an odd look on Jim's face. "I know her." An indecipherable look, though I wouldn't have called it complimentary.

"In my conversation with Luna I got the impression she was into

189

blackmail, maybe not for money, but definitely for gain." Jim's face was getting redder. "I gather that a lot of information comes her way, and I surmised that she might be somewhat unscrupulous in her use of it."

He grunted.

"I threatened to blow the whistle on her. She didn't like it much. It was largely an empty threat, though, I can't prove anything."

"No." Jim fiddled with the cows. "Neither can we, but it's not the first time we've heard it."

"The guy who broke in froze up when I hit him with it, but I didn't get anything out of him. Might be worth checking out though—his connection, if any, with her."

"Sure. We'll try it." He got up, casting a last look at the cows.

"I could tell you where to buy them."

"My wife would lose it, lose me, I came home with those." He winked at me. "You going to be all right here alone?"

"Sure." I thought over my evening. "What else could happen?" God, what a pie-in-the-sky optimist.

"Call if you need us." He looked at the windows and the door on the way out and shook his head. "This house is about as secure as a cake box."

"A damp one with loose string."

We both laughed at that one. "You ought to have an alarm system, something more than spunk." He flipped the spring lock—a bad guy, a credit card, and thirty seconds would slip it—and shook his head again. "Next time the gun could be real."

Yes. It could be. There was a thought. We didn't laugh, just said good night. I sprung the lock, on a better-than-nothing theory, and went looking for my unfinished glass of wine.

I taped a piece of cardboard over the broken window, then I filled up my wine glass and sat down to think it over. Adrenaline and caffeine were charging through my body like little souped-up race cars with their spark plugs tuned, their engines maxed out and roaring, their mufflers blasting, the racing stripes getting ready to blur. My chances of getting any sleep in the near future were slim and none.

Might as well analyze and figure, plot and plan, and two-thirty in the morning is a good time for that sort of thing. There were still some crackers left and the wine bottle was half full.

I thought I'd add things up a couple of different ways. Tonight's events first: possibilities from rational to farfetched, in no particular order.

(a) The intruder was your garden-variety burglar/rapist/whatever who just happened to choose this house, decide I was a pushy broad, and take a dislike to me. Possible, but farfetched. And why had he wanted to "teach me a lesson"?

(b) It was a friend of Luna's trying to scare me off before I had a chance to shove a stick in her spokes.

(c) An associate of Barry's bent on revenge. I thought Barry would be more direct, though, and would have the balls to do it himself, or at least send someone competent. It could be a friend of Stu's too, assuming that Luna had already told him I was a potential problem. I thought Stu would deal with it directly too though, not send someone.

(d) Whoever had tried to shove Toby over that cliff was now trying to scare me off.

(e) None of the above.

Aw, shit.

So that mental exercise was a big success. I filled up my wine glass and tried another.

I pictured a lineup: white wall with feet and inches marked off on it. Then I marched my suspects out, made them stand there looking blankly ahead at the window that was one-way glass, but not their way, hands clasped behind them, guilt hidden deep in eyes and heart, innocence trying and failing to show through.

Black Label Snarl. He remembered Deidre (Deedee) and watched me. Maybe he didn't like women much. Maybe he got his kicks killing female bartenders. He had harassed me in the bar, followed me in the pickup, could have been the fun guy who stomped me in the war games. His eyes said he wouldn't mind killing. I pushed him up against the white wall. Definite possibility.

Luna? Blackmail, yes. Murder? I just couldn't see it. I left her standing there, but didn't really think so.

Chivogny? She was angry, frustrated, and bitter. Big jump from there to murder. According to Tobias, she and Deidre had cultivated a long-term and well-nourished enmity. Would she kill her sister? Tobias said no and he knew her better than I. I didn't let her walk though. Not yet. After all, her husband was having an affair with her sister and she had a .22. Of course, so did a lot of people, up here especially.

Now for the top two contenders: the husband and the boyfriend. I thought back to what Charlene had told me, how Matt had made a land sale Deidre was against, bought an expensive boat, and been seen with a woman, all very soon after Deidre's death. The spark had gone out of that marriage. Deidre had been sleeping with her lover but not her husband. Men had killed for less, a lot less. Would Matt?

Stu was looking pretty good too. He was volatile, hot-tempered, and a rejected lover. He'd admitted in his letter to forcing it, whatever it was, to going out of control. Even more damning were his threats to kill Deidre if she left him. And she had. And he had access to a .22.

Some lineup. I picked up the wine bottle, poured, killed it. And that lineup didn't even include the unknown attacker. I'd had enough of murder for one day. I drank the rest of the wine and went to bed.

27

She put the cookbook down with a sigh. The recipes she wanted weren't in there.

   *Where to find your true love?
   *How to make him love you?
   *How to make love last?

....

The sound of the phone hit me like a cattle prod. The sun was shining, the birds twittering in the ecstatic way that we thought was about life, love, and morning sunshine but was probably really about territorial squabbles, feathering the nest, and whose damn turn it was to go for the worm.

The phone rang again. I yawned and stretched. Nine-thirty. No nightmares. Hot damn! I smiled and picked up the phone, sure as sure could be that it was Charlene. And breakfast plans.

"You owe me big time," I said into the phone.

"Katy? I do? All right. Where are you? What's going on? It took me forever to find you."

My smile faded. I considered going the wrong number route but discarded it. Charity wouldn't fall for it anyway. She had at first, but that was years ago. I sighed.

"Hi, Charity. How are you? I'm out of town on a job. You got my note? Good. So you know I'm okay. You shouldn't have called this number."

"Alma gave it to me. She said it was okay to use in a life-and-death emergency."

My heart constricted in pain and fear. "Alma? Charity, is she all right?" Alma is my eighty-two-year-old grandmother. The bottom would fall out of my world if—

"She's fine. She has a new waffle iron. Belgian, I think, and she wants you to come try out her waffles. With *real* maple syrup, she said. Vermont."

My heart eased. "Life or death?"

"I haven't gotten to that yet."

"What?!" I shrieked. "Who?!"

"Oh, Kat." Charity heaved a heartbroken sigh at me through the wires, like a pie in the face. "Al and I had a fight."

I hung up. The phone rang. I picked it up.

"Go to hell!"

"Kate?" Charlene sounded puzzled.

"Charlene, oh, I'm sorry. I just got an obscene phone call."

And it was true, wasn't it? If someone calls and makes your heart stop in fear and anguish over the safety and health of those you love—that's obscene. Surely. And what about an advice columnist who didn't take her own advice? But that was another question.

"And I didn't get much sleep. Someone broke in."

There was a loud gasp. "Where? At home? Were you there? Are you okay? Kate—"

"Everything's okay, me too, and the police got him."

"Oh!" She sounded stunned, shocked into silence. "Oh. Oh, I don't feel like eating breakfast anymore, do you?" she asked in a small voice. "Do you mind? Oh. I'll come home as soon as I can. I'll bring Steve."

"Good. Does he do windows?"

"Windows? Oh," she said a few more times as I explained, and then she hung up on a final *oh*.

I had a long shower, then sat down to drink coffee, make notes, and wait for Charlene.

The phone rang again. Eleven-thirty. I almost didn't answer, then I compromised on my phone machine voice: "Hi, Charlene and Kate are out shopping, being wild, and breaking new ground in old territory. Leave a message at the sound of the tone." I paused, then bonged.

"Kate. Matt here. It's important. Call me at . . . at . . ." It sounded like Matt and yet it didn't. It didn't sound good.

I changed my voice back. "Matt? I'm here."

"Come over to the Sierra Nevada Memorial Hospital, would you? Could you?"

"Hospital! Matt, is Toby—"

"Fine, yeah." His voice sounded a little better. "It's me."

"Are you—"

"Yes, pretty much. Listen, can I tell you when you get here?"

"I'm on my way." And I was. The phone was ringing again as I shut the door behind me but I paid it no mind.

It wasn't a long drive; the parking was easy; the hospital smallish. So far, so good. It looked and smelled and felt like a hospital though. After I'd been there ten minutes hospitalness had settled into every pore and I felt as though I'd been there for a month. At least Matt's room had a window.

He was sitting up and looked fine, not counting the cast on his right hand, the stitches in his head, and the scrapes and bruises on his face and arms.

"Your pouring arm, too. Shoot. Some people will do anything to get out of a shift."

His face brightened. "Thanks for coming, Kate." His eyes looked into mine steadily, clearly. He was worried. So that made two of us.

I sat down on a corner of his bed. "Tell me about it. No, tell me how you are first."

He looked rueful, or as rueful as a guy his size can look. "Bruised, banged up, bummed."

I nodded. I knew the feeling. "I brought you a Get Well package. I don't understand how anyone can get better on hospital food." I handed my bag over.

He opened it. "Double fudge chocolate chip cookies, pistachios, chips and salsa, chocolate bars, and tacos."

"I brought my favorites." I tried not to drool as I said it. I hadn't had breakfast and now it was lunchtime. "Since I didn't know what yours were."

"Close enough." His lopsided grin was back. "What shall we eat first?"

"Chips and salsa sounds good, then tacos."

"You got it."

"Margarita with that, sir?"

I pulled two little bottles of gold out of one pocket and mix out of another. He started laughing again. I found glasses.

195

A nurse poked her head in. "Hmmmm," she said.

I turned around. "Part of a major national medical study," I said briskly. "We're calibrating the sidereal effects and residual impact of useless, nonnutrient, minimum food value, nonstaple items in counteracting, or at least ameliorating a sterile, antiseptic, and barren environment."

She blinked.

"Have a chip?" Matt offered.

She left. We chowed.

"That was good, Kate." He finished the last chip—the salsa and tacos had been history for a while—and sounded like Matt again. The restorative powers of Mexican food are amazing. "Got another drink?"

I pulled a bottle out of my pocket. "Last one." I dumped some mix in and handed it over. Then I had a cookie and waited for Matt to be ready. It took him three cookies and most of the pistachios. I had the time, I just hoped we wouldn't run out of supplies.

"I was supposed to come back last night. You worked for me?"

I nodded.

"Yeah. Thanks. I had originally planned to drive in, work my shift, then drive back out. There was a big party for the kids the next day, clowns, jugglers, a storyteller. I didn't want Toby to miss it. I wanted something nice for him, Kate."

I understood.

"I didn't want to bring him with me. Trucking a little kid around in the middle of the night is no good, so I'd made plans to leave him with Chivogny and Stu."

I went still and cold, frozen and quiet inside. It wasn't the margarita. "And?"

"I don't know." He frowned at me and then at the margarita. "I took him over there and he just fell apart. He started shaking and crying and clung to me like I was his last hope and he wasn't, sure as hell, letting go. I don't get it."

But Toby did, I thought grimly. I didn't have the whole picture yet but I had just picked up a few more pieces of the puzzle and dropped them into place. It looked like a fit.

"Stress, I guess, and the bad experience of the other day."

Yes, I thought, that would do fine for a start.

"Whatever it was, I couldn't leave him. That was out of the question."

Thank God.

"It would have been impossible anyway, the way he was hanging on.

So I called in, hoping you could cover for me. Then we sat around the camp fire for a while, went to bed early. He woke up crying twice, Kate."

Poor little guy.

"Son of a gun." He shook his head.

"Where is he now, Matt?"

"With the family of one of his favorite preschool buddies. Nice folks. We've known them for a long time."

It's all right, I thought, and the fear eased. "What happened?"

"We got up early, real early. I always do when I'm camping. And Toby's always ready for an adventure." His face darkened. "Well, he used to be.

"We went for a walk. That's when we ran into his little buddy, Jamie, and Jamie's family. They invited us for breakfast and we accepted. Actually, I just had a cup of coffee. Toby was a happy camper, so I asked if I could leave him with them for a bit and take a rain check on breakfast. I was desperate to get away, to try to think things out."

Yes. I understood that feeling. Matt dug into the bag again, found a chocolate bar, ripped part of the wrapper off and offered it to me. I shook my head in a no thanks. He bit into it.

"The thing is, Kate, I've done okay in my life. I own my own business and it's very successful. Until recently I was respected in the community I live in and love. I had a wife and a kid I also love, and a beautiful home. There were problems, yeah. Sure. Nothing's perfect and that's okay. Problems can be worked out and I'm used to doing that. I'm good at that."

His voice was emphatic. I believed him.

"The thing is, I'm used to being in control. Only now I'm not. One day I woke up and everything was different; everything was out of control."

Yes. For sure.

"My wife was gunned down in a parking lot and they never found the killer; my kid is in danger; my business is up and down and because of all this I've become a question mark to my friends, neighbors, and business associates. And there's not a damned thing I can do about it. It's driving me nuts, it's getting to me bad."

Matt balled up the chocolate wrapper, aimed at a wastebasket across the room, let fly, and missed.

"So I went for a ride."

He wadded up the paper bag with the rest of the trash in it, aimed again, tossed, missed again.

"Football? Obviously not basketball."

"Baseball." He smiled, but barely.

"I walked on out to the stables—Reed had invited me to ride whenever I wanted—and picked out a horse, a sweet, high-spirited mare. She nickered at me, kept nuzzling and pushing as I put the bridle on and saddled up. Like me, she couldn't wait to get out into the early morning."

The silence lay between us for a while, easy, soft, and comfortable, not hard and white like the expanse of hospital bedspread physically between us.

"We took it at a relaxed pace. I didn't want to run, I just needed a break. Mostly we walked, occasionally trotted, sometimes sat and listened to the grass grow, watched the birds. It was good."

Silence again. Not so easy. And longer. Hospital sounds pushed at the edge of my mind but I refused to let them in.

"The shot was a surprise, a shock. And very loud in the quiet of the morning. She's a good horse, Kate. It was not her fault." He rolled his shoulders and winced. "She exploded like a bat out of hell, or a firecracker in Jell-O. I'm a decent enough rider but I didn't stay on her."

No, most people wouldn't have.

"A shot at close range will spook the hell out of a horse."

I looked at the cast on his hand, the jagged stitches on his forehead, and thought that it could have been a lot worse.

"I hit a tree on the way down, just missed a nice open patch, slid by a tree stump, and landed on an outcropping of rock. I remember lying there in a fog of pain and thinking I'd made the wrong call. Bacon and eggs beat the hell out of this."

His grin was even more lopsided than usual. I gave him credit just for trying.

"And I was out of fucking control again." His voice was harsh.

"Matt," I started, but then I didn't know what to say. Offering comfort in the form of chips and chocolate had been the best I could do.

"It took me a while to find the mare—she'd been spooked real bad. When I did, I swear she hung her head and looked ashamed, abashed. She's a sweet one, for sure. I managed to climb back on her, not so easy this time."

He laughed a laugh that didn't make you want to join in, or hear it again. It was a laugh that made you want to move on, move over, move out.

"While I was looking for the mare, I called out, looked for the gun and the person who went with it. If it was an accident, if there was an explanation, however crazy, someone should have stepped out, to feel bad, to make lame excuses, to say, 'Damn! I'm sorry.' "

"And that didn't happen?"

"No."

"How difficult would it have been for someone to have left without your seeing or hearing?"

"Easy. I think maybe the fall took me out for a short time too. The light through the trees was different when I started looking around again. But even if I wasn't out, it would have been a snap for someone to get away. There are a lot of trees and brush there and it's easy ground to move on. Fast. Someone could have followed me at a safe distance. I wouldn't have noticed; I wasn't looking. And they could have gotten away even easier than they followed me. I wasn't moving too fast then, wasn't feeling too slick."

"When you got back to camp, was there any way you could—" I thought about it. "No."

"No," he agreed. "No way to keep tabs on that many people moving around."

"And?"

"And I let it go for then. I let it be that the mare was spooked by a snake and I took a fall." He dazzled me with his lopsided grin again. "So, there went my pride, hurt as bad as the rest of me. Hell of a morning, all told."

"And?"

"And I checked up on Toby and then Stu brought me in here, dumped me off and left. Son of a bitch," he muttered. "I just wanted to get my Band-Aids and go."

A nurse, a different one this time, walked in briskly carrying a tray. She smiled at Matt and frowned at me. He smiled back. Me, too, but with a lot less sincerity.

"How are we doing here?"

We. I snorted. She ignored me. I would have, too.

"Here's lunch."

She said it in that bright tone of voice that one uses on terminally deprived unfortunates. I winced but Matt didn't seem to notice. She was pretty, that's why. Overlooking stupidity for beauty is a genetically linked male trait, like male-pattern baldness and hemophilia.

"Eat it *all* now. It's good for you."

She left and we looked at a meal (sic) of beef bouillon, milk, orange juice, dead white fish-eye tapioca, and virulent green Jell-O.

"Bon appetit," I said.

He grimaced, pushed away the tray, then the covers. Bare legs appeared.

"See if you can find my clothes, okay, Kate?"

"No. No way I am aiding and abetting—"

"I would have left with Stu but the bastard was gone. Now I'm leaving with you."

He started to stand up, then thought better of it. I heard a groan but he stifled it pretty fast.

"On one condition," I said firmly, resolutely. I meant it too. Damn right.

"What?"

"I take you straight home and you stay put."

"We pick up Toby first."

"Okay. Good thinking."

The two of us, mostly me, pulled on Matt's clothes, underwear and all. We were both sweating and gritting our teeth by the end. I didn't want to examine the reasons so I just finished tying his shoelaces.

"Can you walk?"

"Yes."

I wanted to write *Farewell,* or *Sayonara,* or *So long, it's been swell* in the Jell-O, but Matt was antsy as all git out. I settled for *Adios!* Short and sweet.

"Kate, come *on.*" See? Antsy.

Walk? Hoo boy, no way. He put his arm around my shoulder and we tottered out. It was slow, but we made it fine. I hadn't said it either and I was pretty proud of myself.

"What do you think, Kate? What's the deal?"

"Murder."

I said it. *Rats!*

Pride goeth before a fall.

28

He plunged into her again and again, desperate to lose himself in her, to find the answers in her. He'd lost the gentleness, the loving; it was all passion and desperation. Under him she moaned, in pleasure or pain, he couldn't tell. And he didn't care, not then.

....

"Attempted murder." I tried to clean it up. "Well, maybe not even attempted murder." I backed down. It was the look in Matt's eyes. And I wasn't sure, I couldn't be yet. "Maybe someone is just trying to scare you." *Big* maybe. I left that out but I thought about working it in later.

"Scare me? What the hell for? Try making some goddamn sense."

Testy, no doubt about it. I waited patiently. An accident that threatens your life, or your child's, that leaves you hurting physically and emotionally is bad enough, difficult enough to deal with, but nothing like and no way as difficult as reasoned attempt, a planned attack. Accidents are random, and that is very different from premeditated violence. That throws your mind and world into disarray. And Matt was still coping with that in Deidre's death.

"An accident," he said finally. "It must have been. And someone saw I wasn't hurt bad and was too embarrassed, too ashamed to come forward. I can understand that." He said it belligerently, his fist, the one not in a cast, clenched.

"All right."

His hand relaxed. "Can't you?"

"Maybe."

"Okay, then."

"Maybe not."

"God*damn*, Kate, you're a stubborn one."

"In the last two days you and Toby have both been involved in life-threatening accidents. I don't think that's a coincidence."

He shrugged. Denial. And looked away.

"Someone broke into Charlene's place last night." His head snapped back. "She wasn't there. I was. He threatened me, told me to back off, said I was interfering. He had a gun." Okay, so it was just a squirt gun. No need to bring that up at this point.

"*Goddamn*, Kate! What—? How—?"

"I got the gun away from him and called the cops. I don't know anything more than that."

"Goddamn."

Maybe it was sinking in. I hoped so. "You've been asking questions, Matt, about Deidre's death." Okay, I had, too. And I was leaving that part out. Again. For now. "You asked me for my help, so I'm in this too. The trouble started after the questions started. Maybe there's a connection here." *Maybe?* Yeah, right. Damn straight.

He looked like he'd been punched in the think tank. Hard. Good.

"If these have been murder attempts, we are not dealing with a very competent person." A determined one, though. *If at first you don't succeed, try, try again.* "If these are attempts to stage 'accidents,' to scare us, then it's working pretty well, I'd say."

"Goddamn."

Under stress Matt was turning into a boring and repetitive conversationalist, no question about it. There was a long silence. It was time to scram out of here. Past time.

"You know, Kate, there's an instant, when you're flying through the air and before you hit the ground, when your mind is working overtime, compressing a lot into that moment."

In case it's your last one, is what we were both thinking.

And I knew that kind of time. I remembered once dialing 911 with someone right behind me, and wondering how fast things would go, wondering if the last time my friends heard my voice would be on the 911 tape as they played it on the news. That would be my fifteen seconds of stardom, only I wouldn't be there to enjoy it. I spun my mind back to business.

"In that instant I was afraid, not so much for me, though that was there, but for Toby and what would happen to him."

"What *would* happen to him?"

"Stu and Chivogny, probably."

Uh-oh.

"Sometimes you have to almost lose something before you realize how important it is, before you decide to fight for it. I've been so busy being mad and sad over things I'd kind of forgotten that Toby and I are a family, that *we* have a future."

Matt rubbed his eyes, looking like a little boy, like Toby, whom we'd already put down for his nap. "My hand hurts, dammit. Could you find me those painkillers, Kate?"

That was my cue. I found the pills, got him a glass of water, and scooted out the door.

Monday night, my night off. Matt's night off now. I walked into the bar. It would be a long night and I didn't even have a cocktail waitress for company. Monday is a slow night. I wouldn't need the help, I would need the company.

That Monday night wasn't slow. It was dead. Monday nights are traditionally slow in the bar business so it didn't surprise me. What did was that I hadn't seen or heard from Stu or Luna.

I had dropped a dime on both of them.

Luna first. She caught her phone on the second ring and spoke in a breathless, shaky voice. Hollywood didn't know what it was missing.

"If you're going to fuck with me," I said pleasantly, no *Hello,* no *Hi, how are you?,* "pick real muscle. You don't send out a Boy Scout to stop a professional."

"What? What are you talking about? Who *is* this?"

Her voice didn't sound breathless and shaky anymore. Or outraged or confused. It sounded scared.

"And armed with a water pistol and an amethyst, for crying out loud. Give me a *break.*"

"An am-m-m-y-what?" she stuttered.

"He said you sent him to 'teach me a lesson.' And I only had to ask him twice before he squealed and told me."

"God*damn* him! That squirmy little weasel."

I thought it over. Yeah, weasel was pretty close. I didn't usually think of weasels as blond, though, or well-built.

"If you paid him, you didn't get your money's worth."

"I didn't pay him. I—I don't know what you're talking about." She took a deep breath. "Who *is* this, anyway?"

I laughed. "Your timing's off, Luna. You're supposed to play innocent before you admit you're involved, not after."

"I *hate* you!"

"And it didn't stop me. All that trouble for nothing." I *tsk*ed. "The cops have your pal and I'm still talking to Stu."

"No-o-o—"

I hung up in the middle of her word. She could stretch a vowel out longer than anyone I'd ever met.

Stu wouldn't be such a patsy. And he was a lot harder to find. No one at home, although the phone machine at their residence obligingly gave me his car phone number. He answered on my fourth or fifth try.

"Stu, this is Kate. I—"

"Kate, hey! Look, I'm jammed right now. Can I call you back? Good," he said, without waiting for my answer, and hung up.

I shrugged. When you can't do anything else, you might as well be philosophical.

That's how I felt at the bar that Monday night, philosophical. And bored. Matt told me to close up whenever business warranted it. Like now. I looked at the clock. No, I'd only been there fifteen minutes. I decided eleven o'clock was it.

At eleven-one the doors were locked and the front lights out. I'd done my cleaning and stocking, what little there was to do, light years ago. I poured myself a glass of wine and sat down at the bar to count my meager drawer.

I heard the deadbolt lock slide on the back door, heard the door open and slip shut. There had been no one here but me. The door had been opened from the outside, not the inside. I had just checked the locks, I was sure of my facts. I finished wrapping a roll of quarters, took a sip of wine, and waited.

"Hi."

A familiar male voice, a familiar smile.

"Am I too late for a drink?"

"Pretty much."

"Aw, c'mon. I don't have to twist your arm, do I?"

Stu came around the bar and sat next to me. There was something about the way he'd said twist. He smiled again, a nice smile. Okay, my imagination was working overtime. My imagination, my paranoia, and my investigator instincts? At the same time? No.

"What are you drinking?"

"A beer would be fine. Corona, maybe?"

I got the beer and sat down again, finished counting the money and bagged it.

"How long has this been going on, Kat?"

I flashed on ALERT!! Something was wrong but it took me a moment to figure it out.

Kat, not Kate, that was it.

"What?" I asked, deciding to try for accident, happenstance, or ignorance, though I'd be as surprised as anybody if it worked.

"The snooping around."

It didn't work. I wasn't surprised. And I didn't like the way he said *snooping*. He said it in the tone of voice that one would say sewage or slime, pornography or pederast. It made my skin crawl. I looked at him again. Something else was making my skin crawl, too. I would have picked a different time and place for this conversation. Definitely.

"Why are you here?" It seemed as good a time as any to change the subject.

"Just felt like a nightcap. I saw your car and knew you were here, thought I'd come by and keep you company."

Well, golly, wasn't that thoughtful. "We're closed."

He sucked on his beer. "Not to me."

Evidently. "You have a key." I made it a statement, not a question. It was, after all, a fait accompli.

"Yes."

"Why?"

"May I have another beer?" We were both playing the change-the-subject game.

"Sure." I stood up to get the beer, went behind the bar, popped the top off a Corona and handed it to him.

"I like you, Kate. You're a nice gal."

From snoop to nice gal. And from Kat to Kate. Go figure. But progress at least.

"How come you have a key, Stu?"

"Precaution. Backup."

"I don't think so. More likely from the construction project here last fall—kitchen remodel, wasn't it?" He looked at me, then drank his beer. I suspected my status was slipping from nice gal back to snoop. Such are the vagaries of life.

"Maybe."

"Matt would have given you a key so you could come and go even if the restaurant was closed, if there was no one here to let you in."

"Yeah." He looked at me steadily.

"And Deidre would have given you a key so you could meet her here nights when she was alone and closing. Stolen moments."

Shoot, I sounded like a country song. *Stolen moments, broken hearts, and cheap red wi-i-i-ne.* Stu held my eyes for a beat or two, then looked down at his beer bottle. Both hands were on the bottle, and clenched. What a duo we were. I sounded like a country song; he looked like one. Heck of a deal.

I wanted out of here. Bad. Fast. I listen to a lot of country music. I know how these songs end and I knew I didn't want my evening to end that way. I left the bar to stash the money where Matt had told me—I didn't have the combination to the safe.

Stu was in the same place, hands still clenched on his beer bottle, when I got back. Still looking like a character out of a bad country song.

"Bottoms up, Stu. We're out of here."

"I don't think so. Not yet." He looked up then.

I didn't like his words, I didn't like his eyes, I didn't like the way things were going. And I definitely didn't want to be just another so sad/too bad country music refrain.

I shrugged. "Suit yourself, you've got a key. Me, I'm going home to bed."

"I don't think so."

He reached across to me, quick as a snake, grabbed my wrist and pulled it down to the bar. His hand was warm and heavy on my wrist. The half-full Corona teetered, then fell, spinning around lazily and spilling beer as it spun, an ugly parody of spin the bottle. But it wasn't a game and it wasn't romantic.

"Let's talk," he said. I looked at the hand gripping my wrist. "Please." His grip loosened, but he didn't let go. And the please was only token. I'm a quick study, I figured it right out. "Get me another beer, yourself a glass of wine, and sit down."

Didn't that sound like fun, a couple of old pals drinking and chatting? I mopped up the bar, filled my wine glass, got the beer and sat.

"You're a private investigator, I know that." I didn't ask how but I was curious. He filled my silence up with an explanation. "I ran into Barry over the weekend."

He said it as though that explained it. And it did. Barry, good old draft beer Barry.

"He comes in here now and again. Actually, lately he's been coming in a lot more than he did before. He likes you."

Wrong. *Used* to like me.

"He told me a story." Stu paused and chugged at his beer.

I nodded glumly.

"About his cousin."

"Yeah. I was a big help in getting him an all-expenses-paid vacation. About two years ago, I think."

"He still there?"

"Damn right. He worked hard for that time. He earned it, he deserves it."

"Whatever. So, the way I figure it is: You're here working. As an investigator, I mean, though it wasn't a half bad idea getting a job as a bartender."

"Actually, business has been really slow. That's where bartending comes in. Salary and tips, it's great."

"Yeah, right. And you came all the way up here to get a job. Tell it to the Marines."

I looked around. "There aren't any."

"Aw, shit, Kate, I'm not buying that bartender bit, so come off it. You're here for a reason, and there's only one thing that connects up with the bar and all of us. Deidre."

Bingo. Give the man a toaster.

"What do you say, Kate?"

"Got any gum, Stu?"

"No. So?"

"Life Savers?"

"No. Kate?"

"Darn," I said.

"Okay, we'll play it that way. I got it figured, anyhow. There's only one person got the curiosity, the stubbornness, and the bucks to do this, and that's the old geezer, Tobias."

Bingo again. And hot-diggity-dog, he won an air conditioner this time.

"So that's it. Tobias is paying you to figure out who killed Deidre and why."

A triple winner! Let's give him a big hand. Girls, show our new winner his brand-new table saw. Now, isn't that a beaut?!"

"Kate?"

"Yeah." I stood up, was taller than Stu who sat on his bar stool still. But not by much. He's a big one.

"Stu, was that you who shoved me through the barn floor Sunday?"

"No." He looked surprised. "No way. That's chicken shit. I got a problem with you, I wouldn't come at you from behind, I'd get right in your face."

He stood up, pushed his stool back, stepped forward.

"I got a problem," he said.

Right in my face.

29

"You won't!" Her cry was passionate, wild.

"I will." His answer was calm.

"You can't!"

"I can."

"You don't dare." She was whimpering. "You don't. Please."

"I do." He reached out for her.

. . . .

"Sit down."

He had stale beer breath. I turned my head and stepped back. Time to go. His hand gripped my arm above the elbow. Hard.

"Please."

Aw, shucks, I just can't resist a polite guy. I sat, before it got less polite.

"You think I killed her, don't you?"

"No."

I thought it was a possibility, though, and not a bad one, not necessarily a farfetched one.

"You think you know what's going on, but you don't, so I guess I better straighten you out, better clean up those misconceptions."

I didn't particularly like the way he said "straighten" and "clean up."

"Okay. Good. Let's do that, and let's do it over breakfast. I'm *starving*. Denny's?" I started to get up.

"No." He put a hot, heavy hand on my arm again. I sat. Wasn't I a regular little jack-in-the-box. "That night, the night she died, was a lot like this night."

He looked at me, his eyes old and hard. I felt the shivers go down my spine, hit bottom, start up again. It was like cold fingers dancing up and down, as if I were an accordion instead of a P.I. who could be in trouble.

"I let myself in with the key that night, too. I'd done it often enough before. She was sitting at the bar, just like you were tonight, counting the till and having a drink. I loved those times. We'd sit, have a drink, talk. It was precious to me, just like she was."

Was.

"I loved the way she would look up from her counting, just like you did."

Damn. I wish he'd stop comparing me to a dead woman.

"She'd see me, tilt her head slightly, smile and lick her lips to wet them. She didn't even know she did it; I asked once. I loved that gesture. She was always glad to see me. Always."

I could see it coming a mile away.

"But not that night."

Just like me, I thought. And shivered. It wasn't the cold. And he was lying. I called him on it.

"You didn't tell the police."

"No. Would you have?"

Not if I were guilty. No way. I'd hope nobody saw, or heard, or guessed.

"You're lying." Kat, the diplomat.

He shook his head. "No, I got no reason to."

I could think of several and I didn't feel like letting it go. Kat, the private investigator. Hot, heavy, threatening hands do that to me. I didn't feel like Kate anymore and the kid gloves were off. To hell with caution.

"Letters are admissible as evidence, no question. Handwritten ones are particularly valuable since a person's handwriting is individual and easily identified."

"So?"

"So the letters you sent to Deidre paint a different picture, tell a different story. When someone dies you can rewrite the past, change events, conversations, change what happened, how it happened, and why. You can do that easily if there's no one around to dispute your version. Or a written record to refute it."

"You have the letters." His voice was slow, hard, mean.

I had the letters. True. "I mailed them to an associate for safekeeping." Not true, but I wanted to keep the excitement of midnight break-ins to a minimum.

"I want them."

"No doubt. And people in hell want ice water."

"I get what I want, Kate."

He sounded like a schoolyard bully. Bullies aren't always bluffing, of course.

"That wasn't the only written record. She left a journal." More lies.

"Aw, shit."

Yeah. That tore it all right, or would if it were true.

Stu put his head in his hands. "What'd it say?" His voice came out slightly chagrined, or maybe just slightly muffled.

"A lot." False. "Enough to put you in deep water." False. There was nothing I could really nail Stu with or I would have already. Before now, and in a time and place more to my advantage.

"She wasn't always glad to see you, was she?"

He picked up his beer bottle, put it down, picked it up, put it down. Nice sense of rhythm. I watched, waited.

"Deidre wasn't always *anything*. You never knew her. She'd blow hot, then cold. And sometimes she'd change so fast it'd make your head spin. I'd try to talk to her, reason with her, but mostly it wouldn't work. Deidre was real smart, real quick, but she didn't think like other people. You couldn't figure out what she was going to do, or how to change her mind. I sure couldn't."

"So you forced it, forced her?"

Stu looked at his hands, flexed his fingers. "I felt so helpless, so out of control. She wouldn't listen to me, listen to reason. I couldn't get to her. It made me mad."

He was looking at his hands, not at me, speaking to them, not to me.

"She wasn't a very nice person sometimes, you know. She wanted me, and then when she had me, she didn't want me anymore. But I still loved her, wanted her. She could be so mean, so—"

He shook his head slowly, heavily.

"She taunted me beyond endurance, so I took her. I *made* her love me."

"Took her? Sexually? You raped her?"

"Not raped her, no, took her. I forced her to have sex."

"That's what rape is."

"No." He glowered at me. "Not rape. I would never rape a woman. It wasn't rape. Payback, maybe."

The words made me cold and afraid. If that was how he defined rape, I wondered how he defined murder. *Not murder, no, just payback.*

"Taunted you beyond endurance?" I asked.

"Most of us know how to get to someone, to make them mad. With Deidre it was an art form. You ever see a bullfight?"

"No."

"Me, either, except on TV. They send a guy out first to get the bull going. He doesn't hurt him, doesn't draw much blood, but he aggravates the crap out of the poor animal, dancing around like that, sticking him. Stick, jab, cut. Deidre would do that. She'd use her words like a sharp knife, jabbing you, cutting you, hurting you. She drew blood, for goddamn sure she did."

"That's not beyond endurance."

"She laughed at me. *Laughed!* She told me I was a pawn in the game against her sister."

Payback. Perhaps you can't outrun payback any more than you can sorrow. Stu couldn't. Deidre hadn't.

"She said she never really loved me, she just used me to get back at Chivogny. She said that Chivogny had always taken things from her as a child, her favorite things, her most precious things. She told me about a doll, a *goddamn doll* that Chivogny had taken and broken. She cried about it. A goddamn doll that was broken twenty years ago. She said Chivogny hadn't even wanted it.

"She laughed at me again and said now it was her pleasure, she used that word—pleasure—to take away what was most precious to Chivogny."

"Like you."

"Like me. So that was when I took her. I wanted to make her love me, not just use me, love me. I wanted control of the situation. I took what she wouldn't give."

"Raped," I said, "not took."

"Yeah." He said it quietly, and after a long pause. "Yeah, raped. Afterward I told her how sorry I was but she wouldn't forgive me, wouldn't talk to me, wouldn't have anything to do with me."

No. I could understand that.

"I called. I wrote. She hung up on me and wouldn't answer my letters. I couldn't let go. I was a fool, obsessed, a madman. The woman had told me she didn't love me and never had and I couldn't stop trying, couldn't leave it alone. It was her death that freed me. Thank God for it."

Thank God and who else? God didn't need a .22 to take someone out.

"That night, the night she was killed, I came down here. She didn't know I still had a key. I told myself I had to talk to her. If I could just see her in person, *make* her listen, then she would see, would understand, would realize. I told myself, I promised myself that if it didn't work out I was through with it, with her. One way or another, I was through with it."

One way or another. Death was one way.

"I was quiet. She didn't hear me come in. She didn't know I was there until she saw me. She wasn't afraid. She told me I had to leave. I said we had to talk. Then, oh, God, I poured my heart out to her, all my love and—" He shook his head in disbelief at the memory. "Everything. Shit. Everything." He thought about it. Me, too. "You ever done that?"

"Everything? No."

"You'd think it would make you feel good, or relieved, or something. But it doesn't, it didn't. Not with Deidre."

No. Not with Deidre.

"She told me that she didn't love me, that she never had and never would. She said I had never been anything much to her but something to use to get back at Chivogny. She said she was through with me and to get out. All the while she sat there looking so beautiful, and out of her mouth came these incredibly horrible and vicious things. It was hard to believe."

"Did you believe it? Believe her?"

"Yeah. Finally."

"Did you get out?"

He stared at me. "You know, this has gone on too long. We have to stop it."

"It?"

"You." He flexed his hands.

3 0

She listened in fear to the pounding at the door. She had
always believed that locks would keep her safe. She believed
in hope and promises, in manufacturers' guarantees and in
living happily ever after. The pounding continued. The door
shuddered and the lock gave way. She cried out in terror.
What would happen now? Who would save her now?

....

He didn't move fast enough. And I can move fast when I want to, when I'm
scared. I was scared. I wanted to stay way ahead of a man who had just
confessed to rape and told me that he was maddened and obsessed.

The only lights that were on were in the bar area and I hit them as I
flew past. Stu swore as the darkness dropped around us like a shroud. I
slipped into the kitchen where the smell of stale grease cut through the
smell of detergent and disinfectant. There were no windows there and the
darkness would have been impenetrable except for the pilot lights on the
stove.

I moved carefully, slowly. I didn't want Stu to hear me, to guess where
I was. The plan was to slip through the kitchen, out another door into the
restaurant, double back into the bar, grab my keys and blast out of there.

The plan. Yeah.

"Kate, what's the matter with you? Huh?" There was a crash and a mutter that sounded like profanity. "What the hell happened to the lights? Let's finish our talk. We can go to breakfast if you want."

Sure we could. I could see him flexing his hands again. Breakfast. Yeah, right. What was for breakfast? Me?

"Kate?"

His voice was closer. He was gaining on me, moving faster than I was. Everything in me screamed at my feet to pick up the pace and fly. *On Dasher, on Dancer, on Prancer, on . . .* I moved slowly, deliberately, sliding my hand along the counter for guidance and support. The kitchen crew had pulled up the rubber floor mats at the end of the night and the floor was slick with grease and spills, slippery and treacherous. I'd fallen, or almost, on floors like this many times.

"Kate?"

His voice was pleasant and mellow. An old bad guy trick. And close. Too close. *This little piggy went to market, this little piggy stayed home, this little piggy . . .* This little bartender needed to . . . *Okay, feet, don't fail me now.*

There was a shout and a fair amount of noise as Stu went down. Then a lot of noise as he started swearing. The worst thing about going down is not bumping your knees and elbows, it's landing on, and then slipping around in the grease and scum.

Knife racks hung over the counter that I was passing. I thought about it. Seriously. And then I decided against it. I don't know what I'm doing with knives and Stu's reach is longer than mine. A weapon that you don't know how to use is one that can be taken away from you, that can be used against you.

Where the hell was the other kitchen exit? I should be there. Almost. Soon. The noises in the background continued. Stu didn't sound mellow and confident anymore; he sounded pissed. I kept moving.

Things take longer in the dark and are scarier. Reality bends in situations like that, and slips, and changes. Still, there was an exit. Somewhere and soon. Reality doesn't bend that much.

"Goddamn motherfu—"

Stu's mood was slipping. And his hands were slimy now, from scrabbling on the floor. Slimy fingers flexed in my imagination and reached out for me. The door? Where the hell was the door? I almost fell through it. I almost sobbed in relief. But that was before I fell over a trash can. Damn!

Behind me it was suddenly silent, and then I heard a chuckle. It didn't

215

make my day. Stu was probably right there, laughing and flexing slimy fingers. I shivered. Bastard. And moving in my direction. Dirty, *rotten* bastard!

I was making time now, moving rapidly and soundlessly on carpet across the restaurant, dodging tables with chairs stacked high on them. I couldn't hear anything. Stu was behind me, but where? I stopped and listened, held my breath. Nothing.

In my mind I heard Stu chuckle again. He was the kind of guy who thought war games were fun. I shivered. Then I made myself stand for a minute in absolute silence. I counted. I had to; it was the only way.

Otherwise I would have thought a minute was a month, because waiting is a hard thing to do. Very hard. Most people can't do it. I'm with most people. Every nerve fiber in my body shrieked at me. Every cell in my brain willed me to run, to fly, and to do it fast.

Mind over matter.

My nerves were winning when I heard scrabbling, scraping, almost skittering sounds. Stu? Rats? That rat Stu? It stopped, then started again. In the kitchen, I thought. I forced myself to breathe normally.

The plan.

The plan was to slip through the arch into the entryway, then back to the bar, grab the keys, and scram. Piece of cake.

The plan.

I slid along the wall up to the arched passageway where once again I stopped and listened for a full——count 'em, 58—59—60——seconds and then slipped through. Looking good.

"Boo!"

I didn't have to ask. I figured it out just like that. It wasn't Halloween. It wasn't a merry little prankster or a ghost. It was Stu. With slimy hands, a bad attitude, and a penchant for obsession, anger, and rape. And now: *Tag. I was It.* I remembered hitting the barn floor and being stomped through, falling into darkness and black widows. I hate being It.

Hands grabbed at me as I pulled away in a reflex action. Hands with flexed fingers. They couldn't hold on. Too slimy probably. I dropped back, back where I had been, in the relative safety of darkness. I started sliding along the wall and headed back toward the kitchen. I was considering the knives more seriously now.

I froze when the lights went on, standing there like a deer on the highway in oncoming headlights, or a bunny at the wrong end of a flashlight beam. Unfortunately my camouflage was no better than theirs. The primary control panel for the restaurant lights was behind me, toward the kitchen. Stu was there. I headed the other way, toward the front door. To hell with my keys. I'd walk to wherever I was going. Or run. The police station was close; that sounded like a nice place to visit.

"Where are you going? The party's just started." Stu was behind me.

I turned around. "Call me a party pooper, I'm out of here."

"You won't make it out the door before I make it to you, Kate." He was smiling.

I smiled back. "We'll see. Did you know there's a large rat behind you?"

I asked it in an easygoing yet thoughtful voice that I had practiced on numerous other dubious occasions—so I got it right; it sounded convincing. I even winced and squinted up my eyes ever so slightly. A nice touch, girlish but not ridiculously so. He fell for it. He looked.

That was when I threw the first chair.

The chair was heavy and it knocked him pretty squarely on the shoulders and head. He reeled under the impact but didn't go over, knuckle under, or fall down.

So that was when I threw the second chair.

When he came to, I had almost finished my piece of chocolate amaretto cheesecake. Really good stuff. The Pioneer was famous for it. I chased the last few crumbs around the plate and set it on a table. Then I sat and watched Stu as he tried to figure it. I was sitting on a heavy straight-backed wooden chair, like the ones I'd thrown at Stu.

He lay on the floor, his hands over his head around a post and securely taped at the wrist. Not flexing, not now. His ankles were also taped. Duct tape—a thousand and one uses—no home or business should be without it, although this one was now. I'd have to remember to tell Matt we were out.

"What happened?"

"Sheesh, Stu, what a cliché. *Every*body who gets knocked out says that when they come to."

"Kate?"

"Comfy?" I inquired solicitously.

I'd tucked a cushion from one of the chairs, the one that had taken him out actually, under his head. It was a thoughtful gesture, one showing no rancor on my part, and I was pretty proud of it. His eyes were clearing, his face was getting stormy. I watched in fascination; life is replete with paradox.

He didn't really answer me. Well, not unless you call the way he lifted the lip on one side of his mouth and snarled an answer.

"You've got two choices, Stu. You can talk to me, or you can talk to the cops. What'll it be?"

Yeah, I lied. Probably. It was probably one choice: Talk to me, *then* talk to the cops. Two choices sounded better, though.

He sighed, a you're-breaking-my-heart-again sigh like my dog makes when I won't let him on the couch, even though I have never let him on the couch. I waited. He sighed again. I'll be *darned.* His was better than Ranger's.

"What's the deal, Kate? How'd we get off on the wrong foot like this? C'mon, undo me and we'll go get some breakfast."

"Oh? No, I guess not. I just had cheesecake. Thanks, anyway."

"C'mon, Kate, this is a misunderstanding. Let me go."

"It's a misunderstanding and you're an innocent bystander, right?"

"Right." He said it with forced enthusiasm through clenched teeth. Not that easy to do, actually. I've tried it myself on more than one occasion.

"Wrong. If you were innocent you'd be outraged and hollering up a storm. What you wouldn't be is conciliating, reasonable, and trying to talk me down."

He began swearing in a low, slow, monotonous tone. I interrupted as he was starting to repeat himself for the third time. Nothing makes me more impatient than a mediocre vocabulary.

"You want to talk and I'll listen, or you want me to ask questions and you answer?"

He started swearing again. Same old boring words again. Shoot.

"Okay. I'll ask, you answer. The night Deidre was killed: Let's hear the rest of what happened."

More of the same. I got up. "Right," I said cheerfully. "Have it your way then. I'll call the cops. Can I get you anything while I'm up?"

"Goddammit!"

"No?" I ambled off.

"Hey, wait a minute, I'll talk."

More hackneyed phrases. Someone ought to buy Stu a dictionary of clichés and a thesaurus for Christmas. Not me though, no way. A person could get bumped from my Christmas list for a lot less than trying to kill me. A whole lot less.

"All right, Stu, if you'd just state your full name, date of birth, social security number, mother's maiden name, favorite beer, and how you like your eggs, we're off and running."

"Go to hell, Kate."

"Close enough. So what happened?"

"Not what you think."

"Let's be more specific."

"We fought, like I told you. And it didn't get better, it got uglier, quite a bit. Deidre finished counting and closing up the restaurant, although we didn't finish arguing. We left together and she took the money with her. Kate, I'm damned uncomfortable. Couldn't you—?"

"No. Go on. Why did she take the money? Matt said it was contrary to house policy."

"Yeah, it was. Is. She said that since she was leaving with me, the money was safe. I was good for that much. Nothing more, she added. That was Deidre all over. She'd start out with something that was either nice, or could have been, and turn it into something ugly, something that made you feel like a redheaded stepchild. You never met her, you don't know."

I was getting the picture though. It was coming through pretty clearly.

"All of a sudden, I saw. I saw it wasn't any good talking to her, or arguing, or expecting things to change. She wouldn't, and they wouldn't. Not a snowball's chance in hell. So I walked off. Didn't say anything, just walked. My truck was parked there in back, next to her car. I got in, drove off. No good-bye, no nothing. That was it."

"And Deidre?"

"She just stood there looking at me, smiling a little and silent. Didn't move at all while I was watching her."

"Stood where?"

"By her car, out back where she always parked it. That's where they found it, found her. Didn't find the money, though."

He shifted a little, stretched uncomfortably. "I have a hard time living with that, even after all she put me through. I drove off without seeing her to her car, without making sure she was in it and safe. Someone was there. Someone killed her for the money. I'll never forgive myself for that."

"You were the last person to see Deidre alive."

"Next to the last," he corrected me.

"That was important information the police didn't have and should have had."

"It wouldn't have helped. I knew that. I hadn't done it, but making them see that, see that it was a stranger out for the money, would have been something. So I didn't talk. It would only have gotten me into a shitload of trouble."

Yes. But maybe not as much as he was in now.

31

"Hey!" He grinned at her.

He was a tall, dark, handsome stranger, just the type her mother had warned her about.

"Shall we go?" he asked.

"Yes," she said. She wasn't afraid. But then love is reckless, heedless and careless.

. . . .

People aren't easy to figure out. They don't wear signs; the pictures aren't captioned. That's where things went wrong in *The Scarlet Letter*. You can pin an "A" to someone's breast but it's still only half the story. Maybe less than that. It takes two for adultery. And that's not taking into account the reasons, passions, and emotions behind the action.

It takes two for murder.

So far we only had the victim. And we didn't have the reason. A lot of reasons, yes, but not the reason.

"Someone killed her for the money," Stu said. "She wasn't hurt, she wasn't raped, they just wanted the money."

She wasn't hurt. No, not hurt; just murdered. Murder and hurt didn't connect? Death didn't hurt? The loss of a long life, glimpsed, but unlived, didn't hurt? Stu and I didn't think the same way, that was obvious.

"It could have been anybody, Kate. It probably wasn't even someone who knew her. No. Probably someone who knew the town, the business, but not her. Or someone passing through. Probably that. There are a lot of people like that out there. To them life is cheap and death is easy. Twelve hundred dollars is cheap—too cheap for a life to you and me."

Yes. Much too cheap, way too cheap. In fact I couldn't, wouldn't put a price on life. Not mine, not anyone else's. Stu would. I found that interesting.

"What is death worth?"

"Huh?"

"Or life?"

"Missing the point aren't you, Kate?" He shifted uncomfortably. "Don't get lost in bullshit. Deidre was killed for twelve hundred dollars. You wouldn't do that, I wouldn't do that."

"No."

"Someone would, though."

"Yes."

"So we're in agreement. Get this goddamned tape off me and let's get the hell out of here."

"I wouldn't kill for money, not for ten cents, or twelve hundred dollars, or two million. I wouldn't; I don't think you would either."

"Yeah, you're right. Hey, thanks." His voice sounded relaxed. He sounded pleased. Of course he didn't know what was coming next.

"I do think you could kill for other reasons."

"Aw, shit, Kate!"

"You threatened me tonight."

"No way! I—" He caught my look. "All right. Yeah, I did. I just wanted to scare you off. It's not good, what you're doing. It's making a mess of things here, muddying the water, not helping.

I disagreed. I thought we were getting closer. I was, anyway, stripping off the layers of what *seemed* to be and getting down to what *was*.

"Some guy walked into town, then walked out again, taking with him twelve hundred dollars and Deidre's life. If I thought we could find Deidre's killer, I'd be right in there with you. I'd do anything. But I don't. We can't and that's life. It's not how I would wish it, but how it is. Do you see?"

I saw. Pretty much now, I thought. I walked around to look at the watch on Stu's arm: twelve-fifteen. The night was still young, the morning was new. I felt older, and tired.

"Where's the key?"

"What key?"

"To the restaurant."

"In my right pocket. On the ring, third from the left of the brass Yale key."

I got the keys out of his pocket, took the restaurant key off, then tossed the key ring on Stu's belly.

"Scare me off?" I asked.

"I thought I could."

"How about you?" I squatted down next to him.

"If I was the killer, Kate, you'd be dead by now."

Yes. I'd figured pretty much along those lines as well. Not dead, no, not that, but he would have made a move, a real move. I got up, walked into the kitchen. The knife I came back with was pretty scary looking. Stu looked nervous but he didn't say so, didn't say anything as I cut the tape, first on his legs, then on his arms. He rubbed his wrists and ankles.

"I underestimated you," he said.

I nodded. I agreed.

"I don't know what to say. I reckon I'll just go on home."

I nodded again. I agreed with that, too.

"You ready? I'll see you to your car."

I laughed at that, at the irony, but Stu didn't.

"I guess it's funny, sort of, but Deidre— Aw, shit, I'm not a bad guy, Kate."

No. He wasn't. Not at all. He saw me to my car.

"Take care," he said.

I laughed again. I still couldn't help it. He smiled wryly. And left. I climbed into the Bronco, locked the door.

He smiled. I could see even in the darkness and the moonlight and then the smile turned into a leer as he kept coming coming, wouldn't heed my warning. Stop! *I cried.* I'll shoot! *My voice was loud in the night but he had kept coming. Too close, nowhere to run, leering, threatening. He had killed already, would kill again, too close, no choice. I shot. Hands reaching out for me still, grasping, grabbing, trying to get to me, to get to the gun, to kill me. Another shot. Blood. Death. His, not mine.*

The nightmares were mine.

I sat in the parking lot behind the Pioneer, in a cold car, on a cold

223

night—a night like the one Deidre had died—put my arms on the steering wheel, laid my head down, and wept.

I had killed in self-defense and was not charged, was found innocent of wrongdoing. Innocent, except in my heart. There I stood condemned, stood in the blood.

Guilty. Guilty. Guilty.

Like Deidre, I longed to rewrite the past, longed for the impossible, sought release in fantasy, in an identity that wasn't mine, and in a life, Kate's, that wasn't mine either. Like Deidre I was terrified of the future.

Dear God.

It was time to accept reality, that I had had no choice, that I had done my best. I did not want to live a life like Deidre's, playing a part and dreaming up fantasies, an existence that was a pale, sad reflection of what could be in order to escape what was. It was time to let go of the past.

There was a new moon. I saw it when I looked up. I saw a lot. Finally. Clearly. And without blood.

You can face sorrow, but not outrun it.

Like me, Kate who was Kat, nothing and no one was what it seemed here. Stu was not a faithful, loving husband, but a lover betrayed and angry. Matt, too, had betrayed, and was betrayed. Luna was a blackmailer, not a spiritual consultant. Chivogny, under the facade of a loving wife and sister, was a bitter childless woman.

The world's a stage, and we the players on it?

Deidre? She was the center of the drama, an ever-changing chameleonlike creature. A woman obsessed with what she couldn't have, looking, longing to fill the holes and blankness in her days and in her soul with chimeras. She wrote romances where love conquered all and everyone lived happily ever after.

Everyone but her.

For romance novels and fantasy are not love and life. Dreams are not reality. She had played parts, assumed personas until there was no telling which was the actor, which the role; until there was no knowing which was the original, which the copy.

Deidre's fantasies and dreams had not freed her, they had damaged and limited her. They had killed her.

I saw it now.

I turned the engine on and the heater up to full blast as I shivered in the cold. I had watched a lot of nature programs as a child. I remembered a female bird, a mother, fluttering, hopping, doing an imitation of a wounded creature with a broken wing to lead a potential predator away from her nest, away from her young.

Stu, a bird with a broken wing, flapping, fluttering, hopping? And I was to be the gullible predator following the "wounded" bird away from the nest, away from the prize.

When the "wounded" one got far enough away she would cock her head, arch her neck, straighten her wings, and fly swiftly, gracefully into the sky, into safety and freedom. And the predator would stand there dumbly, stupidly, his mouth gaping open, staring at her retreating form, saying good-bye to dinner.

That's what happened in all the nature programs.

32

*Shortly after leaving her job as a bartender at the Amble Inn,
Alice Barnet was fired upon. She managed to climb in her car, lock
it, and then began blowing the horn from a crouched position on
the car floor. Several shots were fired, one passing through the
window of Barnet's car.*

*Neither Barnet, nor others who eventually responded to the con-
tinued blaring of her horn, saw anyone. Barnet did hear tires
screeching and a vehicle leaving the area. "It sounded like a
truck," she said, "but I'm not sure. I was too scared to look."
Officer Pursky of the Colfax Police Department said, "The bullet is
apparently from a .22 handgun."*

*Pursky declined to comment on whether this shooting attempt
was linked to a similar incident last December when owner/bar-
tender Deidre Durkin was robbed, shot, and killed as she left the
Pioneer Hotel in Grass Valley alone late at night.*

*Officer Pursky also declined to comment on the possibility of a
serial killer preying on women bartenders. The Colfax Police Department is requesting information on vehicles seen in the downtown area around 2 A.M. Tuesday.*

....

The headline was stark and shocked, a small-town newspaper reporting a
big-city crime. I read the article through twice, had another cup of coffee
and finished my muffin. Blueberry, thank goodness, not a Luna-bran type.
Then I looked up a number and picked up the phone. Someone at the
Amble Inn answered.

"Is Georgie there?"

"Naw, lady, there ain't no Georgie here." He hung up.

Luckily for me, as God knows what I would have had to say to him. Or her. It was ten-thirty in the morning and the Amble Inn was open. I was on my way.

The phone rang before I got out the door. Luna. Luna running scared and asking me to meet her for lunch.

"You buying?"

"Oh. Well. All right."

I ignored the lack of enthusiasm or graciousness. "Great. Same place we had tea. One o'clock."

I hung up and left for the Amble Inn.

There are bars like the Amble Inn all across the country and they fit a generic description. They are dives: long, narrow, smoky, dusty, dirty and with the sour smell of alcohol, of spills not quite wiped up, urine, things gone rotten, hopes gone bad. No windows, no ventilation, and very little light. Decorations are mostly liquor signs, many old and outdated, and shabby and tattered pictures and photographs of a time when. They are bars you want to leave before you sit down.

Bars that open at eight or ten in the morning make no pretense. They are bars for losers, losers who have admitted it, who no longer try to hide it. They are what they are. They are drinking at eight in the morning, drunk at eleven, drunker still at four.

I walked in and sat down. The bar in front of me was sticky. I placed my hands and elbows carefully. No one looked up, not even the bartender. Finally he meandered over. He was drinking too.

"Help you." His eyes were uninterested. I didn't fit here but he didn't ask, he didn't care.

"Coke, please."

I would have had an orange juice but I didn't trust it. I didn't trust much in a place like this. Something in a bottle, no glass, would have been best, but it was too early, for me at least, to drink beer.

He placed the Coke in front of me, centered on the sticky spot as though it were a napkin, took my money, brought my change back, and would have left but for my question. I put away all my change except for a dollar which I placed near the glass. His eyes strayed to the dollar and back again. I tossed out a conversational gambit.

"That was quite something, what happened the other night."

"The shooting? Yeah, we're not used to that around here. Guys might

227

bust things up a bit with their fists, but guns? Naw. We hunt, we don't shoot."

"A boyfriend, maybe? Or an ex-husband?"

"Naw, she got an old man and they git along fine. Have for some time now."

"Maybe it was a disgruntled customer?" He looked blank. I rephrased it. "Some guy was pissed off, or maybe some guy she turned down?"

"Naw, I was here drinking after work that night and I didn't see nuthing. Haven't heard nuthing about any other time neither, and I would have. She ain't no looker, anyway. You want anything else?"

The conversation was over. I'd gotten whatever I was going to get for a dollar.

"No, thank you."

He walked to the other end of the bar and turned on a radio, tuned it into Big Band and nostalgia. I put the dollar on the sticky spot, the untouched Coke on top of it, and left, heading back to Nevada City.

The Amble Inn made Luna look good. That was something. For sure.

I ordered a deluxe sandwich. The muffin and tea still rankled. Then I ate. This was Luna's dime; I waited for her to drop it.

She bit delicately into an all-vegetable with extra sprouts on whole-grain bread sandwich and chewed slowly, deliberately. Her black eye and bruises were healing, going slowly from black-and-blue to yellow-and-green, which was not nearly as attractive with her coloring and purple outfit. After a week or so of chewing she swallowed and cleared her throat.

"I'm so glad we could meet. I'm afraid you might be under a misapprehension and it's been preying on my mind."

I bit back a sarcastic comment.

"When I thought over our last meeting, it was *obvious* you misunderstood. I remember you used words like extortion, *blackmail.*"

Her eyes widened in shock and surprise; her hand pushed at the air as though the word hovered there, garbage about to drop on purple perfection. Luna took another bite of sandwich and chewed for another week.

"Blackmail, oh!" She shuddered in a ladylike fashion. "As if I would *ever* stoop to blackmail. As if I would even *think* about it!"

I bit back a sharp crack.

"No, never ever. Stu and I are friends and *naturally* friends want to help each other." She looked at me.

"Naturally," I agreed, although in my experience friends didn't charge for that help.

"I wanted Stu to have those letters. Of course I did. I mean, he wrote them and he should have them. And he wanted to help me move."

"Has he offered to help you now that you no longer have the letters?"

She flushed a becoming shade of fuschia. "I guess it's been a hard month for him. He—I—"

"Is that a no?" Go ahead, rub it in, Kat.

She hesitated, looking at her sandwich carefully. Then she rearranged some sprouts, took a bite, and finally nodded. After the chewing routine she spoke up with more spunk and confidence.

"Stu worries when he needn't. I mean, it's not as though Chivogny doesn't *know.*"

"Know what?"

"Know that something went on between Stu and Deidre."

"What does she know and how does she know it?" I wanted to make sure we weren't on some kind of an all-things-are-connected spiritual plane.

"Or suspects," Luna qualified. "I'm not sure really, but I know she does."

"How?"

"Just from, well, things."

"Has she ever said so?"

"Not in so many words. But she does, I know." The divine certainty was back in her voice. "So you see," she continued brightly, "Stu doesn't have a *thing* to worry about from me, and neither do you, of course."

She stretched a smile across her bruised face.

"After that *odd,* that strange phone call from you—I don't know," Luna said innocently. "I don't understand. You *can't* think . . ."

But I did. I was that cynical. A cynical private investigator? Hey, go figure.

She was worried about me, that was clear. And that was justified. I did nothing to dispel that worry. I thanked her for lunch and started to get up.

"May the blessings of the All-Knowing be upon you," she intoned a bit nervously.

"Ditto," I replied and waved good-bye.

———

Since I was in the neighborhood I wandered over to Chivogny's store to say hey, and poke around in family secrets. Hers, not mine. She wasn't there and I didn't recognize the person who was.

I left a message: that I'd come in to say hi; that I'd talk to her soon. Stu wasn't the only one who could fake a broken wing.

33

She lay on the bed. Only a wisp of lace, pale, ethereal, and exquisite, separated her from him. She slept easily, peacefully, as yet unaware of his passion, of the desire, the fierceness that would not be denied. He reached out for her.

. . . .

I called Matt when I got home. He was there, was glad to hear from me. We went through the motions; had to, I guess. He said he would come to work; I said I refused to consider it.

"No way, José," were my exact words.

"You've worked the last two nights for me, I can't ask you to—"

"You're not, I'm telling you. I work or you fire me, take your pick." Silence. "How's Toby, Matt?"

"Fine. Look, thanks, Kate. I accept."

"You're welcome. Take care of yourself." I started to hang up.

"Hey, the news, did you see that a bartender, a woman, was shot at in—"

"Yes, don't worry, I'll be careful. I won't leave alone."

"No heroics, Kate, promise me."

"No heroics."

It was a promise I had no problem giving and every intention of keeping. But there you go. You know what they say about the road to hell.

It was last call, last chance, time to go time. Charlene was antsy and her boyfriend, Steve, alias Mr. Tough-Guy-On-Alert, kept flexing his muscles every time anybody moved or the door opened. Nobody was going to kick sand in our faces, by God.

He'd been doing this all evening. By eleven, by last call, we all had a bad case of the jitters. And Steve was going to have some seriously cramped muscles by tomorrow. I was on my way to lock the front door when it opened.

Steve jumped up, kicked back his chair, and crouched in a fighting stance, fists clenched. He looked like a gunslinger at the OK Corral, minus the guns, the corral, and the reason to fight. Charlene huddled behind his muscled bulk and—since no one could see—I rolled my eyes slightly. Chivogny strolled in.

"Hi, guys." Her voice was cheerful. "What's up?" Her puzzled eyes swept over Steve and Charlene and landed on me. Naturally. I was the only rational-looking person there. She lugged a briefcase of stuff over to the bar, dumped it on the floor and climbed up on a stool. "Everything okay?"

Steve went into relaxed mode, which meant that he looked exactly the same except that he sat instead of stood. I thought that he had moved into overkill in his assumed position of defender-of-the-delicate-female, but so far Charlene was eating it up.

"Hi, Chivogny. After the shooting at that bartender in Colfax last night, everyone here is a bit edgy."

"Shooting? Oh, that's right, I did hear something about that."

Charlene accidentally bumped her tray and Steve started to come out of his seat again. Charlene smiled apologetically and he sank back into his chair. I locked the door.

"Am I too late, Kate? I've been doing inventory at the store all evening. I can hardly see straight, so I thought I'd pop over for a break, have a drink and then finish the rest at home."

Steve twitched. I looked at him more closely, checked out the muscle definition. Steroids? Could that be it? 'Roid rage?

"No problem. What would you like?" I asked Chivogny.

"A Jamaican coffee, please?"

I went behind the bar to make it.

"Kate." Steve's voice wobbled a bit, then steadied on a deep tone. "Shouldn't we be closing up."

He made it a statement, not a question, forgetting who was in charge. Me, not him. Was it steroids or the male ego? Hard to say, tough to call.

"Why don't you kids run along? I'm almost through here and Chivogny will keep me company."

I looked at her and she nodded.

"Sure thing. I'm in no hurry to get back to bookkeeping."

They protested but I shoved them out the door and onto the next challenge, the next romantic interlude, the next OK Corral, the next steroid supplement. I'd have to have a chat with Charlene, I decided.

Behind the bar I poured myself a cup of plain coffee and piled on the sweet, heavy cream I'd gotten out for Chivogny's drink, then sprinkled cinnamon on it. I was through now. It was drinking time, home time.

"Are you in a hurry, Kat?" Her eyes smiled at me. "Could I have another?"

"Sure." I let my eyes smile back, *made* them smile back, made another drink. Kat, not Kate. We drank in a silence punctuated by Chivogny's murmers of contentment.

"Do you have a sister, Kate?" Kate, not Kat.

"No." I thought of my little sister who had died, and knew I wouldn't have wasted a lifetime in hatred, jealousy, and regret as Chivogny and Deidre had, as Chivogny was still doing.

"You're lucky. I remember the first time I heard the story of Cain and Abel and I thought—they've got it wrong: It shouldn't be brothers, it should be sisters."

"And the sisters' names would be?"

"Cinderella and her wicked stepsisters, or Deidre and Chivogny," she said softly. "Isn't that sad?"

"Deidre's dead, Chivogny. Let it be, let it go." There was an almost imploring note in my voice. I heard it in wonder.

Chivogny raised her coffee cup and saluted an imaginary audience over my shoulder. "Friends, citizens, bartender, lend me your ears. I came to bury Deidre, not to praise her. The good that men do oft is buried with them, the evil lives on. On," she said, "and on, and on."

Steroids, mangled Shakespeare, melodrama, and possible gunshots: How was that for an unusual and fun-filled evening? I yawned, body language, not fatigue. I started to open my mouth to suggest that we leave. It was time to pick up the pace. Past time.

"What do you think evil is, Kate?"

I guess Chivogny wasn't fluent in body language. Instead she leaned to tough philosophical questions that were difficult, impossible even, to answer. It was a subject I wasn't fluent in so I didn't try to answer the question.

"Suppose something happens, something bad, wrong, evil, and because of it another wrong, another evil is committed. Except for the first wrong, the second would not have happened. The second is a reaction. Surely it cannot be evil, or as bad?"

I didn't answer. I couldn't. There were too many variables, too many levels, too many answers.

"Kate?"

All right, I would try. I picked a simple one. "If someone steals from you leaving you hungry, then you steal from another to feed that hunger, you are both guilty of stealing. Legally and morally. After all, there are other choices you could have made."

"What about murder?"

Murder, yes, let's cut to the chase. All right, I'd try that too. I knew about that one. All too well.

"If you kill another in the defense of your own life, the law does not find you culpable."

"Suppose that person is threatening you, not physically but inside, is tearing up your heart and soul, biting off pieces, sucking out the blood, spitting it in the dirt and trampling upon it? Suppose that!" Her voice was shrill, harsh.

"The law does not recognize such a threat as it does a physical threat. If you kill another in defense of your heart, your soul, your honor, or integrity, it is not deemed self-defense."

"Murder?"

"In some degree, yes. Much depends on the circumstances."

"They say you have to drive a silver stake through their hearts."

It takes more than a non sequitur, however intriguing, to divert me. And it was time to move on from alleged hypotheticals.

"The one murdered was Deidre, the one who murdered her—"

"You don't know!"

The interruption was quick and fierce. I let it stand.

"And I won't tell you!" The same quickness, the same fierceness. "No, I won't, I wasn't, I didn't, I—"

"I am not accusing you, Chivogny, not jumping to conclusions of any kind. You were there, that's all."

234

A siren wailed, close, then gradually farther away, dragging my mind, my attention along with it, screaming up and down into the ugly hollows of someone else's unknown pain. Sometimes the unknown is preferable to the known.

"I know," I said to Chivogny, though I didn't know, I only suspected. "I *know*."

"Yes," she whispered finally, and so low I had to lean forward to hear her. "I was, but it's not what you think."

That again.

"Tell me."

"Stu left the house. He thought that I was asleep, that I wouldn't notice, that I didn't know. But I did. Not just that time, all the times before as well. I tried to pretend that it didn't happen, or that it was nothing, nothing important. But it *did* happen. It *was* important. To me it was!" She looked at me imploringly. "And it hurt me."

"Yes."

It would. It had to.

"That night I followed him. Not right away. I had to get up, to get dressed first. I didn't think, even, that I would find him. I just had to do something. I couldn't lie sleepless in our bed any longer waiting for him to come home, pretending then that I was asleep, and that I didn't notice the way he thrashed and groaned in bed. I had to do something, even if it was only driving around and looking for him."

"You found him?"

"Yes, here at the restaurant. It was closed. His truck was here; Deidre's was the only car here. I waited out back where their cars were. I had parked where they couldn't see, wouldn't know. It was a long wait and I got cold, and angry, and afraid. I wanted to leave, I wished I could, but I couldn't. I had to see, had to know.

"It seemed a very long time, though I don't suppose it was really, less than an hour, I think, and then they came out together and arguing. I knew. Right then I knew. There is a kind of arguing—I can't explain, except you don't argue like that, raw and ugly, unless you have been intimate."

"And?"

"And it was that kind of arguing."

She stared in her coffee cup, picked it up, and sipped from it. Finally she met my eyes.

"My husband was my sister's lover."

Her eyes fell first, then the silence all around us, cocooning us in a way that was stifling, not comforting. "In that moment I wanted to kill. I understood for the first time why people can do that. I understood what a crime of passion is."

"Wanted to?"

"Yes. Wanted to. Thought about it. That's all. I am a civilized person." She made a wry face.

"Was it just the way they argued that made you assume they were lovers?"

She shook her head, her hair gleaming in the light, the French braid disciplined, beautiful, complicated. "No, but I wish it had been. Then I could have lied to myself afterward, pretended that I was wrong, or that it didn't happen that way. I could have done that. It's not that difficult. I know, I've done it before.

"This time, when I had to face it, I had to admit that it had been going on for a long time, that I had seen things, that I had known, or could have known. But I didn't choose to see. I never chose to. They made me." There was a whiny, victimized note in her voice.

"You chose to follow Stu," I reminded her.

"Oh. Well, yes, I did." Admitting the fact, but not the principle.

"What did you overhear?"

"They were fighting, as I said, arguing."

"About what?"

Chivogny's color deepened. She put the fingertips of her hands to her cheeks and her eyes had an "oh my" expression.

"Chivogny?"

"Stu wanted to see her and she was refusing. She laughed and told him it was over, that anyway it had been nothing but a way of getting back at me. She told him to get a clue, to get a life.

"He begged her. *Begged* her. My husband *begged* my sister. 'Once more, just once more!'" Her voice was drawn with pain; her eyes were clear and dry.

"And?" I asked gently.

"Deirdre just laughed as though it were funny, as though another's pain could ever be funny."

She stumbled over the words there. Had she and Mabel laughed at a younger Deirdre and her pain? Had Chivogny remembered? But she gave no sign.

"Stu left." Her voice was bitter like sour grapes, unripe apples, nasty medicine. "He left to go home, I guess, to toss and turn in *my* bed, to bump up later against *my* body, warm with sleep, and think about hers, hot with passion and desire. Life isn't fair, is it?"

But maybe it was. Maybe the sorrow Deidre couldn't outrun had been a heinous and corrupted gift from Chivogny, a gift that now was handed back to her. Maybe there was a terrible fairness in that.

"And you?"

"Me?" She looked puzzled.

"What happened? You didn't leave then."

"I meant to, meant to leave without either of them ever knowing I'd been there, leave without that last humiliation. But then she laughed again. A wild, high, excited laugh. She was so filled with joy and exhilaration—no, more than that, exaltation and ecstasy. I—"

"You?" I prompted.

"I was confused and angry and more even, more that it was difficult for me to define, or even understand. Not then, not now. So—"

I prompted her again after a moment of waiting. "So?"

"So, I didn't leave."

"What did you do?"

"I stepped out of the shadows. She saw me before I could say anything. And she laughed. Peals of laughter, like a small-town church bell gone crazy. I stood there amazed. And then she got the hiccups. She used to get the hiccups when she laughed too hard but I hadn't seen it happen since she was a child.

"Finally, when she stopped, she spoke. 'Oh, dear God, this is perfect,' she said. 'I couldn't have wished it, or planned it any better.'

"I didn't understand what she meant. When I asked her, she made fun of me. 'You don't know? You don't see? What a fool you are, Chivogny. Wake up and smell the coffee, Sis,' she said. 'Tune in your brain, girl.' She flashed her eyes and flaunted herself and her words at me. Oh, how I hated her."

She taunted me beyond endurance.

"It was beyond bearing. I . . . I'm ashamed of this but I wanted . . . I started to slap her."

Chivogny looked at me, her eyes deep pools of contrition, of shame, of something else that I couldn't readily decipher. They begged me to understand.

I was trying. "It's not a reaction that anyone would be surprised by, Chivogny. Not laudable, but understandable. I would have felt the same, perhaps done the same." I said it seriously. I meant it. *Unbearable. Beyond*

237

endurance. Push someone far enough, hard enough, the result is often violence.

Chivogny wasn't comforted. I don't think she even heard me; she was listening to the past.

" 'Your husband is mine for the asking,' my sister told me, taunted me. 'Mine, mine, mine!' She started laughing again. I was crying, I couldn't help it. 'Mine,' she said, 'only I don't want him, so you may have him back.'

"She spoke that way! She spoke about giving me something that was already mine!"

No. You can't own a person, or stake out love, or get guarantees on the future. We wish that; we don't have it. I looked at Chivogny's face. It didn't seem the perfect moment to make the distinction.

"I lost it. I tried to hit her again, but I couldn't see through the tears. I missed and she laughed and laughed, those church-bell peals again. I realized how much I hated her, and how I had for some time now.

"And then, thank goodness, I realized in a moment of sanity how much I hated myself. I was what I didn't want to be—angry, unhappy, bitter and regretful about what I couldn't have and others, like my sister, did."

She drew a long sobbing breath. "That realization sobered me. That awful night could have ended there, if only—"

"If only Deidre had stopped," I finished. "But she didn't."

"No." Chivogny said it sadly. "She didn't. She couldn't. 'And that's not even the best part,' Deidre said. 'Not the best part at all.'

"I said nothing. It was pain, more pain, and I knew that.

" 'Don't you want to know what the best part is?' Deidre asked me.

"But I didn't. Dear God, I didn't.

" 'Don't you? Don't you? Don't you?' she shrieked at me."

Chivogny covered her eyes with her hands, tried to cover the pain in them.

34

His lips closed over hers and he pulled her into him as a starving man would a shred of food. His body hungered, lusted after her. He tried to slow down, to be gentle, but his passion and need were overwhelming. The fire in him threatened to consume them both.

. . . .

"Finally I asked, as she knew I would," Chivogny continued. "It would be bad, I knew. I couldn't know it would tear my world apart."

Chivogny moved her hands away from her eyes. The pain was raw, graphic, and garish as neon on a starless night.

"Deidre stood in front of me, suddenly still in the dull white of the streetlight and the moonlight, and then she . . ."

Chivogny mimicked the action. In that moment she was Deidre, and I the watcher, silent, dumbstruck, horror-struck, cold in the anticipation of what was coming, as Chivogny gently rested her hand on her belly. " 'It is a singular part of a woman's body, don't you think?' she asked me. 'Congratulate me, Chivogny,' she said. 'I'm pregnant.'

"Oh, *God*, it was a struggle to congratulate her, to feel happy for her. I wanted so desperately, had tried so desperately to have a child. But I swallowed all that, the envy, the longing, the hurt. I congratulated her.

"Then she smiled, leaned forward, and touched my cheek. 'I am carrying the baby you can't have.' And the laughter again. 'Not yours, *mine.*' She danced in front of me, her hands on her belly."

The silence in the bar was sudden, sullen, heavy. I could hear a faucet dripping, like the anguish, the heart's blood that must have been squeezed out of Chivogny that night.

"What did you do?" I asked into the quiet.

"I left," Chivogny said. "I felt all broken up inside. I wanted to hit her but I couldn't, I didn't, not with the baby. I left, I just left. Can we leave now too, Kate? I'm so tired."

"Yes."

It wasn't over, but we would leave.

I turned off the dripping faucet, turned on the alarm, and we walked out together. Both of our cars were parked in the alley behind the restaurant. We walked that way, then stood there talking. As we moved and talked, I watched her: another bird with a broken wing. Another partial truth.

Take a walk on the wild side, Kat. Don't be a candy ass. I took a deep breath and dove into the mud, the muck, and the lies.

"You didn't leave then; it was not like that."

"Yes. Yes, I did, And someone must have come by right after I left. And killed her. And robbed her." The "broken" wing stirred the air; I felt the breeze on my cheek.

"No."

"You know this, too?"

"Yes. If I didn't know, I would have guessed. A fight between the two of you couldn't end that way."

"Yes." Her voice was dreamy, far away. "Yes, that's true. There was more, and I wanted to hurt her as badly as she had hurt me."

"So you killed her."

"Oh, *no.*" Her voice lost its dreamy quality, became solid, everyday, matter-of-fact. "Oh, no! But I pushed on her. Too hard, perhaps. We knew how to do that, you see."

She smiled at me. I recalled her comment about being civilized. I had been wise to discount it.

"She stopped laughing then, and patting her belly, but she couldn't stop my words and the hurt. She couldn't stop it and I wouldn't."

"How did you hurt her?"

"Hmmm? Oh. The old things: how no one had wanted her or loved her, and how she could spend her whole life trying to make up for that or change it, but she never would, or could. We had never loved her and we never would. I didn't stop until—"

Her hand covered her mouth. She had almost gone too far. I took the next step.

"Until she pulled the gun."

And guns have a way of stopping conversation. Conversation and life.

"Yes." She looked puzzled. "But you couldn't know that. How did you?"

I had traced the registration on the .22 in Chivogny's bedside table. It was Deidre's gun.

"A lucky guess?" she asked.

I let it go at that.

"Or investigator stuff? Stu told me what you are, what you're doing."

Yes, it was that too.

"What happened then?" I asked. More questions. More investigator stuff.

"We fought. Before it had just been arguing, quarreling, hurting with words. The gun changed that. We fought for the gun. And then, oh, *God!* I don't know how it happened." There were tears in her eyes. "The gun went off. It *killed* her."

It did. The gun had killed Deidre, not Chivogny. Okay, I got the picture. Tears spilled down her cheeks.

"I *know* I said over and over how I hated her, how we hated each other. And we *did. I* did. But not enough to *kill*, to take her life and the child's."

"Why didn't you get help?"

"It was too late to help Deidre."

No. Another lie. Diedre hadn't died instantly. The coroner's report had told me that. I looked in Chivogny's guileless eyes. They were not a window to her soul. They lied. It had taken Deidre long minutes to die.

"It was too late to help her. She was dead. There wasn't any triumph in her eyes then, or joy. There wasn't any anything in them, just death."

There wasn't any anything in Chivogny's eyes either, except the hurt and innocence I didn't believe. I was still looking, still hoping. I was wrong. It was a waste of time.

"Kate, I was scared. I had no proof, just my story. I was so afraid no one would believe me, that they would think I shot her on purpose. But I *didn't*. It wasn't murder; it was an accident. And I was a coward and a fool. I ran. Don't think I haven't hated myself for that!"

Did she? Did she hate herself for leaving her sister there alone and dying, getting colder as her lifeblood slipped away, a corpse that would be found by strangers in the morning? Or had she waited until Deidre died, waited and made sure another shot wasn't needed?

"It was awful, horrible of me to leave her there! I know that, I pay for it every day. Believe me, I do!"

I didn't believe her. I was that cynical. "When you left, you took the gun and the money?"

"The money? Oh, no!" Another flap of the "broken" wing, another lie.

"The gun and the money," I repeated.

"I was such a fool." A tangent, a feint.

"Why did you take them?"

"So they would think—so it would look like robbery. I didn't take the money for *me*, you can't think that. I put it aside for Toby, for a college fund. I mean to add to it, to help build his future."

She smiled self-deprecatingly. Toby had a college fund instead of a mother and I was supposed to congratulate his aunt on her thoughtfulness. I wasn't up to it.

"I've handled this badly, I know, but I didn't *mean* it that way."

Just an innocent bumbler. An innocent, charming bumbler, but not a murderer. *Don't be a candy ass, Kat. Take another walk on the wild side. Go for it.*

"Anyone would understand how you felt," I said.

"Would they? Do you?" She asked it eagerly, wistfully.

"Of course. How could you not have hated someone who first took your boyfriend—"

The breeze picked up and hit me, hit us. It was cold and unfriendly and I longed for a fire, a smile.

"Boyfriend?"

"Matt. You were dating him, you cared for him. Deidre took Matt away from you."

Her face darkened, even in the moonlight. She said nothing.

"And then she took your husband. Even when Deidre was through with him, he wasn't yours. He still thought of her, longed for her."

"Yes." The word came out on a sigh. "It wasn't the same ever again."

"But the baby, that was too much, wasn't it?"

"Oh *no*, I was *happy* for her. I wished it was me, mine, but I was happy for her—"

"No. She took your boyfriend, and your husband, and then she told you that she was pregnant. Not with Matt's baby, but with Stu's. Her child was fathered by your husband."

Chivogny whimpered. "You can't know that."

But I did. The coroner's report had stated that Deidre was pregnant and that the blood type of the fetus was incompatible with that of the dead woman's husband. It was a jump from there, but not a big one. Stu himself had suggested the truth.

"It was too much to take, wasn't it?"

"Yes." Whimpers again. "It was."

She taunted me beyond endurance.

"I was only taking back what was mine," Chivogny said. "She had no right . . . It was only fair, only just. She took the love of Matt and Stu from me. She had the baby that should have been mine. I just took it all back, what was mine. It was justice. Now I have it and she doesn't."

A smile peeked out sweetly, coyly, bashfully through the whimpers.

"She's dead, Chivogny. She doesn't have anything."

"I have it. She doesn't."

She was sweet, coy, stubborn. And off track. Badly. I hoped to God that she wasn't pregnant, that the sorrow that this family couldn't outrun would end soon, end here in this generation.

"Kat, I'm *so* tired." She yawned, covering her mouth delicately with a hand. "Let's go, shall we?"

She reached into her purse, fishing for car keys. I moved quickly, closing the distance between us. Quickly, but not quickly enough. She pulled something out of her purse.

Not car keys. A .22.

"Another bartender killed after work." That shy, sweet, beguiling little smile again. "A serial killer. How *awful!* How *scary!*"

The gun was steady in her hand, was pointed at me.

"Curiosity kills the cat. Have you ever heard that, Kate?" She smiled. "Kat?"

Oh, yes. I nodded glumly. I'd heard it more than once. And ignored it. There was after all, I reflected, something to be said for being a candy ass. It was a premise worth reconsidering. I hoped I would have the chance.

"It wasn't an accident, was it?"

"With Deidre?"

"Yes."

"What does it matter now, Kat?"

"Humor me."

"No, it wasn't an accident. And this won't be either. I'm sorry it got to this point."

I raised my eyebrows in polite disbelief.

"No, I am. I was hoping it wouldn't, needn't come out at all, the fact that I was there that evening. But you figured it out. Then I hoped you would believe that it was an accident, would just let it be. Let bygones be bygones."

"*Let bygones be bygones.* What a quaint way to refer to death and a cover-up."

She grinned, or leered. The moonlight and the shadows were distorting things now, playing tricks on me. So was fear. My fear.

Blood.

"Stop now, Chivogny. If you kill me, it's murder."

"Oh? I don't think of it as murder really, but as silence."

I let it go. It was no time for semantic squabbles.

"Deidre pulled a gun on you. The two of you struggled for it and it went off. Or, even if you shot her intentionally, it was self-defense, not murder. No jury would find you guilty. They'd understand."

I was lying. They wouldn't, anymore than I had. Especially if she smiled at them the way she'd smiled at me. Coy, sweet, and beguiling didn't cut it much with juries.

"You'd walk," I stated firmly.

"Do you think so?"

"I'm sure of it. Positive. No question at all."

It's okay to lie in some situations. Like: *Can you help me move next weekend? Oh, I'd love to, but I'm going to be out of town on business.* Or: *Do have a tofu, carob, molasses, sunflower seed brownie—yummy and so good for you. Thanks, too full.* And: *I've got this* great *guy I want you to meet. He's thirty-seven, an accountant, and lives with his mother. Sheesh, if only I'd known, but I'm booked solid for the next two years.* All these lies are okay, are essential even.

Blood.

And the times I've said I was a meter reader, a high school friend, or a census taker to worm out information? That was okay too. Almost.

Small potatoes. Small stuff. Small time.

When your life is on the line is when you *really* lie. And then it's *really* okay.

Anything to stop the blood.

"Self-defense is everyone's right. Maybe even duty," I expanded. "You needn't let yourself be hurt, victimized, or killed. You have the right, morally and legally, to defend yourself." I took a long step toward her. "Put the gun down. You're not a murderer." I hoped. A cat cried somewhere close. Probably a stray raiding the dumpster for dinner.

"Stop! Don't come any closer." The gun was pointing squarely at my chest. "Maybe what you say is true—I think it might be—but I think maybe I should have come forward at the beginning." Her voice petered out.

Damn straight.

"And I shouldn't have made it look like a murder scene and hidden the truth."

Yeah, no shit.

"Now they won't believe me."

Depends. You get a jury that believes that pigs have wings, you're set. Otherwise . . . aw, shucks, you're in trouble, by golly.

"They will, yes. You were in shock. You acted foolishly, even stupidly, but understandably. Everyone's done that. Everyone understands that."

"You think so?"

Another cat cried. A young one, a kitten perhaps. It sounded forlorn, lonely, and hungry. Almost like a child, a baby.

"Yes." I took another step toward her.

"Stop it!" She started to back up. "Stop it right now!" She raised the gun as she backed up.

"Watch out!" I hollered. "There's a kitten right behind you."

It was a crummy lie. Shoot, a dull second-grader could have done better. But it worked. And that was a surprise, because why bother about stepping on a kitten when you've snuffed your sister and her unborn child?

It broke her concentration for an instant and I dove for her knees. It was tackle, not touch time. We went down. The gun went flying. I heard it land on her car, skitter along the metal, and slide off into the darkness and dirt somewhere.

We were in the dirt, too. What would Luna have made of it: physical reality mirroring the metaphysical?

I had Chivogny securely pinned and was prepared to do her serious damage if I had to, prepared and tempted. I'm not a cop; she didn't have any rights with me. None that she hadn't first violated, then given away in threatening to kill me. I was also in a frenzied and savage mood with adrenaline, anger, and thoughts of violence pumping through my body with each heartbeat.

Blood!

I tried desperately to decelerate.

"Kate! Oh! You're hurting me, Kate!"

"Aw. Break my heart," I snarled through clenched teeth, but I eased up.

She started to cry. My heart didn't even melt slightly, or crack—never mind break.

"I'm sorry. I really am."

She looked sorry. Against my better judgment I almost believed her. She wasn't a cold killer; she didn't have the guts or stomach for it. She'd waited too long to shoot me and she hadn't fought back with any spunk or conviction; now she was sniveling like a teenager whose date to the prom had stood her up. And struggling to get away.

"Hit the dirt, Chivogny. Hug the ground," I snarled. I wasn't taking any chances.

Still crying, she followed orders, dirt and tears giving her a mud pack look. Her French braid was tousled and disheveled. I got duct tape out of the Bronco—twice in twenty-four hours, that did it, I was writing the company—taped her wrists behind her, then belted her into the passenger seat of the Bronco. I left the gun where it was, for the cops to find, and drove to the police station, then sat in the parking lot leaning on the horn.

It didn't take long. As a couple of cops spilled out of the station, Chivogny turned to me and whispered.

I got off the horn. "What?"

"Thank . . . you . . . for . . . stop . . . ing . . . it. . . ."

The cops yanked the car doors open.

That *thank you* played in my mind for a long time. I didn't fully understand. I never got to ask her.

I didn't leave the station until almost dawn. Chivogny didn't leave at all. By then she'd stopped crying and had tried charming. It hadn't worked. It takes a lot, more than she had, to charm cops off a homicide.

Good-bye charm, hello expensive lawyer.

I went home to sleep.

But it wasn't over, and it wouldn't be for a while.

35

"How do you get used to it?" she cried out.

"What?" he asked.

"The wanting. And not having." Her voice was a desperate ache. "The wanting, and wanting, and never having," she sobbed.

"Soon. I promise you," he said.

She fell into his arms.

. . . .

I heard the noises in the background but I didn't pay attention. The dream was with me still. It had started out with my nightmare, with gunshots, shouts, and blood. And then the blood faded into pink and dissolved into a new dream sequence. There Deidre Durkin sat staring into the clear river and faces were reflected back at her: Chivogny, Stu . . .

It wasn't until Charlene touched my shoulder that I opened my eyes.

"Kate, Stu's here. He's real upset and says he has to see you. I told him to come back later but he—"

"I have to talk to you."

His voice was hoarse with tears, anger, or violence, I couldn't tell. I sat up, swung my feet over the edge of the bed and stared him down. I'm good at that kind of macho shit. Still, I'm not at my best in the morning after a night with homicide cops and four hours of sleep.

"Okay, Stu, I'm going to have a shower while you go get muffins, or croissants, or something like that for breakfast."

"The *hell* I—"

"Play it my way, Stu, or don't play at all."

My voice wasn't hoarse; it was hard, mean. It was how I felt. I hide from disillusionment and broken ideals in hard and mean. It fools almost everybody. Not Alma, or Hank, or Lindy, or Charity, or me, but Stu? Yeah, no problem.

Charlene was wide-eyed. *"What's* going on?"

"She's an investigator," Stu said. "A private eye. Chivogny's been arrested for killing Deidre."

"Kate! Oh, my God! Chivogny?"

"Kat," said Stu. Hoarsely.

Charlene looked at me.

"Yes," I agreed. "Kat. Kat Colorado, private investigator." *For crying out loud,* I sounded like a two-bit gumshoe in a B-grade movie.

Charlene's mouth opened and closed. "A private eye?"

I nodded and turned back to Stu. "Blueberry muffins, almond croissants. Scones are good too." And I headed for the shower. Still two-bit. Still B-grade. Still tired. So it goes.

I finished a scone with my second cup of coffee and started on a croissant. Stu played with the salt and pepper cows and a crumbled up, uneaten blueberry muffin. He was having trouble putting things in order. I didn't blame him.

"Kate . . . Kat . . . uh . . ."

"You knew, didn't you?"

He shook his head, rearranged the cows.

"Don't kid yourself anymore, Stu. It's time for some honesty around here."

A cow shattered from the force, the pressure in Stu's hand. He looked at the pieces without expression, then carefully put them down and brushed the salt off his hands before he spoke.

"Okay. Yeah, I knew. Chivogny was snapping. Badly. I couldn't make sense of what she was doing, of the way she was thinking and talking. She hated Deidre, kept telling me that she wanted to take everything away from her."

"This after Deidre died?"

"Yes." His voice was miserable, choked. "Yes."

"So you helped."

He didn't answer. He clenched a shard of the broken cow, a sharp point pressed against his thumb. I could see blood.

"Chivogny wasn't the only one snapping." I stated it flatly.

"I don't know what you mean."

But he did. I could see it in his eyes.

"What does it take to push a child into a ravine, Stu? Into almost certain death? What does it take to kill a child?"

"It wasn't like that; it wasn't like that at all."

I stared at him in disbelief.

"It wasn't to kill Toby that I did it, but to save Chivogny."

It wasn't rape, just payback.

It's not attempted murder; it's rescue. Not death, but life; not bad, but good.

Sure.

"I thought it might bring her some peace if she knew that Deidre didn't have a child, either."

But dead Deidre had nothing, nothing but flowers on her grave.

"I felt so badly that I'd hurt Chivogny, betrayed her with Deidre. I love her. I wanted to make it up to her, make it better for her."

Make it better by killing a child?

"You see, don't you? You understand?" His voice pleaded with me.

I saw. What began years ago in childish taunts had ended in death. No one had had the courage to resist the seduction of evil, that easy, ugly joy that comes with bitterness, anger, and hate. Hatred and blame are easier than love and responsibility and evil is a communicable disease. Yes, I saw.

"You understand, don't you?"

My mind did, not my heart. I turned back to finding out what had happened. The truth, but not Stu's truth.

"The shots at Matt? The graffiti? The shots at the woman bartender in Colfax?" The bird with the feigned broken wing. "It was you, wasn't it? A distraction, a one-man crime wave to shift the focus off Deidre's death and away from Chivogny?"

He nodded at his hands.

"Look at me! Say it!" It pissed me off. To hell with broken wings and rationalizations.

He finally met my eyes. "Yes, it was me. I did it."

There was something deeply ashamed, broken in him. He was an adult who had tried to harm a child, a child he knew and loved. A man who protected a woman who didn't merit that protection. His shame was earned and justified, not something to be shed easily.

"Chivogny isn't pregnant, is she?"

"No."

"That was another reason why she hated Toby and the child Deidre was carrying at her death. *Your* child."

"Yes."

"A child of rape."

Not a love-child, a hate-child.

Crimes fell like rose petals around us, leaving only the hard, dead brown center of the spent flower. There was no beauty in it, only a remembrance, a suggestion of what had gone before and now was not.

"Why did Chivogny lie about the pregnancy?"

"I don't know. I've heard of it happening to women when they want a child and yet can't have one. I don't know."

I didn't either. Perhaps we never would. It seemed a small thing compared to why she had killed her sister and her sister's unborn child. To me it seemed a small thing. To her, perhaps, it had been everything: a note of hope, the future, a new beginning. If it had been real—but it wasn't.

Murder was.

And attempted murder.

More sorrows Chivogny could not outrun. Or Stu.

"What will happen to her?" Stu asked finally.

"I don't know. Get the best criminal defense lawyer you can afford."

"You did this!"

Stu picked up a scone and pulverized it. The fragments of things, muffin, scone, the salt-shaker cow lay on the table before us. He opened his fingers, crumbs clinging, flexed them, then made a fist in front of me while his eyes held mine.

It was a threat. I'm a detective; I could tell. I didn't react. I'm a tough detective.

"You did this," he repeated, sullen and menacing.

"No. Chivogny did. And before her Mabel, Deidre, and that family. And you. And more that I can't see, and don't want to know about. I only opened the window and let in the beginning of truth."

The spring sunshine poured into the kitchen and danced around, bouncing off the yellow cupboards with stenciled birds and flowers. A bowl of fresh unblemished fruit sat on the counter. Life and joy spoke in many voices, but not in Stu's.

"Without you, this wouldn't have happened." There were flecks of foam in the corners of his mouth.

I stood. "Get out."

He followed my direction and lumbered heavily to the door.

"Stu."

He didn't turn, but he paused.

"Learn to live in the light, or the darkness and the past will take bites out of you as it did of Deidre and Chivogny."

As it and the nightmares, the blood, had of me.

"It will cripple you, destroy you."

He walked out, leaving the door ajar.

I cleaned up the mess, then crumbled up the remaining muffins and scones, throwing them outside for the birds. I watched from the window for a long time. The bright, greedy blue jays tried to scold the others away and little dusty brown fast and fearless ones darted in and out and feasted. There were many birds, eating, flying, chattering, not in harmony exactly, but in coexistence.

In the sunshine.

No broken wings.

Hank was out when I called; I left a message. Tobias was in; we spoke for a long time. I said I would come to see him very soon. I called Matt then and told him I was on my way over. It was too much to handle on the phone; I didn't even try.

If I were a bird, I would have flown.

36

Experienced bartender wanted.
Tues. thru Fri. nights. Apply
days only. Pioneer Hotel.

....

The ad had gone in the paper this morning. Tonight, Friday, was my last night. We were in Matt's office at the restaurant, he sitting at his desk, me sitting on it swinging a foot in time to Marvin Gaye singing "I Heard It On The Grapevine."

"You got a lot done in two weeks, Kate. Kat," he corrected. "I'm not used to it, yet. Anyway, you still look like a Katy to me."

"I am."

He laughed out loud.

"Just to my family and friends, though."

The laugh ran down like a junker car and Matt looked at me clearly, steadily, that lopsided grin too shy to appear, to presume.

"That's you, Matt. A friend."

There it was: lopsided, sexy, gorgeous.

"Anytime you want a job, Katy, it's yours. Or a boyfriend."

That grin again. Damn good thing he didn't have dimples. Damn good thing I was spoken for.

"Auntie Kate?" Toby pushed open the door with a grubby little hand and walked in gnawing an apple. "Daddy said to say I was sorry."

I looked at Matt. "Did he now. What for?"

"For hitting you. I'm sorry." He kicked Matt's desk.

I thought about the little boy who had hit me this morning. Matt, Toby, and I had gone to the cemetery. Toby pulled all the petals off his flowers and scattered them across the grave and in the wind.

"Mommy," he said, "I miss you and I love you and God bless you and why did you have to leave? I miss you really really really much."

His voice rose on each *really* until it was high and excited.

"You're a *bad* mommy for leaving me. Bad bad *bad* and I hate you." He stomped his feet on the petals and on the grave. "I hate you I hate you I *hate* you."

He turned then and his fists battered my thighs and belly, my arms as I reached out to him. "I hate you too Kate I hate you *I hate you* you're leaving me too."

I scooped him up and held him tightly, his arms around my neck and pounding my back as he shouted, "I hate you I hate you I hate you" until, worn out, he collapsed. A tear-streaked cheek pressed up against mine. "I don't *really* hate you," he whispered.

"I love you," I whispered back.

"Luv you too." It came out on a hiccup.

"I'm going away, but I'll be back. And you and Daddy and Tobias—"

"Granpappy?"

"—and Granpappy are coming to visit me soon, remember? We're having a big family picnic."

"Really?"

"Really."

"Tell me."

I told him all about it. For the fourth time that day. "You'll meet lots of people, kids too. We'll have yummy things to eat and a pony you can ride, and dogs and my kitten."

"Really?"

"Really, little guy."

He thought about it. *"Big* guy."

I kissed him. "Big guy."

That was this morning. Now he gazed at me and repeated himself. "I'm sorry. Can I still call you Auntie Kate?"

"Yes. And Toby?"

"What?"

"It's a good thing to say your feelings to other people like you did this morning."

Don't hold them in and go crazy, wild, and off track over them like Deidre and Chivogny. Or like me, for a while. Don't go the way of blood and death.

"But Daddy's right, it's better to say them without hitting."

Or lying. Or killing.

"Thank you for saying 'I'm sorry.' "

"Okay." He smiled. It was a little lopsided. Look out world, here comes another one. " 'Member how you said I could help name your kitty?"

"Yes."

"I'm thinking hard." He wrinkled his forehead at me, then stuck his tongue out at us and bounced out of the room.

"I'll need your address, Kat."

Good. Back to business.

I gave Matt a business card after writing my home address and number on the back. "Two weeks to my family picnic, Matt. I'll call and give you directions on how to get there."

"I'll mail you your check."

I frowned.

"Do you need it now? I can approximate."

"Does Toby have a college fund?"

"Deidre and I started one. Why?"

"Matt, I've never heard you say Deidre's name before."

"No. I couldn't. I was consumed with anger, with bitterness. That's gone now and I have you to thank for it. The sorrow's still there but that's okay, that's as it should be."

"And you started a college fund?"

"We did, Deidre and I." He spoke her name in a gentle loving way.

"Good. I'd like to make a contribution. Whatever I made working for you."

"Katy, I can't let you—"

"Being paid for a job once is about all I can handle, Matt. Tobias is paying me well. And hey, don't forget you promised me time and a half for —for something, I forget what." We grinned at each other. "Every cent into the college kitty."

He walked over, put his hands (technically hand and cast) on my shoulders, and kissed me. So much for business.

"Uh-oh." I was looking at the clock as I said it, not that that was the uh-oh. "I'm late for my shift and the boss will raise hell."

Reluctantly, Matt let go of me. "Go on then. I'll take Toby home, get him settled in, and come back to close with you."

I laughed. He looked puzzled.

"Yo, Matt. You think I'm working? Ha! It's goof-off night, fun night. It's last-night, party-night tonight."

"Go for it."

Good. I was planning to.

I walked out to the bar, where Charlene met me with a frown. "What's the matter?"

"Vodka splash seven, bourbon water, Scotch soda, two whites, a Miller, and three drafts. Steve."

"What'd he do?" I iced up the glasses and poured.

"Not what'd he do, what'd he not do?"

"What'd he not do?"

"That great bod," she mused. "You'd think he'd know how to use it."

"No?"

"Phooey. Ooops, here come the Trasks, add on two gin tonics, one with a splash of lime. Doesn't know, or isn't interested. All show, no action. Phooey."

Steroids. I was right.

"You think I'd be good behind the bar, Kate?"

"Yes, I do, but you'll have to toughen up. Can you do that?"

She looked a little dubious, a little determined.

"Or, hey, marry Steve, buy a brand-new microwave, matching washer/ dryer, and—"

We looked at each other. "Nah!" And laughed. After all, it's only in math that two negatives equal a positive.

"C'mon back," I said. "We'll start training you right now. Easier to find a cocktail waitress than a bartender any day."

"Should I? What about the customers? What will Matt say?"

"The customers can come to the bar. And Matt? Shoot, what's *he* going to do, fire us?"

She giggled. "Hot damn!"

We had fun. Everybody had fun. We packed 'em in. A little more practice and Charlene would be a good bartender. She mouthed off at everybody all night, the guys at the bar coaching her in the art of being tough. *Hot damn* was right.

The draft beer walked in. Barry. I asked Charlene to serve him though

255

he sat at my end of the bar. I didn't want to talk to him, to deal with any grief. It was my last night and I'd dealt with enough these past few days. She did, but he caught me later anyhow.

"Sorry if I was outta line the other night. Guy breaks the law, he oughta go to jail, and the rest of us oughta be glad that's where he is." He stuck his hand out and we shook.

Later I saw him flirting with Charlene. She flirted right back. Good for her. On the life scale you could slot Charlene under Bounce-Right-Back.

Matt came in early. He looked a little puzzled—at the crowds, at the two of us behind the bar. We explained the situation: he hadn't lost a bartender, but a cocktail waitress. He got into it right away. So then there were three of us behind the bar, goofing off, having fun.

Some guys bought me a bottle of champagne. Matt opened it and we started drinking. No rules tonight.

It wasn't a champagne celebration exactly—things were too complicated still. More of a toast to the future, to a lot of futures and to a bunch of people I'd come to care about. I invited Charlene to the family picnic. We all toasted friendship.

It wasn't just friendship for me. It was more, it was family. I don't have any family of my own, so I adopt. First Alma, Charity, and Lindy. Now maybe Tobias, Toby, Matt, and Charlene. Maybe. I hope.

Then I drank to life and love and dreams, sweet dreams. The nightmares were over now, and the blood. I had let the past go.

"Hey, bartender," someone snarled. I hadn't seen him come in, but I knew who it was. Black Label Rocks. I turned around.

"I'll have a drink."

I smiled. "Will you?"

"Yeah. Double."

"Not here, pal. I don't serve pukes."

It was pretty quiet when I said that, a lull, and I said it pretty loud, payback for scaring me that night he'd trailed me in his truck. A lot of people heard it, enjoyed it. I had a bunch of friends there; he didn't have any.

"Well, shi-i-t, I'll have your job!"

"Matt." I spoke without raising my voice, without turning around; I knew he was standing right behind me. "This guy wants me fired."

"You the boss?" Black Label asked.

"No." Matt's voice was even. "She's the boss. I'm the muscle. You're out of here."

So that was that, and pretty fine. Those moments of denouement are all too rare.

Right after that, Tobias called. I took it in Matt's office. He was upset. Very. Chivogny had called from jail.

"She wants me to help, Kat. The girl wants help. Now, what the hell am I going to do?"

"I don't know," I said, and I didn't. I didn't even want to think about it. Hurt, dread, and fear were still in my way, in the way of rational thought. "Follow your heart, Tobias."

There was a dense heavy silence on the line, like old, cold, gluey, disgusting oatmeal.

Pease porridge hot, pease porridge cold, pease porridge in the pot nine days old. . . .

"Matt and the boy okay?"

"Yes. They need you, too."

"You're a good woman, Kat."

"I come from good stock. You're going to meet her."

"Her?"

"Alma, my grandmother." Adopted, but why quibble over details? I chuckled inside at the thought of playing matchmaker. "You're a good man, too, Tobias. You'll figure it, what's right, what's best."

"Thank you kindly." His voice was gruff and country.

"See you in two weeks at the picnic. Slick up now, Alma's a sucker for a pretty face."

He hung up on a sputter. I hung up on a grin. And went back to the bar.

Charlene kept pouring us champagne. Matt kept opening more bottles. We worked, danced, drank, played the jukebox.

I had one regret. Elihu. I still hadn't seen the ghost of the heartbroken gold-rush miner or heard the faraway tinkle of the honky-tonk piano he listened to night after night as he drank whiskey and smoked cigars. But I'd be back.

I tossed down another glass of champagne and wished my friends were here.

Be careful what you wish for; it could come true.

A stranger walked in.

It was like the entrance of a hero in a western movie. *Hot damn!* The place got sort of quiet. They didn't know the newcomer. I did. They didn't know the script. I did.

"Yo!" I said, as I walked across the barroom floor.

"Hey, Katy!" Hank grinned at me.

I let out a whoop and jumped him. He caught me, held me tight. Hank's good that way.

37

The pornographic pictures were under the bed, the stuffed bird sang silently in its cage, a moth fluttered in the dimmed bedside lamplight. I stood in Hank's arms.

I was unbuttoning things: jackets, shirts, blouses, Levi's, those kinds of things, and as fast as possible. I had most of our assorted things off when he caught me by the elbows and held me tightly, stilled my frantic, frenetic movement.

"It's over?"

"Yes. It was the dead woman's sister, and hate and ugliness fostered— even lovingly nurtured—over the years and generations and lives."

I trembled. It was cold without many clothes on. And hate, hate was cold too; it ran hot at first, then turned to ice. I moved closer into the warm circle of Hank's arms.

KAREN KIJEWSKI

"Hank, I remember speaking to a winemaker once. He said that sometimes a vat of wine will go bad, that there is no apparent, no logical reason for it. Is love like that too?"

"No." His eyes crinkled up. I loved the way they were white in the bottom of the wrinkles where he had squinted too often into the sun. "Love doesn't do that; hate does." His hand touched me with love.

"For all that I found out, I still don't completely understand. Deidre lived in fantasies, was a different person to everyone I spoke to. She was a mystery; she still is. And her name—Deidre? It's Gaelic and it means sorrow, complete wanderer. How well it fit her, how sad that is."

"It's over, Katy?" Hank asked me, used to mysteries and sorrow.

"It's over."

His hands played up and down my arms, across my back, on my neck, a touch on my cheek.

"Really over. I saw the choices that Deidre and Chivogny made—the loathing and malice, the evil—and the strange joy they took in those choices." I trembled—from the closeness of evil, not cold. "I've made mistakes but I've never chosen evil."

"No more nightmares?"

"No more. And I'm glad to be Kat again."

"And blond?" He touched my hair, my face, kissed my eyes. I held onto him.

"And . . ." I started, stuttered to a stop.

"And?"

"Nobody else died, nobody got hurt. No blood. I just . . . helped."

"You always do, Katy." He said it gently.

The phone rang. Hank looked at me.

"Will you answer it? Please."

He did and spoke and laughed and hung up. "Charlene's not coming back tonight and said to look on the kitchen table."

Half naked, I walked downstairs and into the kitchen. Pink flamingo salt and pepper shakers winked saucily at me. I felt the tears in the back of my eyes. I love pink flamingos—the tackier, the better. The tears weren't because of that.

"See, Katy?" Hank stood behind me.

"What?"

"Who you are, what you do—the help, the love." He kissed the top of my head. "You smell like bars and cigarette smoke."

"Yes. Yuck. You, too." I danced in place. "I did it, Hank! No more

260

twisting in the wind, just pink flamingos!" The thought made me laugh in delight. "Let's have showers. You go first."

His breath was gentle on my cheek. "You did it, Katy. Congratulations." We kissed.

"*You* go first," he said, and we both laughed.

It wouldn't matter who went first, we'd both end up in the shower together. My hair would get wet, we'd use up all the hot water, and the soap would get away from us.

That wouldn't matter either.

"I love you," I whispered. "Let's buy land up here. For the future."

He couldn't hear me. The hard hot spray pounded down on us.

But I said it.

It was a start.